S0-ANN-071

Saving The Dream

Saving The Dream

Vanessa D. Gilmore

Vanessa Gilmore

Library of Congress Control Number:		2012907081
ISBN:	Hardcover	978-1-4691-2693-7
	Softcover	978-1-4691-2692-0
	Ebook	978-1-4691-2694-4

This book was printed in the United States of America.

To order additional copies of this book, contact:
Xlibris Corporation
1-888-795-4274
www.Xlibris.com
Orders@Xlibris.com
115120

To my son, Sean Harrison Gilmore.

Thank you for your love and inspiration.

Love, Mom

PROLOGUE

When a child is born, there is an instant connection created between mother and child. Some have described it as an invisible string that weaves them together with no beginning and no end. Even still, there are times when a birth mother recognizes and understands that the great love that she has for this new life won't be enough to sustain him and sometimes, out of love, she passes her blessing forward to another mother. In those instances, that child is sometimes fortunate enough to find his earth mother—a woman that is divinely chosen for him through adoption. This is the story of one boy and his two mothers—his birth mother and his earth mother, and the life he might have lived with each and the person he became. It is also the story of how the choices made by each mother impacted his life journey and the lives of the people he touched along the way.

Story A		*Story B*	
Birth Mother		*Earth Mother*	
Andre Parker	Erica Parker	*Anderson Pierce*	*Alexa Pierce*
D'Andre Parker		*Daniel Pierce*	

Saving the Dream

Erica was walking home from school kicking a can back and forth with her best friend, Tanya. The can clinked and rattled against the rough asphalt kicking up rocks and pebbles along the way. Something about kicking the can took her back to a happier, more care free time in her life. Despite the thick pollen that clung to almost everything, it was a beautiful spring day in Texas, but Erica didn't even notice. The words of her school counselor were still echoing in her head. "You are too young to raise a baby. Have you considered adoption?" And even though it had been several hours since they had that conversation, Erica instinctively raised her hands to her ears hoping to block out those words she didn't want to hear—that she was too young to raise a baby. How could she be too young to raise her own baby when she hadn't been too young to get pregnant? Besides, this was her life and her baby. No old woman was going to tell her what to do. Even still, she wondered how she had let this happen. And as if she didn't know, she turned to Tanya and asked.

"How did this happen to me?"

"Because you decided to be impressed by a boy who gave you some carnations. And those aren't even real flowers."

Tanya was right. She was so starved for attention that she had ignored everything her mother had taught her. Although she was only fifteen, Erica was well developed for her age. At five foot seven, she towered above many of the girls in her class. Her long, gorgeous, honey colored legs got her noticed both in track and field and in the hallways of her high school. She had been so flattered when Andre had started watching her run after school while he was at football practice. Most of the boys that flirted with her were young and hadn't started growing yet so she towered over them. Andre was a full six feet already with broad shoulders and wavy hair that he wore a little long. When he finally offered her his football jacket, she felt a connection to him that she had never felt with anyone before. Besides the fact that carnations weren't even real flowers, she had managed to overlook the fact that Andre was seventeen, but only in the tenth grade. It hadn't mattered to her because he had a car that his uncle had given him and when they rode around in it, they were the envy of all their friends.

Their relationship had felt so perfect to her. Andre was always bringing her little gifts of candy or soda. And though the gestures were small, it was enough to make Erica daydream about the way she hoped Andre would always take care of her.

Erica thought back to the afternoon that had changed her life forever. Andre had bought her some teen magazines and surprised her by bringing them to her locker after school. He asked her to go for a ride to the beach. She knew she should go straight home like her mother told her to, but she didn't think a short ride would cause much harm. With the temperature in the seventies, it was a perfect day. They parked along the seawall and Andre took a blanket and his backpack from the trunk.

"Where are we going?" Erica asked.

"You'll see. It's my secret spot. But now it can be our secret spot."

Erica grinned. She liked the way that Andre thought of them as a couple. She knew this was a good sign that their relationship would last. She squeezed his hand and he squeezed back as he pulled her down the beach. Finally, they reached a secluded area where the rocks came together and almost formed a cavelike structure. Inside the rocks, they were shielded from the wind and Andre spread his blanket on the warm sand. As he sat down, he pulled Erica down toward him and gently kissed her. Everything about that moment felt right.

"I brought us a little something to drink," he purred in her ear, as he reached into his backpack with one hand and stroked her back with the other.

"You know I'm not really used to drinking, Andre."

"I know baby, but this will make you relax. Trust me."

He poured some of the sweet liquid into a paper cup and handed it to her. It had an apple flavor and was much more pleasant tasting than she thought it would be. The warm liquid slid down her throat and warmed her stomach. She felt almost instantly relaxed.

"Umm, that's good," she said.

"Umm, that's good too," Andre replied as he sucked on her earlobes.

"Stop it Andre!"

"Just relax baby, and have another drink. I promise you that I'm gonna make you feel so good, you're going to want to holler."

Erica took another big swallow of wine and her head began to feel a little dizzy. She laid back on the blanket to stop the spinning and Andre laid down beside her. Even in her alcohol induced haze, a million thoughts began to swirl inside her head. Erica knew Andre wanted to have sex, but she could hear her mother's voice in her head, warning her not to get pregnant. She knew other girls who had gotten pregnant, but she wasn't like them. They were the fast girls that had sex with everybody. She was a virgin and she thought she remembered hearing somewhere that you couldn't get pregnant the first time you had sex. Still she wondered, should she or shouldn't she? She felt like she was standing at the edge of a dark alley in a scary movie trying to decide which way she should run to avoid the monster. But while she lay there contemplating her options, Andre had already made the decision for her. Andre was arousing feelings in her she had never felt before. He was rubbing against her slowly in a way that made her whole body tingle. She decided to relax and give in to this wonderful feeling. But in just a few minutes, as if she was being awakened from a dream, she began to experience unbearable pain that completely startled her.

"Stop it Andre," she yelled, "you're hurting me!"

"It's ok baby, you just need to relax. Damn, I knew you were a virgin and this is so good to me."

"Well it's not good to me," Erica screamed as tears rolled down her face, but by now Andre was sweating and panting and he wasn't even listening to her anymore. The wild look in his eyes scared Erica to death and even though she was trying to push Andre as hard as she could to get him off of her, every move just seemed to make it worse. The rocks around them that had initially seemed like a shelter from the outside world now seemed to be closing in on them as she looked upward trying to imagine some salvation from this horrible experience. Erica felt a terrifying feeling in the pit of her stomach. Just as she thought that she couldn't take anymore, Andre finally let out a scream that seemed to echo off the walls of the rocks.

"Damn baby, damn, damn, damn."

That's what she was thinking too as she lay there shivering and felt warm tears running down her cheeks. Damn.

It wasn't long before her body began to experience some changes. The first thing she noticed was how tender her breasts were. Not soon after that she was nauseous every day. Her thin frame began to show some extra weight. She had been running track since elementary school, but now when she went to practice, she could barely get around the track before she started feeling faint. Although she suspected the worst, she decided she would just rather not know, so she ignored all the signs.

One day as she was coming out of the bathroom, her mother was standing at the door waiting for her. Erica jumped back startled to see her mother standing there staring at her so intently. Her mother had dark piercing eyes and a gaze that could look right through you. She had been around the block before and she had let Erica know at a very young age that children were not entitled to any privacy in their parents' home. She would regularly go through Erica's purse, backpack and drawers. Sometimes Erica would come home and find some note she had written to a friend in confidence taped to the kitchen wall. It drove Erica crazy, but she knew better than to argue with her mother about it.

"Erica, I noticed that you haven't used any sanitary pads in two months. I counted and there were thirty-six in there in March and it is now May and there are still thirty-six in there! What's going on?"

"Nothing, mama," Erica mumbled as she tried to hold back her tears. But her mother knew her too well.

"Nothing my butt. It's that Andre isn't it—he's gotten you pregnant hasn't he," she demanded.

"No, mama," was all Erica managed to say before the first hot tear rolled down her cheek.

"Erica, I told you about running around with that no-good Andre! I ain't raising no more babies. Hell I'm only 28 years old myself. Ain't no way in hell I'm gonna let you bring a baby into this house. Your grown ass gon' have to give that baby up."

"No mama. Please don't make me give my baby away. Andre loves me and he's gonna help me raise it," Erica cried.

But even as she said the words, she already knew how silly they sounded. She and her momma—who was also named Erica, but went by the nickname Ricky, lived in a cramped two bedroom, broken-dreams kind of apartment in a broken-dreams kind of town in southern Texas. They felt lucky to have a place to stay that her mother could afford on her pay as a waitress at a busy truck stop diner. Her mom was only twenty-eight, just thirteen years older than Erica, but she already looked like life had passed her by. Her hair was braided, but not in one of those pretty modern styles. It just looked functional, as if she couldn't be bothered with trying to fix it every day. And most days she didn't. She just put on her uniform, stuck her braids in a fishnet and went to work so she could keep a roof over their heads. She looked like she must have been pretty at one time—a long time ago. But when she got pregnant at thirteen all her dreams of getting out of this town so she could make something of herself vanished into thin air. It wasn't like she'd had anybody to serve as her role model. Her own mother was just fourteen when she had her and named her after her favorite soap opera star from All My Children. But Ricky was smart and she had vowed to make something out of her life even though she had nobody to encourage her except Bobby. Bobby was Erica's father. But he had been no more than a sperm donor. When Ricky got pregnant at thirteen, he quickly disappeared from her life. For him, child rearing ended with conception.

Ricky had actually been pretty back then and she had a good voice too. The choir director at her church had first noticed how beautifully she sang and had encouraged her to enter a local contest. She won that contest and got a chance to enter a regional singing competition. After winning that with ease, it seemed that she might have found a way to escape her dreary life. But just as it was time to go on a small tour around the state, she discovered she was pregnant and had to drop out. Ricky had so hoped that her mother's fate would not be her own. Instead of the glamourous life she had dreamed of, she ended up, like her mother, just another unwed teenage mother going from one low paying job to the next to keep herself and her child fed and clothed.

And now Ricky was watching her own daughter carry on the generational curse of becoming pregnant before you really had the chance to become a woman just to prove that you were a woman. It made no sense to her now, but she remembered how this circular reasoning had seemed logical to her at thirteen. Even though she was just reaching the age when she should have been thinking about having children herself, raising Erica's baby was the last thing she wanted to do right now.

"Erica, I done been through this myself. And even though I'm glad you're my baby, I ain't going to raise no more babies. So unless you and Andre have figured out how you're going to live on your own, you gonna have to give that baby up for adoption."

Erica looked stunned, but Ricky just kept right on talking without meeting her eyes.

"I'm going to check with a local agency tomorrow about doing the paperwork."

But even as she spoke these harsh words, she couldn't look at her daughter. She could feel Erica's eyes welling up with tears of pain, resentment, humiliation and anger. She knew what she had to do, but she also knew Erica would hate her for it. She wondered if she was strong enough to risk alienating her daughter's love. Her baby, her namesake. She had named her Erica too, mostly because she didn't have enough imagination to think up another name. But she had struggled to raise this girl and she loved her too much to let her go through the same misery and heartache she had experienced as a teenage mother.

She knew what she had to do, and like it or not, Erica was going to have to give that baby up. She had to.

"Mama. I hear you loud and clear. If I want to have my baby, me and Andre are on our own. I'm not worried about that. I know he loves me."

And with that Erica turned and stormed away.

Chapter 2A

Birth Mother

Six months earlier when Andre learned that Erica was pregnant, he felt like a truck had hit him. He could tell that his initial reaction had scared Erica, but he was scared too. He wanted her to know he was going to be there for her though, so after his initial shock, he knew he had to get it together as quickly as he could. He wanted her to feel safe and not afraid. So, despite his initial shock, he picked her up and spun her around and around until she thought she might throw up.

"Stop it Andre, you're going to make me sick!" she laughed.

"I don't care. You're going to have my baby and I am celebrating, even if I have to pay for it later."

"It won't be you who has to pay. It will be me."

"No baby, you don't have to pay for anything. Your man has got this. I'll quit the team so I can start working after school. You'll see. It's going to be fine."

"I know," Erica said hesitantly. She was hopeful but she was still afraid. She was afraid that Andre wouldn't stay with her. She was afraid that she would get fat. She was afraid that they wouldn't have anyplace to live. She was afraid of childbirth itself.

Slowly, her fears began to dissipate. Andre genuinely seemed like he was going to step up and take care of her. And she was feeling good. She had often heard that pregnant women had a certain glow about them and that was certainly the case for Erica. Her hair grew shiny and strong thanks in part to those gigantic prenatal vitamins she had gotten from the family clinic. Her nails were strong and her complexion was smooth and shiny. She gained some weight, but her doctor said that it was in proportion to her size. She had also been lucky to find some cute maternity clothes for free in her church's thrift store.

For Andre, all he could think about was the fact that Erica was carrying his baby. He had done this—and nobody else could get the credit. All his boys were laughing and slapping him five when they found out because it was common knowledge around school that Erica was a virgin. Most of them when they heard she was pregnant said things like "you busted that cherry man" and "your stuff must be strong to knock her up on the first hit". He just laughed and slapped them back five, but in his heart, what he really felt was overwhelming happiness that he was finally going to have something that really belonged to him.

As the months leading to the birth of her child went by, Erica often thought back to that first day that she had told Andre she was pregnant. Andre hadn't been exactly thrilled to have to quit the football team. It had always been his dream to play college football. She thought that having to give all that up would put a lot of pressure on their relationship, but Andre had been very supportive of her during her entire pregnancy and seemed proud that he was doing the right thing by them.

Andre was sure that he was going to be able to take good care of Erica and the baby. His uncle had started teaching him how to repair cars when he was about ten years old. He was good with his hands and now it was paying off. He started working at his Uncle's auto repair shop after school to earn some money for the things that they were going to need. He also fixed up a small garage apartment behind his uncle's house for them to stay in after the baby was born.

His uncle's house was on a short dead end street of small, white, one story shingle houses. Most of the homes had corrugated carports attached to them and old broken down cars were a common sight. The yards were small but usually well kept. The place that Andre and Erica called home was a small upstairs garage apartment behind the home of Andre's uncle. It had a narrow wooden staircase with open slats that hadn't seen paint in about twenty-five years. The stairs ended in a small landing that faced a door with a creaky old screen door in front of it that had the bottom screen torn out. The front door itself was dirty and worn with an old lock on it that didn't work half the time.

Inside, there was a small living room that could have almost been called cozy in some earlier time. It had a large window overlooking the backyard of his uncle's house. From the window they could see the small vegetable garden that Andre's Aunt Muriel was growing. The living room had a green linoleum floor that Andre's aunt had covered with an old throw rug that had begun rolling up along the edges. There was a small kitchen behind a brown accordion door with an old stove and an even older refrigerator. The adjoining bedroom was barely big enough for a full sized bed and the crib. The walls were painted a pale green with paint that looked like it had been left over from painting some school or hospital corridor. Inside the bedroom there was a small bathroom that was kind of dark with one frosted window, a small pedestal sink and a grimy old tub that they had covered with pretty duck stickers. It wasn't much, but it was going to be home.

The first time that Andre brought Erica to see the place, he covered her eyes as he walked her up the stairs. He had worked hard to create a home for them and he was so proud to be able to show Erica everything that he had done to get ready for the baby's arrival. As they walked up the stairs, Erica could hear him grinning as he guided her every step.

For Andre, this was his opportunity to show Erica that he could be the man she needed him to be and that he wanted to be. When Andre finally uncovered her eyes at the top of the stairs and opened the door, she squealed with delight.

To Erica, it didn't really matter what the place looked like. She just loved the idea of them living together as a family, just like a grown man and woman would do. She daydreamed about how she would cook dinner for the two of them and they would eat together as a family. She had gotten a second hand crib from the Salvation Army with some of her birthday money she had saved and some of her friends had chipped in to buy her some curtains and a matching comforter from the little thrift store in their church. She couldn't have been happier.

For Andre's part, he was so glad that he was able to give Erica somewhere to live after her mother had kicked her out. He understood how mad Ricky was and how disappointed she was in both of them, but he was glad he had the kind of family that accepted you and supported you, even when you made mistakes. He knew the little garage apartment wasn't much, but at least it gave them a place they could call their own. Despite her initial coolness about the idea, even Ricky seemed impressed when they brought her over to show her their place. She nodded approvingly and Andre couldn't help but grin when she gave him a little hug.

A few months later Erica was in the county hospital giving birth to her son and waiting for his father to show up. She had told anybody who would listen that her baby's daddy, Andre, was on the way to the hospital to see his baby be born. Even the nurses in the hospital seemed impressed that she actually had a boyfriend who was sticking by her and might actually show up. If only her school counselor could be supportive of her decision. She treated Andre nastily and never had anything positive to say about Erica's pregnancy or her future plans. And although her counselor had been helpful in getting her a transfer to the alternative school for pregnant students, she hadn't been the least bit thrilled by Erica's decision to have her baby. Well, it didn't matter. Andre really loved her and that's what really counted. She could hardly wait for him to get there. She had called him when she was on the way to the hospital and he said he was coming right away, but the baby wasn't going to wait for Andre to get there to make his entrance into the world. But just as their son was ready to make his appearance into the world, Andre burst into the room already wearing his hospital greens, yelling, "Wait for me, wait for me."

Erica didn't know whether to laugh or cry. She only knew that she was happy to see Andre. She hoped that his showing up in the nick of time was a good sign.

"You're just in time," one of the doctors said laughing.

"I knew my baby would wait for me," Andre said grinning.

At that moment, Erica gave one final push and screamed out in pain. As she did, she thought about the fact that so far, sex had only brought her pain. But that same moment, she heard her baby crying and all her fears melted away. She fell back on the bed, but could see that the nurse was already cleaning the baby up to hand to Andre.

From the moment he saw him, he knew he couldn't deny that this was his baby. He had his same full lips and the same light brown eyes. His nose was wide and flat like his momma's but Andre recognized his ears on the baby immediately.

Erica was weak, but she managed to prop herself up on her elbows just enough to see her beautiful baby boy.

"Andre, bring the baby over here, please," she asked. Andre grinned at her and he walked across the room and handed her the most perfect little bundle of brown sugar she had ever seen. And when he bent down and kissed her head, she knew that Andre really loved them.

They decided to name the baby D'Andre after Andre. Andre Parker and D'Andre Parker. And while that made Erica happy, she couldn't help but think that she wanted to be a Parker too. As Erica watched Andre with his son, she knew that this was probably the best time to talk to him about their future together as a family. They had never actually talked about whether they would get married and it was something that she really wanted more than anything—to be Andre's wife.

"Andre, they put your name on the birth certificate like we talked about."

"Good, 'cause this is my boy and I want everybody to know it."

"Well, I was kinda hopin' that I could have your name too."

"What you mean, like get married?"

"Well, yeah, why not?"

"I mean, we kinda young to be rushin' into marriage, don't you think?"

"We kinda rushed into having a baby!"

Andre just hung his head on that point. "I guess you right. If I gon' do right by my son, I should do right by his momma too, I guess. But I don't want it to be no big deal. If we gon' do it, let's just do it and get it over with."

And that's what they did, the very next afternoon in the hospital chapel. It was almost a nonevent. Nobody was there except Erica, Andre, Ricky and the baby. The hospital chaplain hurriedly performed the ceremony that made them husband and wife and Andre went back to work at the auto shop. Erica was a little disappointed that Andre hadn't taken the time to even clean his hands and nails before he came over because she couldn't stop looking at them during the ceremony.

But in the end, she decided to just be happy that he was here and they were getting married. She wasn't going to let a little dirt come between them.

Andre felt apprehensive about marrying Erica, but he also thought he would really feel bad if he didn't marry her. He kept thinking about his own father and he was determined to do a better job. If marrying Erica was going to make her happy, then it was what he had to do. Also, by marrying her he also felt that he had done what he needed to do to show that he intended to do right by his family. In many ways it was a relief for him to know that he had done his part and now he could get back to work.

Chapter 2B

Earth Mother

The county hospital was the kind of place you didn't go unless you had been in a major trauma and needed what you could only get from their state of the art trauma center. Otherwise you stayed as far away from there as you could because there was nothing there but immigrant mothers who used the emergency room for regular health care for their babies, gunshot victims, drug addicts recovering from overdoses and poor, usually unwed, mothers having yet another child. Six months later Erica Parker was right another teenage mother who had come to the county hospital to give birth to her son. Her boyfriend, Andre, hadn't been exactly thrilled to learn that she was pregnant, but he had been supportive of her during her pregnancy. He had quit the high school football team so he could work after school at the auto repair shop and earn some money for the things that they needed for the baby. He was also in the process of fixing up a small garage apartment behind his uncle's house for them to stay in after the baby was born. It wasn't much, but it was going to be home. She loved the idea of them living together as a family, just like a grown man and woman would do. She had gone to the local thrift store and picked up some second-hand curtains and matching comforter for the baby. And some of her friends had chipped in to buy her a used crib.

Even the nurses in the hospital seemed impressed that she actually had a boyfriend who was sticking by her. If only her mother and her school counselor were supportive of her decision. Both of them had told her what a mistake she was making. But, it didn't matter. Andre really loved her and that's what really counted. She couldn't wait for Andre to see the baby. She had called him when she was on the way to the hospital and he said he would come as soon as he got off of work, but the baby couldn't wait for Andre to get there to make his entrance into the world. And so, D'Andre came into the world screaming like he was already mad that his daddy wasn't there to see his grand entrance. Erica didn't start getting worried until she realized that it was already three hours after the time that Andre was supposed to get off work. But just then, the door burst open.

"My grandson is gorgeous," Ricky exclaimed as she swept into the room.

It was the most enthusiastic Erica had seen her mother about anything in years. Erica was crestfallen that it wasn't Andre coming to see her, but managed to say, "Yes, mama, he is beautiful isn't he. But have you seen Andre?"

"No baby. But I did run into his uncle down at the diner today. When I thanked him for letting you and Andre have the place, he said that he hadn't seen Andre since yesterday and he was wondering why he hadn't shown up for work."

"What?! When I paged him, he told me he couldn't come to the hospital with me because his uncle was making him work late. Mama, where could he be?"

"I don't know baby. I don't know."

That night and the next Erica called Andre repeatedly, but he never answered and he never came to the hospital to see her. Some of her friends wanted to stop by, but Erica couldn't bear to see them and have to admit that Andre had not been to see her or the baby. Finally one day when she woke up her counselor was sitting there. All Erica could do when she saw her was break down in tears. But it was clear from the sympathetic look on her face that she didn't come to say she told her so. She looked genuinely concerned and sympathetic about the situation Erica found herself in.

"Hi Mrs. Burke," Erica said weakly.

"Hello, dear," she replied. "How are you feeling?"

"Well, the childbirth wasn't as bad as I thought it was going to be. But . . ."

"You haven't seen Andre, have you?"

"No, and I know he has to know that I've had the baby by now. Mrs. Burke, where could he be?" Erica said, sobbing.

"I heard from one of his friends on the team that he was having second thoughts about all of this. He said he didn't want to give up his dream of playing college football and he actually came to talk to me. Ordinarily I would be prohibited from talking to you about what he said, but in this instance it involves you and he asked me to come see you."

"What? He sent you to come see me? But why, where is he? Why isn't he here himself?"

"Erica, he just couldn't face you. He said he isn't ready to be a father yet. He wants to go to college and play football. He says that it is something he has dreamed about all his life and he is good and doesn't want to give up that dream."

"Well, what am I supposed to do. He told me that we could raise this baby together. And what about my dreams? I had dreams too. I had dreams of having a family with Andre. Why doesn't he want us?"

"I don't think that's it Erica. I just think he wants more for all of you. When you think about it Erica, don't you want the best life possible for you and for Andre and for your baby, even if that means that you won't be together? Right now having a baby with Andre seems like the ideal. But that dream could quickly turn into a nightmare for a young uneducated couple

with limited resources. You once told me that you wanted to run track in college? What happened to that dream?"

"Well, I still want to do that, but . . ."

"But, what? You still can do that if you finish high school and apply to college like we talked about before. But your options are limited with the baby."

"But, Mrs. Burke, I love my baby."

"I know you do, and don't you want the best for him too. Don't you want him to be able to live out whatever dreams he may have too? As the birth mother, you could have a say in the kind of family your baby goes to. You could actually pick the adoptive parents and know what kind of life your child would have."

"Really?" she asked surprised.

"Really," Mrs. Burke said reassuringly.

"I like that term, "birth mother". It seems to at least recognize that I had something to do with giving my child life."

"Exactly, because without you there would be no life. But because of your sacrifice, another couple who really is ready for a baby will be able to have one. There is a couple that my friend Gail from the New Beginnings adoption agency told me about. The lady is a pediatrician—a doctor for kids and her husband is a judge. They wrote this letter to give to the birth mother and prepared this book about themselves so you could see if you like them. If you decide you like them and want them to be your child's adoptive parents, I can let Gail know. Take a look and I'll be back in a little while."

"Ok, Mrs. Burke. I'll do that. I'll see you in a little while."

Maybe it was because she genuinely seemed to care that Erica was receptive to the idea of giving her baby up for adoption. Even though she knew her mother wanted her to give the baby up, it was the way that Mrs.

Burke talked about it that made her believe that doing so was the right thing. She opened the three ring binder that Mrs. Burke had left with her. Inside the front cover was a letter in a clear plastic sleeve that was addressed—"Dear Birth Mother". She took a breath and began to read it.

Dear Birth Mother:

I know that the step you are considering must be the hardest thing you have ever done in your life—giving up the son you love. There is no greater bond than that of mother and child and we know that for you to be considering adoption, you must really love your son and want the best for him. We want to assure you that we are aware of the sacrifice you are making for your child and ultimately, hopefully for us. We want you to know that we respect your decision and your need to know that your child will be going to a good home and that he will have all the things in life that you want for him.

We have been married for ten years, but are unable to conceive because of medical reasons. My husband is a judge and I am a doctor. We are both committed to raising a happy, healthy child and we believe that the love we share between us will be enhanced by the addition of a child to our family. We both come from loving families and can assure you that your child would have not only loving parents, but a loving extended family as well. We live in a lovely neighborhood and have a home that is ready for a little boy.

As suggested, we have enclosed pictures of our home and neighborhood and of the room that we have prepared for the baby. We hope that you will see from this brief snapshot of our life that we are ready to give your baby a happy and loving home. We also hope, that in some small measure, this will give you comfort as you move through the adoption process.

Erica turned the page and saw a picture of a happy, well-dressed couple standing in front of a beautiful, two-story, modern, stucco house. The following pages showed the inside of the house and the room that they had prepared for the baby they wanted. It was painted a pale blue and had stars on the ceiling. There was a blue comforter in the crib with animals on it and a matching mobile hanging above the crib. A comfortable looking glider chair sat in one corner next to a small table with a lamp on it. A changing table was placed against another wall and a matching chest of drawers was on the opposite wall. The rug on the floor matched the star pattern on the ceiling and there was an adjoining bathroom that Erica could just make out. The rest of the house was tastefully decorated and there was a large back yard.

There were also pictures of the couple with other family members. Some looked like reunion pictures. Others looked like vacation pictures. Erica turned back to the picture that gave her the best view of their faces. As she looked at them, she could tell that they seemed honest and sincere. The lady was pretty, but she didn't look stuck up. The man looked kind. They looked like they really liked each other. Everything about them made Erica feel happy and safe. She knew by looking at them that she liked them. She also liked what they said in their letter. They understood that she was making a great sacrifice and that she was doing so because she loved her son. They respected her and they wanted to reassure her. Their kind words had really touched her and she knew that her child would be safe and happy and loved with this couple. She felt that she could see her baby being happy there and decided that they were right for her and her baby.

Erica never would have believed that she would be leaving the hospital without her baby, but three days after her baby was born, she returned to her mother's tiny apartment empty handed. Before she left the hospital she had signed the papers giving her baby up for adoption.

Andre had intended to come to the hospital the day the baby was born, but he just couldn't face Erica. As much as he wanted to be there with her he just knew he wasn't really ready for the responsibility of raising a child. It had been fun playing house for a few months while Erica was pregnant, but when she left to have the baby, he realized for the first time that she wouldn't be coming home alone. He wanted to hang out with his boys. He wanted to play football. He wanted to have the freedom to spend his money as he pleased and not have to worry about diapers and formula. He had finally gone to see Mrs. Burke himself to see if he could find out about giving the baby up for adoption. He knew it was what the counselor had thought was best all along, so after they talked, he decided to let her break the news to Erica.

On the day Andre went to the hospital to see Erica and sign the papers he and Erica held their child together and cried. Their hot tears blended together and fell onto their baby's forehead. He seemed to reach up with his little hands and touch both of their faces as if he was trying to wipe the tears away. Already Erica could tell that he would be the kind of person who would be concerned about other people. She hoped that one day she would be able to tell him that she had let him go not because she didn't want him, but because she cared about him so much.

Chapter 3

Earth Mother

Alexa Pierce was just finishing her morning rounds at the hospital when her phone rang. She couldn't imagine who it could be because she had managed to see every one of her pediatric patients that morning and she wasn't waiting for any lab results. She looked at the phone, but didn't recognize the number.

"This is Dr. Pierce."

"Yes, Dr. Pierce, it's Gail from New Beginnings. We may have a baby for you," her counselor blurted out enthusiastically.

Hearing those words made Alexa's heart stop. Those were words that she had waited to hear for so long, and now that she was hearing them, she was completely paralyzed. She had begun the adoption process exactly nine months before that. It had started with an orientation meeting at a local adoption agency. At that first meeting they were told that there weren't that many healthy newborn infants available for adoption. Alexa and Anderson had naively believed that meant that there were a lot of African American babies available for adoption, but that didn't turn out to be the case. In fact they learned that there were not that many healthy newborn African American or white babies available for adoption anywhere because girls didn't give up their babies as readily as they did in the past. There was no longer any stigma attached to having a child out of wedlock. In fact, they were later told that the majority of the babies available for adoption were mixed race babies from situations were young white or Hispanic women had become pregnant by an African American boyfriend and their parents were unwilling to allow them to keep their baby. Their counselor asked them if they would be willing to accept a mixed race baby. They realized that if they said yes that it would probably improve their chances of getting a baby sooner, but in the end they decided that they preferred to have an African American baby.

Even though they had been very specific about their desire to have a healthy newborn boy, they started receiving calls almost immediately from counselors with C.P.S.—children's protective services—asking them to consider babies in their custody who had been removed from their homes because of abuse, neglect or exposure to drugs or alcohol. Neither of them felt that they were up to that kind of challenge and although they understood that it would mean a much longer wait, they declined the opportunity to adopt three different children that they had been told about, one of whom had fetal alcohol syndrome, one of whom was developmentally delayed because of cocaine exposure in utero and another whose parents had both been incarcerated and had no family members who could take him.

When they finally started getting calls about babies, they had no idea how quickly a situation that looked good at first might change. When they were first told they might be getting a baby, they prepared excitedly only to learn a few days later that the birth mother had changed her mind about giving the baby up for adoption. Another time the baby they expected was born with severe health issues and became unavailable. Another baby that they were told would be given to them was given to another couple instead. They weren't prepared for the roller coaster of emotions that they faced during those long months of waiting.

And now they were finally telling her that their baby was here. At first she called Gail constantly trying to find out if there was any news about a baby. Her counselor was caring and patient and encouraged her to be patient as well. She didn't discourage her from calling, but reminded her over and over that these things just took time. With all the setbacks they had, Alexa was embarrassed by how much she was calling and just decided to do as she was told and wait patiently for the call that would change her life. For a while she thought about it almost every waking moment. But then it was driving her crazy, so she decided she would try to put it out of her mind. That didn't work, of course. She had made the mistake of telling a few close friends and family members. They meant well, but their constant calls to ask if they had a baby yet were nerve wracking. It was hard enough having to wait, but it made it even harder to have to constantly say, "No, we haven't heard anything," or "No, they haven't called us about a baby," or "No, I don't think I want to try another agency". Finally, Alexa had to tell her friends to please stop asking her about the baby. Her response now was that the right baby would come at the right time. And now, apparently, that time had come.

As she held the receiver in her hand, her mind flashed back over her entire life. It was a life, she felt, that was meant to be shared with a child. Alexa Pierce often told people that she didn't know anybody who'd had a happier childhood than she had. She had grown up as the daughter of an Army officer. Her father, Don Patterson, had used the military as a way to get his education funded. Originally, her father had thought he would do the time he needed to repay his military obligation and then quit, but the army offered him an attractive position in Europe and he jumped at the opportunity to take his family overseas. His wife thought it would be a wonderful opportunity for Alexa and her sister Jackie and so the family packed up and moved to Vicenza, Italy when Alexa was only four years old.

Life in Europe was wonderful for Alexa's family. There was a real sense of community there among the military families. Everybody looked out for each other and for each other's children. They attended the American school for the children of military officers and other diplomats and as a result they received an excellent education. The cost of living there allowed them to have a nanny, a housekeeper and a cook. When Alexa was very young, her mother didn't work outside the home and she recalled how wonderful it had been to know her mother would be there every day when they got home.

When the family returned to the states, they lived on the east coast where her father practiced medicine and her mother started work as a teacher. That meant that her mom was off of work whenever she and her brother were out of school and that they could have summer vacations together. It was then that they started a family tradition of spending their summers in Martha's Vineyard. Alexa and her brother spent every summer there roaming the beaches and neighborhoods of gingerbread houses until she went off to college.

Alexa was thankful that she had loving and supportive parents who had encouraged her to pursue medicine and her dream of being a pediatrician. She had always loved children and pediatrics had been the perfect choice for her. And even though she had devoted years of her life to finishing school and her residency program, she had still managed to find the man of her dreams in Anderson. Alexa had been too busy to date when she was trying to finish undergraduate school and study for the entrance exams to medical school. It was the early 80's and women still had to work twice as hard to get half as much and she was determined to be admitted to medical school. She was also determined to find a good relationship but she hadn't meant anyone she was remotely interested in on campus. Finally, she decided to use her network of friends to find her true love. She sat down one day and wrote a letter to her friends which read:

> *Dear Friends:*
>
> *As most of you probably know, I am extremely happy. In fact, I think I am the happiest person that I know. I have a wonderful and supportive family, good friends and good health. I've had a wonderful time in college and now I'm about to graduate and enter medical school.*

I know the years ahead will be grueling and long, but I also know that they will be worth it. Even with all of this, I think my happiness could be enhanced if I had the chance to share my life with someone that has been divinely chosen for me. I know that person is out there looking for me, but we haven't been able to find each other. If you know where he is, would you please let me know. My view of the world is, if somebody wants their name after the word doctor on my medical license, they need to marry me before I become a doctor. My intended is smart, athletic, ambitious, spiritual, self confident and has a good sense of humor. He is on the way to graduate school, like me, and ready for a serious relationship. He may be your cousin, friend, neighbor or the guy you sit down next to on an airplane. Just let him know I have been looking for him.

Thanks,
Alexa

After she wrote the letter, she debated whether she should really send it. She wondered if her friends would think she was crazy, desperate or both. But the truth was, she hadn't met anybody interesting that she thought she could be serious about in college and she was ready for a serious relationship. So she sent the letter to about thirty very close friends and relatives. To her great surprise, the feedback she got was overwhelmingly positive. People wrote, "Good for you. I hope I am the one to find your soulmate." or, "Can I be in the wedding if I introduce you guys?" and even, " I didn't know you were looking. I think I have someone in mind. I'm going to get on it right away."

Not long afterwards, she received a letter from a young man who was the cousin of one of her friends. It said simply, "I think you have been looking for me." His name was Anderson Pierce and he was about to graduate from college and was on his way to law school. Her friend had thought carefully about whether Anderson might be a good match for Alexa and she was right.

They hit it off from the start. That first letter was followed by hours on the telephone and then finally they had a chance to meet over spring break their senior year. The moment that Alexa saw Anderson and he put his arms around her she thought, "I'm going to marry this man". Within the year they were talking about getting married. One of the things that they both were sure about was their desire to have children. They both agreed that they didn't want to wait until they had finished professional school to start a family and so they decided to get married during their first year of medical and law school. Their wedding was the social event of the season.

Before long they were living like struggling, married, graduate students but they had settled into a wonderful life. But try as they might, they never managed to get pregnant. Alexa chalked it up to the stress of medical school for her and law school for Anderson and decided not to worry about it. She believed, as most women of her age did, that she could get pregnant any time she wanted and that when the right time came, it would just miraculously happen. But it never did. Even after they both finished school and began their careers, they were never able to conceive.

By the time she was twenty-nine years old, Alexa was working as a pediatrician in private practice and Anderson, had been elected as a judge after a few years of practice. She and Anderson had great friends a wonderful life and a lovely house. But they both felt that in order for it to really be a home, they needed a child to share their life with. After exploratory surgery, she learned that she had been born with only one fallopian tube and when she lost the other one because of an ectopic pregnancy, Alexa knew she would not be able to have children of her own. They had considered using a surrogate mother and donor eggs, but Anderson felt that since Alexa was not going to have the chance to have a biological child, that he would rather they adopt. And now she was thirty years old and Gail was on the other end of the line telling her that her dream of motherhood was about to become a reality.

"Alexa are you there?" Gail asked pulling her from her daydreams.

"Oh yes, I'm here. I'm so sorry. My mind is racing a million miles an hour Gail. I've waited for this call for so long, and now I don't know what to do first."

"I understand. Well first tell me that you and Anderson are ready to come see your son, and then get in the car and head down here as fast as you can!"

Our son. She was overwhelmed by those words and how happy they made her. They had always wanted a son. As she was going through the adoption process, Alexa was surprised to learn that it was a lot easier to adopt a boy because nobody seemed to want a boy baby. Boys were perceived as more difficult to raise. Girls were perceived as cute and pretty and those stereotypes had an impact even in the world of adoption.

Alexa couldn't wait to call her husband. When she looked at her watch, she realized that he was probably already back on the bench after lunch. She called his chambers and as she expected, his secretary confirmed that he was back in court. But as Anderson had always told her, the good thing about being the judge is that they can't start without you and you get to say when it is time to go. One of the things that she most loved about their marriage was that no matter how busy they were at work, they always made time for each other and if the other one needed something, that took priority over everything else. Whenever she needed to get in contact with Anderson while he was on the bench she just called Jennifer and had her take in a note to him. He liked to say "it's good to be the judge" because he could recess whenever he needed to when she sent him a note. She called Jennifer and told her to tell Anderson that it was an emergency and she had to talk to him right away. She half expected him to call her on his next break from court at 3:00, but she wasn't surprised when five minutes later her phone began ringing.

"Hey baby, what's up," Anderson purred into the phone. God she loved this man. "What's so important? You know people are trying to go to jail up in here."

"Honey I know. And if it was anything else, I would have just left you a message, but this is too important. Gail called and they want us to come to the county hospital to pick up our son. He's two days old and the birth mother isn't going to take him home and Gail thinks the situation is perfect for us and I want to go right now and bring our baby home," she blurted out without taking a breath.

"Whoa honey, slow down."

"I know, I know. It is just that I am so excited that the baby we have waited for so long is finally here. Can we go get him please?"

"Absolutely. Why don't we meet at the house in thirty minutes so we can pick up the car seat and some things for the baby and then we can ride to the hospital together."

Odd as it may have seemed, Alexa had started preparing the nursery for the baby ten months ago when they began the adoption process. She was a firm believer in the law of expectation. For years she had read the books of an author by the name of Florence Scovill Shinn and had applied those teachings to her own life. In her book, "The Game of Life and How to Play It", Shinn discussed among other things, the law of expectation—how you had to prepare for the life and the things you were expecting to have. She knew that if she asked God for something that she had to live as if she was expecting it to happen and not live as if He was not able. Over and over in life she had seen examples of people who lived and prepared to receive the blessings they had asked of God. If you asked for a new home, you needed to start packing. If you asked for a child, you had to prepare a place for him in your home and in your heart. And so she had prayed for their child and then prepared for his arrival. And now, he was coming.

Chapter 4A

Birth Mother

Andre had asked his Uncle for the afternoon off. He told him he could leave as soon as he finished the car he was working on because a customer was expecting it. Andre was mad. Finishing that car had almost made him miss the birth of his son, D'Andre. From the moment he saw D'Andre he was in love. He couldn't explain it himself. Sure he had been upset at first when he learned that Erica was pregnant, but he was determined to be a better father to his child than his own father had been to him.

Andre's dad had been in prison for as long as he could remember. He didn't even know exactly what he had done, but it had something to do with drugs. When he was very young, he remembered his mother dragging him and his brother on a long bus trip clear across Texas to have weekend visits with his dad. The same sad but hopeful women and children were on the bus every time, going to see their husbands, fathers, uncles and brothers who were incarcerated for various reasons. The prison even had a small playground area where the children would play while their parents had a chance to visit. Andre hated going there as a kid. Going through that barbed wire fence always gave him the creeps. And once they were inside, they had to sit on hard metal benches or play on the broken down playground equipment while his mother and father talked. When they got hungry, they got chips and drinks from the vending machines. At the end of the visits they would all hug awkwardly and say their goodbyes. His mother always left there crying. For days afterwards she was depressed. Finally, she got tired of it too and stopped taking them to the prison to see his dad. Andre wasn't really sure if they ever got divorced or not. All he knew is he didn't have to get on that bus any more and go clear across Texas to visit a man that he felt he barely knew. By the time his father finally got out of prison, his mother was living with another man and he hardly ever saw his dad anymore.

His stepfather hadn't exactly been the fatherly type. He and his mother got along, but that was mostly because she turned her head and looked the other way when it came to his indiscretions with other women. She was mostly just happy that he was a good provider. What he didn't make legally during the week, he managed to make up for gambling on the weekends. He and his buddies had a Friday night crap game where they would shoot dice half the night. He knew his stepfather wasn't above using loaded dice when they needed a little extra money. He had even taught Andre how to slip the loaded dice into a game. What Andre really wanted though was a dad who would go with him to his ball games on Saturdays, but his stepfather was always too hung over from the night before and was never able to make it. Andre had vowed to himself that if he ever had a son that he would do his best to be a good father.

When Erica told him she was pregnant, he knew right away that he wanted them to name the baby D'Andre, after him, if it was a boy. He wanted to be the kind of father to his son that his father had never been to him. Andre intended to work hard and bring home the bacon and go to his son's baseball games and teach him how to swim. He knew it would be difficult without a high school education, but he was determined to make it work.

The day that Erica was scheduled to be released from the hospital, he arrived there bright and early. They didn't have insurance, but he had been saving his money so he would be able to pay the bill for the delivery. He had carefully tucked seven hundred dollars into his jacket pocket. He didn't know how much the bill would be, but he was sure it couldn't be more than that. When he got to Erica's room, she and the baby were ready to go.

"Hey Andre, how you doin' honey?"

"Good baby. How are you and my little man doin'"

"We're ready to get out of here."

"Well, let me go take care of the bill and I'll be right back.

"How much is it?"

"Don't worry about it. Your man has got it covered."

"Ok. We'll be right here, " she said, smiling proudly.

Andre made his way to the billing office to pay the bill. He was really proud that he was going to be able to take care of his family. When he arrived at the office, he knocked on the small window where the cashier was sitting.

"Hi, I need to pay the bill for Erica Jackson, she just had a baby."

The cashier looked up sleepily, barely acknowledging him and started typing into her computer. "Here it is," she said. Erica and baby boy Jackson"

"No, it's D'Andre Parker. I'm his dad, Andre Parker."

"Whatever. I was just trying to see if that is who you were talking about," she said in a monotone voice.

"Yes, that is right. How much is it?"

"You don't have no insurance?"

"No, but I have the money to pay in cash."

"Ok, well then that will be one thousand, two hundred twenty-nine dollars."

"What?! Twelve hundred dollars."

"That's what I said."

"Well, I only have seven hundred dollars on me."

"You can make a partial payment and then sign a payment guarantee for the rest of the bill."

"Ok," Andre said dejected. "Where do I sign."

He walked away completely disgusted. He had actually believed he might have a little of that money left over after paying the bill. In fact, he had counted on it. Instead of being able to pay the bill and take home some money, he was now in debt for the first time in his life. He was determined not to let Erica find out that he hadn't been able to take care of the bill. He was the man and it was his responsibility. But, he knew that it was going to be hard to find the money to pay that five-hundred dollar balance. When he got back to the room, Erica was in a wheelchair, holding the baby.

"Ready to go?"

"Yes," she beamed back at him.

He started pushing his family down the hall toward the exit. He was so proud. When they got to the door, a nurse asked him if they had a car seat for their baby. Erica hadn't thought about it but she looked at Andre hopefully.

"Baby, did you get a car seat?"

Andre couldn't believe it. Once again he was unprepared. "I'm sorry, but I didn't think about it. We can get one later."

"Well, sir we can't release the baby without a car seat. You can borrow one from the hospital if you sign a guarantee that you will bring it back."

Another guarantee, he thought. But what choice did they have. "Ok, where do I sign?" Andre asked, dejected.

"Just right here," the nurse said as she pointed to the bottom of the form. "Now follow me to the office and I'll get one for you."

Andre followed the nurse to a small office where he saw old car seats stacked in a corner. He tried to pick one that didn't look so ratty, but when he lifted it up, it smelled of urine. He couldn't believe that they were actually lending these smelly things out to be used by newborns. When they got back to the car, the nurse told him that she would help him get the seat in the car. How difficult could it be, he thought. But by the time he finished struggling to pull the seat belt through the tiny openings on either side of the car seat and get it strapped in, he was sweating profusely and was now in a foul mood. Finally they were on their way, but it hadn't been the kind of pleasant home going experience Andre had hoped for. To top it off, Erica picked at Andre the entire way home. She wanted him to drive slower, drive faster, change lanes so he wouldn't ride next to an eighteen wheeler.

"Look baby, you got to let me drive. You makin' me nervous with all that backseat driving, especially since you ain't got no license!"

"I know, I know," Erica laughed. "I just don't want anything to happen to the baby. Erica didn't seem to notice Andre's foul mood or that she was really getting on his nerves. She was just happy to be going home with her baby and her husband. As they walked into the house, Erica thought things couldn't have been more perfect.

Chapter 4B

Earth Mother

Alexa and Anderson got to the hospital in record time. They had met at home and strapped the new car seat into the back of Anderson's new SUV right in the middle as the instructions suggested and with the seat facing backwards as was required for newborns. They had even gotten one of those mirrors to hang above the baby's head so they could still see his face from the front seat. They had put some pull down baby shades on the side windows to block the sun from his face. Before they left, they carefully packed a bag with diapers, a receiving blanket, a onesie for the baby to wear that had a matching hat, a bottle of formula, some cloth diapers and some wet wipes. Then they double checked their list to make sure they had everything.

"What are you going to name him," the social worker asked when they arrived at the hospital?

Alexa had always liked the story of Daniel in the lion's den. In it Daniel was thrown to the lions, but God saved him and let him live so that he could be a blessing to others by showing them the right path. In a way this baby seemed like Daniel to her. He had been born into a challenging existence. He was now being given a chance to have a different life, a better life. God was delivering him in many ways. He had already been a blessing to her and Anderson. She could only pray that he would also be a blessing to others.

Looking up at Anderson, she smiled and said, "We're going to name him Daniel."

"That's a wonderful name. It sounds strong," said Gail. "We just have a few details you need to take care of before we release the baby to you."

"Can we see him first?"

"Normally we don't allow the adoptive parents to see the baby before the process is finalized. We provide you with the medical and other information from the birth parents and ask you to move forward on the basis of that information. We really don't want people accepting or rejecting the baby based on the way they look."

"I understand," Alexa said laughing, "but believe me, as a pediatrician I know that all newborn babies look like wet rats, so if their parents were going to make a decision based on how they looked, nobody would take their baby home."

"You are so right," Gail replied laughing. "Well, come on, let's go look in on Daniel."

They walked a short distance to the window of the nursery. The entire way there, Alexa held her breath and Anderson's hand. She knew her nails were digging into the flesh of his palm, but she was so nervous. Every cell in her body was tingling with excitement. She knew that her life would be forever changed the moment she looked in Daniel's eyes. As they approached the glass, she knew instantly which baby he was. It was as if he was expecting them. He looked right at her and as their eyes locked, she fell in love. The space between them seemed to disappear. From the first moment Alexa felt a circle of love radiating from Daniel to her and back to him. She imagined the force as a continuous figure eight that had no beginning and no end. The feeling was so overwhelming that she began to weep. Anderson pulled her close and said, "Let's go do what we need to do to take our son home."

They took care of all of the outstanding hospital bills and signed all the adoption papers right there at the hospital. They received a lengthy detailed questionnaire from the birth parents with all of their medical information as well as their family history and medical information on both sets of grandparents. They got the lab results from a number of genetic tests that had been performed on the baby, as well as hearing and vision tests, and the baby's Apgar score, which Alexa knew was helpful in determining a child's physical condition at birth. Daniel's score was high which meant that he was in no apparent distress at birth and had not needed any special medical attention. Most importantly to Alexa, there was a letter from Daniel's birth mother. She knew that this letter would be important to him later on when he had questions about his birth family and why he had been given up for adoption. She carefully opened the pale pink envelope and unfolded the letter.

> *Dear Son:*
>
> *If you are reading this letter, you are probably a grown up man. As I am writing this letter, you are only two days old. I am sure you probably have many questions about who I am and why I would give you away. I hope that reading this answers some of those questions for you.*
>
> *I am a fifteen year old unwed mother. My boyfriend, your father, and I are both in high school. We thought we were ready to take care of a baby, but we both realized we were just too young. We love you and we want you to have a good life. The kind of life that you could not have with us right now. We didn't give you away because we didn't want you—we gave you up for adoption because we wanted so much for you. It is our dream that your adoptive parents will give you a happy and loving home and that all their dreams for you will come true. One day when you are ready, we hope you will come and find us too.*
>
> *All my love,*
>
> *Your Mother, Erica*

There was a return address and phone number on the bottom of the letter as well as a social security number for Erica and the birth father, Andre Parker. Alexa was very moved by the letter. She planned to keep it in a safe place and hoped that it would bring Daniel some peace one day. She had already learned in her adoption classes that many children experienced a phenomenon called adoption rejection during adolescence when their hormones and thoughts about their own identity converged. During that time, she knew that Daniel might experience a sense of loss about being given away and a strong desire to reconnect with his birth parents. She was told that she should assemble a scrap book regarding his adoption with pictures of his birth parents and their medical information as well as the letter she was holding in her hand. She reached into the bottom of the large brown envelope the letter had been in and found a picture of Erica and Andre holding the baby. It looked like it must have been taken in the hospital room because Erica was still wearing her gown. Her hair was neatly combed and Andre had his arm around her shoulder. Alexa could tell from the picture that they really cared about each other. She hoped Daniel would see that too and realize that they had both loved him very much.

It had been pouring down rain the entire time they were in the hospital, but when they finally got Daniel and prepared to leave, the showers suddenly stopped and the sun popped from behind the clouds to light up the sky. It was as if the earth was rejoicing in their happiness and was preparing to receive Daniel. They strapped him into the car seat and he drifted off into a contented sleep. Alexa was nervous the entire ride home and kept fussing at Anderson to slow down.

"Honey, if I drive any slower, I'm going to get a ticket for holding up traffic!"

"Ok, ok, well just be careful," Alexa complained. But she knew he was being careful and that she was just being a worry-wart. She couldn't wait

to get the baby home and when they finally pulled into the driveway of their house, she let out a sigh of relief.

As they walked into the house, they both thought things couldn't have been more perfect.

Chapter 5A

Birth Mother

The first several weeks of D'Andre's life seemed like a blur to Erica. It was an endless stream of diapers, formula and washing clothes. She had trouble at first getting used to the near constant demands of her young son. What made it even worse was the feeling that she was doing it alone. Andre was always working these days. He took as much overtime as he could get just so they could make ends meet. It wasn't exactly the life she had envisioned.

Formula for the baby was so expensive. She was surprised at first when she discovered that the stores in her neighborhood kept formula locked up in a glass case to cut down on theft. Every time you wanted to buy some, you had to track down a store clerk with a key. One day while she was trying to find a clerk to help her, she started up a conversation with another customer who was pushing her own small child in a baby stroller.

"I am so irritated every time I come in here to buy some formula and then have to run all over creation looking for somebody to unlock the case!" Erica complained.

""Yeah, I know what you mean girl," the woman replied. "That used to be me too until I found out about the WIC program and started getting my formula from there for free."

"What's the WIC program?"

"Girl, don't you know? It's the Women, Infants and Children program. They help by giving you formula and food for your baby and they got all kind of information about free health care and some other stuff too."

"For real? Where is it located? I need to do that."

"It's down on Main Street near that dollar store."

"You mean the one with the sign that says, 'If you have a buck, then you're in luck'?"

"Yeah, that's the one."

"Oh, that's not far."

"And while you're over that way, you might want to check out the fire sale store in the same strip center. They have the best rummage sales and bag sales in town. You never know what you might get in one of those bags of clothes for sale, but the price is good and there is always something in it you can use."

"Thanks girl."

"No problem. We sistas have got to stick together and share the information that will help us take care of our children. Lord knows these no good men ain't gonna help us."

Erica just nodded her head at that last statement. She didn't want to disagree with what this woman was saying, but she also couldn't really relate to it. She knew Andre was doing the best he could to support her and little D'Andre, but everything was so much more expensive than either of them had thought it would be. And with both of them having dropped out of high school to take care of the baby, the prospect of a decent paying job was very slim.

Erica knew that she needed to go to work as soon as she could. Andre was working hard at the automotive center, but he wasn't bringing in enough money to take care of all three of them. Erica wanted to get a job, but Andre didn't want her to work. She figured that the least she could do was figure out how to get some free formula. That very afternoon Erica went down and enrolled in the WIC program. She had been using about a case of formula a week. The savings would be wonderful for them. She hoped it would help with their finances enough so that Andre wouldn't have to work so much. She was so excited about this new discovery and she couldn't wait to tell Andre about it when he got home that night.

Andre came into the house, as he often did these days, in a foul mood. Erica knew it was because he had to work so hard to take care of them. She hoped her good news would cheer him up a little.

"Hey baby, you hungry?"

"Yeah, I am. Did you cook something?"

"Yes, there's some spaghetti on the stove."

"Spaghetti again? When you gonna learn how to cook some real food?"

"I know baby, but it's cheaper to cook spaghetti. But I've got some good news."

"What?" he asked sullenly.

" I met a lady at the store today who told me about the WIC program for mothers and children and I went and signed up for it and now we can get formula for free," she said grinning from ear to ear.

"What!" he almost screamed. "You went and signed up for that welfare program for women who ain't got no man? What, you think I can't take care of my own family? Or maybe you don't want a husband no more. Maybe that woman you met was a dike and you want her?"

"No, Andre!" Erica screamed as she jumped up and ran toward him. "I was just trying to make it easier for you, for all of us, so you wouldn't have to work so hard," she pleaded as she tried to put her arms around his waist.

Andre twisted and pushed her away. As he did, he noticed a small candle sitting on the counter.

"What's this crap?", he demanded, picking up the candle in a votive holder.

"Just a little scented candle I found at the dollar store. I thought it might help with the musky odor up here."

"See this is why we don't have any money, because you keep buying crap we don't need."

"No honey, that only cost fifty cents."

But Andre wasn't listening. He had already latched onto something to be mad about to hide his own feelings of inadequacy. No matter how hard he tried, he just didn't feel like they would ever get ahead. From the day that they came home from the hospital the bills started pouring in. First there were the bills from the hospital for the delivery. Then they had to go out and buy a new car seat to replace the one that they had borrowed from the hospital. Even though they weren't paying rent, they had to pay for electricity and gas and water. Since they didn't have money to go out most of the time, he felt that they had to have cable so he could at least watch t.v. After a while, it seemed like every penny he made went right back out the door. As he thought about it, his eyes grew red with rage. He looked down at the small votive candle that he was still holding in his hand. Erica looked too and she realized almost the same time that Andre did that he was going to throw it at her. She turned and started to run, but everything seemed to go in slow motion. She was halfway across the small living room when the glass votive caught her on the side of her temple exploding as it made impact. She closed her eyes against the flying glass which caused her to trip and fall over the small coffee table and hit her head on the corner of the couch. She lay there bleeding and stunned. It was the first time Andre had ever done anything to hurt her. She knew he couldn't have meant it to happen but it had. She knew he was sorry. She knew he would come over and help her up, right up until the time that she heard the front door slam shut. She brushed her eyelids to make sure there was no glass, then looked around frantically. Andre was gone. Just then D'Andre woke up and started crying. She didn't have time to think about her injuries. She had to see about him.

"Here comes mommy, baby. I'm right here," she said as she stumbled into the bedroom.

She reached down and picked up D'Andre. As she hugged him close, a small drop of blood dropped onto his cheek. It mingled with his tears making it appear that he was shedding tears of blood. She reached up and touched her temple. She knew she needed to take care of her own injury, but she had to deal with D'Andre first. She would worry about herself later. Right now she had to go give D'Andre a bath.

After she had gotten D'Andre settled back into bed and cleaned up her face and the living room, she sat down in the dark on the sofa to wait for Andre to come home. As she sat in the darkness, fatigue finally came over her and she drifted off to sleep. She was awakened, not by the sound of Andre at the front door, but by D'Andre crying from the back room. Startled, she jumped up trying to remember where she was and what had happened. She tripped over the coffee table again, but caught herself before she fell.

As she got to the room and turned on the light, she could sense from D'Andre's cry that he was in distress. She reached down to pick him up and realized immediately that he was hot. Although she felt momentarily panicky, she knew she should take his temperature to see if it was too high. She held her breath as she waited for the thermometer to beep. When she saw the temperature was 102.5, real panic set in. She grabbed the baby and her purse and rushed down the narrow stairs. There were still lights on in the living room of Andre's aunt and uncle, but she knocked on the door before bursting in. His aunt, Muriel, turned with a startled look and said, "What's going on Erica?"

"It's D'Andre! His temperature is 102.5. I think he's real sick."

"Oh goodness, give me that baby," she said reaching for him. "You're right. We got to get to the emergency room. Where's Andre?"

"I don't know," Erica said hanging her head.

It was then that Muriel noticed the cut on the side of Erica's head.

"Lord, have mercy girl. Is he beating you?"

"No, Auntie M. Really, he just got upset and threw something by accident."

"Girl, let me tell you, whatever way you start out is the way you gonna end up. If he's already beating you, that ain't never gonna be over. But we can only deal with one drama at a time, so let's get this baby to the hospital."

After they got checked in at the emergency room, they were asked to have a seat in the waiting area for what was sure to be several hours. Like many of the young mothers here, Erica had no insurance and D'Andre had no pediatrician. Preventive health care was practically out of the question since it often took weeks to get an appointment at the county health clinic. Sick care generally meant a trip to the emergency room at the county hospital where children suffering from viruses sat in the same room with drug addicts suffering from overdoses. Because serious emergencies like gun shot wounds and accident victims had to be triaged first, it meant people with sick and crying babies usually had to wait for hours to be seen.

Erica knew she had a long night ahead of her, so she decided to call Andre. The first time she called she used her own cell phone and he didn't answer. She waited few minutes and borrowed his Aunt Muriel's phone and called again. This time he answered after the first ring.

"Hey, Aunt Muriel," Andre said using his most pleasant voice that Erica could tell was a big front.

"Andre, it's me, don't hang up. D'Andre's sick and we're at the emergency room," she said as fast as she could hoping he would actually hear what she said.

"What? What's wrong with him?"

"I don't know yet. His fever is 102.5 degrees and Aunt Muriel said we had to come to the emergency room. We've been waiting for a while, but the doctor hasn't seen us yet."

"I'll be right there. And baby?"

"Yes," she asked hopefully.

"I'm really sorry."

"I know," she said almost smiling to herself. That was all she had wanted to hear.

Andre hung up and drove to the hospital as fast as he could. The whole way there he was cursing at himself for being such a jerk. He hadn't meant to hit Erica, but he had been so frustrated. It seemed like no matter how hard he worked, they could never get ahead. He wanted to do so much for Erica and D'Andre, but it seemed like every time they got a little bit of money, some unexpected bill came up. By the time they had finally managed to pay the bills from D'Andre's birth, they had to spend three hundred dollars to fix the plumbing in the bathroom of their little garage apartment. After that, the refrigerator went out too. By the time they got that fixed, they had to spend the little money they had managed to save to get the carburetor fixed on his car. He had been able to do the work himself, but he still had to pay for the parts. He knew Erica was just trying to help, but it upset him to think that she knew he couldn't take care of his family by himself. Instead of thanking her for trying to make things easier on them, he had acted like a fool and taken his frustrations out on her. All his life he had dreamed about how he wanted to be a better father to his own child than his father had been to him, and now he was screwing it up. He knew he had to do better and he intended to do whatever he could to make things right and give Erica and D'Andre everything they deserved.

By the time that Andre got to the hospital, they were already in with the doctor. There hadn't been that many gunshot wounds that night since it was a weeknight, so it only took about and hour and a half for them to be seen. The doctor spent about two minutes examining D'Andre before he quickly diagnosed him with an ear infection, handed them a prescription for some antibiotics and sent them on their way. After all the time they waited to see the doctor, they spent less than three minutes with him, before he left the room.

"But how long will it be before he gets better," Andre asked Erica after the doctor had left.

"I don't know. I'm sure that he'll be ok as soon as we get him this medicine. Let's go get the prescription filled."

They went from the hospital right to a pharmacy in their neighborhood. Fortunately medicaid paid for most of the expense of the prescription. They got a syringe from the pharmacist and gave D'Andre the first dose of the chalky pink liquid as soon as they got in the car, but that night and all the next day, D'Andre continued to cry uncontrollably. They kept giving him the antibiotics, but it was three or four days before D'Andre finally seemed to get better. Although the doctor hadn't mentioned the need to see D'Andre again, Erica began to worry that maybe she should take him back in for a checkup. Unfortunately, it took her another week and a half to get an appointment at the county health clinic since D'Andre wasn't really sick at that point.

"I'm taking the baby to the doctor today to make sure everything is ok," Erica said to Andre as he was getting ready for work.

"It's been two whole weeks. I'm sure he's fine. What are you so worried about?"

"I don't know. It just doesn't seem like he's himself since the ear infection. He doesn't seem as cheerful and happy as he usually is. I just want to make sure he's ok. Can you drop us off at the clinic on your way to work? We'll take the bus home."

"Ok, baby."

Erica loaded D'Andre into the back of Andre's car and climbed into the back seat to sit next to the baby. She gently stroked his head as Andre drove them into town. D'Andre cooed and grinned up at her showing off his four little teeth. Erica, leaned over to kiss the baby and just as she did, two cars collided loudly right in front of them. She jerked her head up just in time to see that the car in front of them had run a red light and hit another car broadside. What startled her even more, however, was the fact that the baby seemed to show no reaction at all to the noise.

"Wow did you see that baby," Andre asked.

"Yeah, yeah. I did. But the baby didn't seem to even notice."

"What?"

"Never mind. Just go see if anybody is hurt. We'll wait here."

Erica felt a sense of panic creeping into her stomach. The crash had happened right in front of them and the sound was tremendous, but the baby had shown no reaction at all. She snapped her fingers near his ear, and he looked up and grabbed her hand. She couldn't be sure if he had actually heard her snap or just seen her hand. She looked up with relief when Andre got back into the car.

"What's happening?" she asked.

"Bad accident, but everybody is ok. The police are on the way, and I gave the guy who got hit my name and number in case he needs a witness. Let's go ahead and go."

"Ok," Erica said, relieved that they could be on their way.

When they got to the clinic, it was so crowded that Erica couldn't find a seat at first. Finally a young woman about her age and her little girl, got up after their name was called and Erica and D'Andre managed to get their seats. It took nearly another hour before the doctor called them in. She scooped D'Andre up and took him into an examination room. Even after they got a room, they waited another forty—five minutes before a doctor finally came in to see them.

"What seems to be the problem, today?" he asked without even saying hello.

"Good afternoon doctor," Erica said with a smile.

"Oh, good afternoon. Sorry, it's just that I'm so busy sometimes that I forget common courtesies. What can I do for you and this handsome boy today?"

"Well, he had a real bad ear infection recently. I gave him all of the medicine they gave me, but I still think something is wrong because he doesn't seem to be able to hear very well."

"Was the infection very bad?"

"Yes, we had to go to the hospital. He had a really high fever and was crying a lot."

"And what kind of medicine did they give you?"

Erica reached in her purse and showed him the empty bottle from the prescription. The doctor could see the remnants of the chalky pink medicine D'Andre had taken. When he did, he just shook his head.

"What is it?" Erica asked.

"Well, the likelihood is that if your baby was as sick as you say he was, he needed a stronger antibiotic than this to get the infection under control. Usually when a child presents with a really bad ear infection and high fever, I give them an injection of a really strong antibiotic called rocephin right away. Often when you give the oral antibiotics, it takes too long to get the infection under control. Sometimes that can result in damage to the ear drum and even deafness."

"Do you think that's what happened to my baby?"

"I can't be sure until we have his hearing tested. Let me give you a referral to the ear, nose and throat clinic to have his hearing checked."

"Doctor, why didn't they give my baby the medicine he needed?"

"I hate to tell you this, but it's because medicaid won't pay for the more expensive medicine."

Erica was heartbroken at the possibility that D'Andre might have some hearing loss. It took her another three weeks to get an appointment at the ear, nose and throat clinic, and when she finally got there, her worst fears were confirmed. D'Andre had lost nearly 60 percent of his hearing in one ear and his hearing in the second air was compromised about 30 percent. Because his hearing had been damaged, the doctors told her that she should expect some delay and trouble with language development as well.

Andre felt completely helpless when Erica broke the news to him. It seemed no matter how hard he worked to try to take care of his family, they just couldn't catch a break. Now his son had to grow up suffering with hearing loss. He knew that meant D'Andre would have to fight the rest of his life to make people understand that he wasn't stupid, he just had trouble hearing. It was just so unfair and he was frustrated that there was nothing he could do about it.

Chapter 5B

Earth Mother

Alexa had been to so many weddings and baby showers in the years before Daniel was born that her friends often joked about how much they would owe her if she ever had a baby. And sure enough, when Daniel arrived, her friends reciprocated with an embarrassment of riches. Her friends gave her several showers and even designed her birth announcements. Another friend who had also had a child through adoption arranged an adoptive mother's tea so that these special mothers could come together to share their adoption experiences. Daniel had more toys and clothes and baby paraphernalia than two children needed. Alexa also felt lucky to have gotten so many great books. She loved reading the child development books about early brain development in children. Having studied this many years, it was good to finally have a chance to see it in practice. She was acutely aware of all of the studies that talked about how important it was to speak to your children constantly to promote the development of a large vocabulary. She was happy to see that research incorporated into so many of the childhood development books she received. She and Anderson decided early on that they would limit the amount of television time in their house so they would spend more time talking to Daniel.

Alexa's favorite book that she received was called "Teach Your Baby to Sign". The book revealed that parents could teach children beginning at about nine months how to sign using American sign language. Alexa was delighted by the idea and started working with Daniel early. By the time he was eighteen months old they had learned approximately thirty-five signs that they used regularly in communicating with each other.

Interestingly to Alexa, people would frequently stop her on the street when they saw her signing with Daniel to ask if he was deaf. She would just laugh and say no, he just couldn't talk yet and they would invariably walk away either confused or embarrassed. It didn't matter to Alexa because being able to communicate with Daniel cut down on a lot of frustration for both of them. It also had another unexpected benefit that Alexa hadn't anticipated. One of the signs that Alexa had taught Daniel was the sign for pain. That turned out to be useful very early because Daniel awoke one morning screaming and red. When Alexa picked him up he was burning with fever.

"What's wrong baby, what's wrong?" Alexa asked not expecting any response but more crying. But Daniel stopped crying, focused his full attention on his mom, made the sign for pain and pointed to his ear.

"You have an ear infection?" Alexa asked. Daniel nodded his little head as if he were actually answering his mother and she laughed and hugged him tight.

Anderson came in the room about that time and asked, "What's wrong?"

"Daniel said he has an ear infection. I'm going to take him in to see his doctor today."

"It's good to have a doctor in the family," Anderson said smiling.

"It's good to have a child who can communicate," Alexa replied.

Daniel's pediatrician was one of his mother's former classmates. When they got to her office, they were given an exam room right away. The two old friends greeted each other warmly.

"What's wrong today Alexa?", Dr. Norris asked.

"He has an ear infection."

"Did you look at his ear already? How bad is it?"

"No, no. He signed to me that his ear hurt and he has fever, but I haven't looked yet."

"Get outta here. Well let me see."

When she looked at Daniel's ear, however, she could see that he had a terrible ear infection.

"You're right, or should I say, he's right. It's a really bad infection too. We don't have time to wait for an oral antibiotic to kick in. I'm going to give him an injection of rocephin. How does that sound?"

"You're the doctor." Alexa said smiling.

By that evening Daniel's fever was down and he was almost back to being his normal self. When Alexa put him to bed that night he looked at his mother and made the sign for happy and pointed to himself.

Chapter 6A

Birth Mother

Andre decided early on that no matter what happened, it was his responsibility to take care of his family. Most of the time money was tight and he and Erica barely managed to make ends meet but he still didn't want her to work. Andre felt that Erica should stay home and take care of D'Andre. He told her that he was worried about somebody else taking care of him because of his hearing loss, but in reality, it just made him feel more like a man to be able to provide for his family. So for the first two years of D'Andre's life, Erica spent all her time caring for him.

At first she felt happy that Andre wanted to take care of her, but it wasn't long before she started feeling cooped up in their little apartment with nothing to do. Most of her friends were still in school and her and her mother hadn't really gotten along since she had the baby. After she fed D'Andre and cleaned up a little, she had nothing but the t.v. to keep her company. Most days Erica left D'Andre in his crib for hours while she stared blankly at the television set watching one game show after another until the soaps came on and then she spent most afternoons watching the judge shows. The feeling that was starting to take shape inside of her practically crept up on her. One day it wasn't there and the next she knew she was probably depressed.

Now that he was nearly three, Erica felt like it was time she got a job and put D'Andre in daycare. For one, she was tired of just staying home taking care of the baby. She wanted to get out of the house and see people again. And secondly, she just wanted to do what she could to ease the financial burden on Andre. But every time she brought it up, he just got mad and refused to discuss it with her.

Finally one day Erica decided that she would just go out and get a job. She figured it was easier to ask for forgiveness than it was to ask for permission. Finding a job turned out to be easier than finding childcare for D'Andre. Erica got hired on at a local grocery store the same day she applied. They assigned her to a day shift when she first took the job, but they made it clear that there were no guarantees she could keep it and that it was likely she would have to work evenings from time to time. An occasional evening wasn't a problem, it was just that she needed to have some certainty so she could figure out what kind of childcare to choose for D'Andre.

Erica wanted to find someplace nice for D'Andre to stay while she worked. There was a place at the end of the street that they lived on just before the bus stop. It was in a strip shopping center that contained a beauty supply store and an auto parts store. The playground area in the back was fenced in, but it backed up to a restaurant in the next block and there always seemed to be strong odors coming from the rear. That childcare center was convenient to get to, but the hours didn't work. You had to pick up no later than six o'clock in the evening and there was a stiff penalty if you were late. With Andre working and her hours varying from week to week, that just wasn't a schedule that worked for her.

Then Erica considered her neighbor who lived just a couple of blocks away. She had a licensed daycare center in her home, but Erica knew that she routinely took in way more children than she was authorized to handle and last year, another neighbor's child had been accidentally burned when she pulled a cup of coffee onto herself. Erica knew she hadn't meant for the baby to get hurt, but she just didn't have enough help.

Erica had even considered asking her mother to help her with the baby, but Ricky had made it clear from the beginning that she wasn't trying to be that kind of grandmother and even occasional babysitting wasn't something she was interested in doing. The last time Erica called, Ricky cut her off before she even had a chance to ask.

Finally, Erica went to talk to the people at her church. They had a typical daycare program for working mothers, but when she told them she needed something with more flexibility because of her erratic hours, they suggested that she check out a day care center at a nearby mega-church that had a variety of programs including an overnight child care program. This progressive idea was begun by Sister Deloris, the first lady of the church, and was designed to help parents who did shift work, but still needed a safe and secure environment for their children. When Erica went to visit, she was blown away by the facility. It was a large center that was divided up by age group. There was a central television area that had couches and other homey touches, but when the children weren't in that area, they had specific rooms and activities that were appropriate for their age group. Each area had cots neatly stacked against the wall and bedtime for each age group was posted on the door. The two and three year old kids had to be in bed by 7:30 p.m. Erica thought that was perfect for D'Andre. There was also a play area and another area where they could have their meals.

Erica was nervous that she wouldn't be able to afford such a nice looking child care center, but when she went in to see the director, she was pleasantly surprised to learn that the cost was calculated on a sliding scale based on income. She signed up immediately, and left there feeling happier than she had in a really long time. When she brought D'Andre back the next day she was nervous because she thought he might not adjust to an environment with so many other children. She sat him down and then waited nervously to see how he would respond. D'Andre ran off to play, but stopped short and came back to kiss his mother. Then he said the words that let Erica know that everything would be ok.

"Mama go bye-bye."

Chapter 6B

Earth Mother

Alexa had begun researching child care options almost as soon as they had started working on the adoption. She knew that she would be able to take some time off to spend with the baby, but that she would have to get back to work in very short order. She began her research with local childcare agencies. It was her hope that she could find someone willing to live in during the week who was Spanish speaking. She had minored in Spanish in college and being able to speak Spanish had been invaluable to her in her work as a pediatrician. Anderson, on the other hand, had taken French all through junior high and high school and had done a semester abroad in France during college. He preferred that they hire a French speaking au pair for child care and had been looking into agencies that had french speaking nannies. In the end, Alexa convinced Anderson that Spanish was much more practical for a kid who was going to grow up in Texas, but her one concession was that she would encourage their son to take French as soon as it was offered and she would allow him to do a French exchange program one summer.

Once they had agreed that they would concentrate their efforts on hiring a Spanish speaking nanny, their work began. The agency sent over a nice young lady, but Alexa decided fairly quickly that she had on way too much lipstick for her taste. She wasn't interested in bringing temptation into her house, especially after hearing about that star that had an affair with the nanny. Several tries later, they finally found a mature woman who was Spanish speaking, but also completely fluent in English. Alexa decided that was their best option especially since she had been reading books by the psychologist JoAnn Deak that suggested that children should concentrate primarily on the language in which they would be taught at school before age three.

As soon as Alexa's neighbor found out that she and Anderson had adopted, she came over to give them some advice on applying for schools. It made Alexa's head spin, but Kate insisted that if they wanted to have the option of getting into the best private schools available, that they would have to get their applications in right away. She had thoughtfully brought over applications for St. Matthews—the best school in town that started with preschool and went all the way through twelfth grade as well as the private parochial school close to them that went through the eighth grade. Kate had told Alexa that in order to have any chance of being considered for admission, she would need to apply before Daniel was even a year old. Most of the best schools only took a limited number of applications for each year and when they hit their limit, that was it.

Alexa sat down one Saturday with the stack of applications and her check book. Each application also required an application fee of one hundred dollars. By the time she finished four hours later, she had writer's cramp and had written checks for six hundred dollars. Some of the schools only wanted basic information about the family, others wanted your life history. All of them suggested that early preschool attendance was considered almost mandatory for admission to their kindergarten program. That meant that the next step was to try to get into the preschool program at St. Matthews or somewhere else.

Of course Kate had several suggestions for preschool programs, but since it had been a few years since her own children had attended preschool, she also gave Alexa the name of two of her friends whose children were enrolled in good preschool programs in their neighborhood. Both of the ladies were happy to talk to Alexa about the programs in which their children were enrolled. One had two children in a Montessori program and the other had a son in the preschool at St. Matthews. The first lady, Cynthia, couldn't stop talking.

"Now, my eighteen month old is in the infant program and it is doing wonders for him. He is becoming very verbal and his sleeping has even gotten better. I think it is because he is so tired by the time he gets home from a full day of playing."

"Really, that's wonderful," Alexa said, trying to get a word in before Cynthia started talking again.

"And my older child, well she is just loving the primary program, but I am concerned that she spends most of her days doing the same thing . . . polishing silver. Every day I ask her, "Courtney, what did you do today , and every day, she says, silver polishing. Now I realize that is supposed to help with their fine motor skills and everything, but come on. How much silver polishing does one kid need to do. I told her teacher, now , no offense, but my daughter is not going to need to know how to polish silver when she grows up so can you move her onto something else, but they said that this is Montessori so she can do whatever she wants as long as she wants. But I think since I'm the one paying the bill for this expensive ass school, I want them to make her move onto another activity, even if it's only table scrubbing. You know what I mean."

"Yes, so . . ." Alexa tried to interrupt.

"So, all I can say is that this school is great when they are young, but if your child needs a little more pushing to try new things, like mine apparently does, then by the time they are four, you better be ready to look for something new."

"Oh, ok, well thanks for the advice."

"No problem. It was great talking to you. Call me anytime."

Alexa hung up, laughing to herself. She was almost afraid to call the next woman whose number Kate had given her, but she picked up the phone and dialed anyway. A very pleasant woman answered and she and Alexa had a wonderful conversation. It wasn't until she had this conversation though that Alexa realized how important references could be in the admissions process. She hung up shaking her head and called Anderson.

"Hey honey," she said as soon as he answered.

"Hey, baby, how goes the great school hunt?"

"Well, it is a lot of work. And I just realized that I need to get some references."

"References! This isn't college honey, it's preschool."

"Don't you think I know that? But apparently, there are some schools that look at your application more favorably if someone you know already goes there. So I was wondering if you could call your former law partner, Jonathon Smith, and see if we can put him and his wife down as a reference on the St. Matthews application."

"Ok, I'll call him right now and I'll see you for dinner."

"You better bring something home. I've got to get back on the phone and try to talk to a few more people," she said laughing.

"All right, I'll call you when I'm on my way to see what you have a taste for tonight."

What Alexa soon discovered was that among her friends and her friends', friends, there was no shortage of people willing to talk about their children and their school choices and experiences. Everybody had an opinion and a story. She learned what the difference was between Montessori schools and more traditional schools. She heard about how some private schools nickeled and dimed you to death with a fund raiser every other week for something. She empathized with the working moms who complained that the private schools seemed to give more deference and respect to the moms who didn't work outside the home. She heard success stories about children who got into the high schools and colleges of their choice and horror stories about those who didn't. Alexa contemplated and explored enrollment at the Greek school, the Baptist school and the schools that incorporated French or Mandarin language programs into their every day curriculum. By the end of her research, she was suffering from information overload, but she had narrowed her decision down to two top choices.

When she finally settled on the preschool she wanted, she made arrangements to take a tour. When she called for the appointment, she was extremely pleased at how quickly they were able to schedule her to come by. The day of the tour, she and Anderson showed up early so they could observe the comings and goings of the students for a little while. The students were well dressed and well behaved. The older children wore uniforms, but the preschool kids were in regular clothes. When the bell rang, they all filed orderly into the school. The little ones held hands as they made their way down the hall.

The receptionist greeted them warmly and called someone to take them on their tour. Since they were interested in the preschool program, their guide took them to see a preschool class that was in session. The students were happily working in their separate work areas. Some of them were working with numbers and others were working with letters while still others were cutting paper. Their guide told them that the cutting area was used to develop the fine motor skills of the children. As they were watching, the teacher suddenly went to the middle of the room to get the attention of the children. She raised one hand and said in a calm voice,

"One, two, three, eyes on me."

Immediately, the children responded in unison,

"One, two, eyes on you."

Then they all turned their attention to their teacher while she gave them some instructions on what they should do next. They all picked up their work and put it away and moved to the floor to sit in a semi circle.

"Wow, " Alexa exclaimed, "They're only three years old! Are they always like that?"

"Absolutely. We expect the best from our children and they understand that and live up to our expectations."

"Does that make it hard on the boys who tend to be a little more lively."

"Oh, no. We expect our boys to be lively and we give them plenty of outlets for that energy. Unlike many public schools, you will find that we don't pressure our parents to medicate their children to keep them calm. We make sure that the student-teacher ratio is small enough to give the children the individual attention that they need. That includes finding creative ways to let boys be boys without disrupting the learning that is going on."

They later went to another part of the school and observed the older kids. One of the teachers explained the discipline system which involved a series of escalating warnings before they were sent to the principal's office. They also had a reward system to encourage good choices. They told Alexa and Anderson that children were never told they were bad, but instead they always talked to them in terms of making good choices or making poor choices. There were consequences for poor choices and rewards for good choices. The children seemed to respond very well to this system of discipline. In the younger grades the student teacher ratio was ten to one. Each preschool through kindergarten class had twenty children and two full teachers. The children really seemed to benefit from the extra attention that they got.

Their guide gave them information on the dates for preschool testing. By the time the testing day came, Alexa and Anderson had talked to Daniel several times about what to expect. He knew that some people would come into the room to take him to do some special work and that he should go with them when they came to get him and do his best on the work. When they got to the school that day, there were several families already there, playing on the floor with their children. They found a spot on the floor and began to play with some of the toys with Daniel. Before long, the woman who was head of the preschool program came forward and announced that in a few moments the teachers would enter the room in unison. Each was assigned a specific child to pick up. They expected that your child had been told already that they were to go with the teacher. The process was known as flight. If your child went willingly, they would be considered for admission, if they did not, they would probably encourage you to try again when your child was more "mature". Seconds later, the teachers swooped into the room and started picking up children like they were prey.

Alexa and Anderson held their breath as a teacher came and picked up Daniel. He turned to look at them and smiled and waved goodbye. A boy who had been sitting a few feet from Daniel responded with an absolute look of terror on his face and began to scream uncontrollably. They tried to take him anyway but his wails could be heard all the way down the hall. A couple of minutes later they brought the still sobbing child back and in hushed tones suggested to the parents that they try again the next year. Alexa and Anderson waited for what they felt like was forever. Finally a teacher brought Daniel back to them. He was grinning and holding a piece of construction paper that had a project on it he must have completed.

"How did he do?" Alexa asked nervously.

"Just fine, just fine," the woman replied.

"Do you think he'll get in?"

"Well, I am not the one who makes that decision, but I would guess that we'll be seeing Daniel in the St. Matthews preschool program very soon."

"Does admission to the preschool program guarantee his admission to kindergarten here?" Anderson asked.

"It is not a guarantee, but any child who completes three years of preschool at St. Matthews is well prepared for acceptance into the kindergarten program. Don't worry."

They tried to take the woman's advice, but they were on pins and needles while they waited for a letter from the school. Finally, a few days later, they got their letter of acceptance for Daniel and he was on his way.

Chapter 7A

Birth Mother

Bright and early one Saturday morning, D'Andre jumped out of bed. Sleeping on the living room sofa meant he always heard his mother when she got up to fix breakfast. His dad had usually left for work long before he and his mother got up. He couldn't believe his mother could still be asleep this late. He pushed open the door to her bedroom without knocking and ran and threw himself on the bed.

"Mama, mama, get up. I'm going to be late for school."

"Today is not a school day, baby," his mother said groggily.

"Is it church today?"

"No, baby."

"Well, what day is it?"

"It's Saturday, baby. It's laundry day."

And so began another Saturday for D'Andre and his mom.

They had a nice rolling basket that was usually just big enough to fit all of their dirty clothes in. D'Andre really liked helping his mom stuff it full of clothes. Before they left, they sat down for a breakfast of sugar frosted flakes. D'Andre had a cabinet that he could reach where he kept his box of cereal and bowls and spoons. His mother always kept a carton of milk on a low shelf in the refrigerator for him. While she got dressed, he ate his cereal and watched the cartoons that kept him entertained every morning.

"D'Andre are you ready to go?"

He smiled back at his mom and said, "Yes momma."

"Well put your bowl away and let's go."

He jumped up from the couch and picked his bowl up off the t.v. tray. He was almost skipping as he went to the sink thinking about spending the day hanging out with his mom.

As they got ready to go, D'Andre took his place a couple stairs down from his mom so he could help her lift the laundry cart down the stairs. When they got to the bottom he grabbed her free hand as they made their way down the street to the laundromat. They stopped at the corner convenience store where his mother picked up a box of overpriced laundry detergent and some fabric softener. Although she tried to hide it, D'Andre also saw her buy a lollipop for him for later. When they got to the laundromat, there was the usual assortment of mothers already hard at work and children already hard at play.

"Momma, can I go play with Tommy and his brother?" D'Andre asked grinning.

"Where they at?"

"Outside on the side of the building. They playing marbles."

"Ok. But don't go nowhere else."

"Ok, momma, I won't."

Erica smiled. D'Andre had never given her any trouble and she was grateful for that. He gave her so much joy. She just wished she could do more for him. Erica had been lucky to find a job as a cashier at the grocery store. At the beginning she had to work different shifts all the time which meant she often had to leave D'Andre at the childcare facility. But now that she had been working there a couple of years and had some seniority, she was able to pick a daytime schedule. That new schedule enabled her to walk D'Andre to school every morning and be there when he got out in the afternoon. Now that he was seven and in the second grade, he was in school until 3:15 in the afternoon. That meant Erica could work from 8:30 to almost 2:30 in the afternoon and she was grateful for the extra money that gave them.

Last year she had managed to save up enough money for them to be able to take a trip to San Antonio to go to Sea World during the summer. It was the first vacation they had ever taken as a family and thinking of it still made her smile. A friend from work had told her about an inexpensive hotel that was close to Sea World and she had called and made reservations for them. She had also managed to find some coupons for some discount admission tickets. Both she and Andre had been able to get a long weekend off and their car was running good enough to make the three hour drive to San Antonio. When they had told D'Andre about their plans he jumped with joy and hugged them both so hard that they could barely breathe.

The trip had been perfect. They had been able to get to San Antonio on less than a tank of gas. Andre drove and she was the navigator. They found the hotel with ease. Although it wasn't anything fancy, it was clean and it was cheap. As soon as they checked in they went right to Sea World and purchased their admission tickets with the discount coupons Erica had gotten. D'Andre had so much fun seeing the dolphins and the whales and the sea lions. They rode all the rides they could find and watched all the shows that the park had to offer. In the afternoon D'Andre ran through the sprinklers and then laid in the sun to dry off. They stayed until late in the night and D'Andre was so worn out from all the fun he had that Andre had to carry him to the car. Since he was already five by then, his long legs dangled down almost to Andre's knees.

Another night they went into downtown San Antonio and rode the river boat cruise on the San Antonio river. Afterwards they strolled along the river walk looking at the shops and listening to the music of local musicians who played at many of the outdoor restaurants. They found a reasonable place to have dinner and sat and watched the other tourists strolling by all evening. Sitting there under the stars along the river watching the twinkle of the lights and listening to the mariachi music had been one of the best nights of Erica's life. Even now as she thought about it all she could do was smile.

Her daydreaming was interrupted on this day by the screams of one of the women at the laundromat. When Erica looked up, D'Andre was running toward her with his eyes wide from fright.

"What happened, baby?" she asked as she grabbed D'Andre to her.

"Momma, those big kids came again. The ones you told me to stay away from."

Erica knew D'Andre meant the boys that usually came around trying to sell drugs. It was a constant problem in this area.

"What did they do?"

"They were talking to us and then Tommy's mother came out there and saw them. She started yelling at them, but they got mad and pushed her."

"Oh my God, I'm going to go see if I can help. You stay here D'Andre."

"No momma. Don't go. One of those boys took out a knife and stabbed Tommy's mother because she pushed him back."

At that moment Erica looked up and saw Tommy's mother, Ruthie, stumbling into the laundromat. Her white shirt was covered in blood and she was holding her side. Tommy was screaming and crying and his little brother was clinging to his mother's other arm. Somebody must have had the presence of mind to call the police because suddenly there were sirens and police everywhere. One of the officers grabbed Ruthie and sat her down in a nearby chair. Erica grabbed a towel out of a nearby laundry basket and pressed it to her side with one hand while she called for an ambulance with the other. People were running around all over the place screaming and crying and the whole place was in total chaos.

Finally, one of the officers yelled for everyone to sit down and be quiet. Officers spread out in the laundry room and started talking to everyone there about what had happened. Erica wanted to leave, but she still had clothes in the washing machine so she sat down and waited for their turn to speak to the officers while she finished her laundry. When they finally got to them, D'Andre was sitting there holding onto her for dear life.

"Did either of you see what happened here?" the officer asked.

"My son did. He was outside playing with Ruthie's boys when it all happened."

"What did you see son?"

"Well, those boys that my momma don't like came 'round trying to show us green stuff in some plastic bags."

"What kind of green stuff?" the officer asked.

"It looked like grass. They said it would make us really happy and they asked us if we had any money and if we wanted to be happy."

"Then what happened?"

"Tommy's mom came outside and when she saw those boys, she started yellin' at them to leave us alone. They told her to shut up and then they pushed her. But Tommy's mom was mad and she pushed one of them back. Then he pulled out a knife and stabbed Tommy's mother and ran away."

"The boy who stabbed Tommy's mother—do you know what he looked like?"

"Yeah, it was Jimmy Jackson. He lives over on Third Street. He wears his hair in corn row braids and he has a diamond earring in his ear."

"Do you remember what color shirt he had on today?"

"Yeah, it was black and it had a picture of Martin Luther King on it."

"Martin Luther King?" the officer asked. "Dr. King would be rolling over in his grave if he knew somebody was going around stabbing people while they were wearing a shirt with his picture on it."

"Why?" D'Andre asked.

"Because Dr. King believed in non violence. He didn't think that people should act in a violent way even if somebody did something to them first. He would be very sad to know that Jimmy stabbed Tommy's mom just because she was trying to protect her son from the dangers of drugs."

"Is she going to be ok?" Erica finally asked.

"Yes, ma'am, I think so. She's on her way to the hospital."

"Thank goodness," Erica sighed.

They finished their laundry and then they left to walk home. All Erica could think about was how lucky she was that D'Andre hadn't been hurt. Living in this neighborhood, she was constantly worried about his safety. She couldn't even let him go outside to play in the yard for fear that some thug or criminal might try to talk to him. Those predators seemed to be everywhere. Standing on the corner in front of the store, hanging around the laundromat even at the park where she sometimes took D'Andre to play in the afternoons after school. Until now, she had believed that they wouldn't do anything to the moms who constantly yelled at them to leave their young children alone. It was like a show of some respect. They would sometimes scowl at them, but if a mother asked them to move along, they usually complied. None of them had ever been pushed let alone stabbed by the beat boys as they called them. If this small social code had been broken, then what kind of trouble could they expect next?

On the way home, they walked quickly, pulling their basket of clean clothes behind them.

They were only two blocks from their house when a tall lanky boy stepped out from between two buildings and blocked their path. Erica recognized him as one of the beat boys that usually hung around the park after school. She immediately sensed trouble and pulled D'Andre behind her.

"Wassup little man? Don't hide behind your momma."

"Leave us alone," Erica said, her voice trembling slightly.

"I don't mean no harm. In fact I want to leave you alone. I just want to be sure that if I do, that you'll leave me and my boys alone too."

"We don't even know you. Why would we bother you?"

"Well, I just wanted to make sure that nobody starts flapping their lips about what happened down at the laundromat today. Do we understand each other?"

Erica was trying to figure out what to say, but at that very moment one of the police cars that had been at the scene drove by slowly. It was the officer who had interviewed them. He rolled down his window and asked if everything was ok. Before Erica could answer, the tall boy had disappeared between the two buildings again.

"Uh, I just live two blocks down the street. Could you keep an eye on us until we get home please?"

"Of course," the officer said.

The officer drove slowly behind them as they made their way down the street. When they got to their house, they went into the yard and locked the gate behind them. By the time they were making their way up the stairs of their garage apartment, the officer had waved and was pulling away. They quickly went inside and locked the door behind them. Erica pulled back the shade and looked outside. There was nobody there, but she couldn't shake the feeling that they were still being watched. She just couldn't help thinking how vulnerable and unsafe she felt in her own home.

On Monday, Erica walked D'Andre to school to make sure he was safe, but she looked over her shoulder the entire way. She had a feeling that those drug dealers were still watching them. The one thing that she knew was that she wasn't going to let D'Andre cooperate with the police. They were going to have to find somebody else to help them make the case against Jimmy. When they got to the school, Erica watched until she made sure that D'Andre was inside the school before she began her walk home.

D'Andre was glad that his mother had walked him to school that day. He had a feeling that those boys would still be looking for him if he was by himself. When he got to school, he saw Tommy.

"Hey, Tommy. How your momma doin'?"

"She awright. But she scared. She said she can't believe them beat boys stabbed her."

"Yeah, I know. My momma said the same thing. She real scared too. But she walked me to school today."

"You lucky man. My momma can't get outta bed since they stabbed her on Saturday."

When they got to their homeroom class that morning, their teacher had already heard about what happened.

"So I understand you boys got into a little trouble this weekend?"

"We ain't get in no trouble," D'Andre replied, "Trouble came lookin' for us."

"Yeah, that's right," Tommy chimed in, " Wasn't our fault them beat boys come after us for nothin' We be mindin' our own business and they still wanna mess with us."

"Will you people ever learn how to speak the English language?" the teacher said indignantly as she walked away.

"What that bitch say?" Tommy asked. "Man, fuck her. What the fuck she talkin' about we can't speak english. What she think we speakin', Chinese?"

"I don't know. She crazy if you ask me."

"Hey, I think we better stick together today when we walk home from school. Wha' you think?"

"I think you're right, " D'Andre replied. "I'll meet you by the flagpole right after school, ok?"

"Yeah, I'll be there. Later."

"See you."

After school that day, D'Andre stood in front near the flagpole. The front yard of the school was landscaped but the grass had disappeared years ago and the front lawn was now just hard packed dirt that flew up and stuck to your socks and shoes. There were a few planters surrounding the yard, but they were mostly full of trash and weeds. The little grass that was still left grew in tufts and spilled over the edge of the grass onto the sidewalk finding every crack and crevice and creating a mosaic pattern where there should have only been cement. The students barely noticed though, as they poured out of the school at the end of the day to catch their buses, rides or to walk home.

D'Andre looked around nervously for his friend, and to his surprise, he saw his dad walking toward him.

"Hey Daddy," he said with a big grin on his face. "What are you doing up here?"

"Hey yourself. I came to see if you might want a ride home?"

"Yeah, I sure do! But can Tommy ride with us too? I promised him we would walk home together and here he comes now."

Andre turned to see Tommy approaching them. He had a worried look on his face.

"Hey D'Andre. You going with your dad?"

"Yeah, but you can ride with us too, right Daddy."

"Right. But we gon' have to stop on the way home 'cause I got something I need to take care of."

The boys didn't care where Andre needed to stop. They were just happy to be getting a ride home from school. They chatted happily in the back seat as Andre drove and they didn't look up until the car pulled to a stop in a strip shopping center.

"Where are we daddy?" Andre asked.

"I just need to run in here and take care of something for your uncle Willie.

D'Andre looked up and read the sign above the door. "B-A-I-L B-O-N-D-S, bail bonds. What is that Daddy?"

"It's a way to pay some money to help a friend who is in trouble get out of jail."

"We know somebody in trouble?"

"Yeah, your uncle Willie got picked up for drunk driving and he's in jail. We need to pay his bail bond so he can get out."

"How does it work?" asked Tommy.

"Well, the judge tells you how much the bond is, in this case it's five thousand dollars. Then I have to pay 10 percent of the bond in cash. Do you know how much 10 percent of five thousand dollars is?"

"Ooh, ooh, I know," yelled D'Andre. "It would be five hundred dollars because ten times five hundred would be five thousand."

"That's right," his dad said proudly. " Now you boys come with me and sit quietly while I take care of this business and I'll take you to get some ice cream later, ok."

"Ok," they said in unison.

After they left the bail bond place the boys squirmed excitedly in the back seat anticipating their trip to get ice cream. But instead, Andre pulled the car to a stop at a local park.

"Where are we daddy? I thought we were going to get ice cream."

"In a little while. I have to take care of one more thing today. I'm getting' a surprise for your momma."

"Ooh, I like surprises," D'Andre replied.

Andre walked the boys hurriedly toward a picnic table set far back from the street. After they sat there for a few minutes, a man came and sat down at their table.

"Hey man, you got it?" Andre asked.

"Yeah, right here," the man replied gruffly.

He reached under his shirt and passed something under the table to Andre. The boys eyes grew wide with surprise and finally Tommy couldn't stand the suspense. He looked under the table just as Andre grabbed a gun.

"Ooh, it's a gun."

"Shut up Tommy. We wouldn't have to be getting' a gun if your momma hadn't been messin' with those beat boys," Andre said.

"Man, y'all talk too much," the man said. "You want it or not?"

"Yeah, I'll take it," Andre said passing the man a wad of cash under the table.

They left there and went to get ice cream. Then they dropped Tommy off at home. When they got home, Erica was already there fixing dinner. D'Andre wondered when his dad would give his mom the gun, but he didn't have to wait long.

"Hey baby, I got a surprise for you," Andre said.

"I love surprises," Erica replied turning to face him.

Andre reached under his shirt and pulled out the gun. With his other hand he reached in his pants pocket and pulled out some bullets and placed them both on the kitchen t table.

"This is for you and D'Andre to protect yourselves when I'm not here. Put it somewhere safe."

Erica was stunned. She didn't want a gun. But she could see in Andre's eyes that he felt proud about doing something to protect his family. Finally, she mustered up a response.

"Thank you, I think."

And with that, they sat down together as a family for dinner.

Chapter 7B

Earth Mother

Daniel felt the sunlight streaming through the plantation shutters on his windows before he saw it. But when he finally opened his eyes, he was surprised at how bright the sunlight was. Usually when he woke up in the morning, it was not quite light outside and the sun didn't get this bright until after he was at school. He couldn't imagine why the sun was already so bright, but he had every intention of finding out.

Daniel jumped out of bed and headed for the door. The only thing that stopped him and turned him in his tracks was the sudden realization that he needed to use the bathroom. He turned back and hurried into the bathroom that was inside his bedroom. He loved this room almost more than he did his bedroom. His mother had painted it a pale blue and put a wallpaper border of little trains along the top. The little floor rug in front of his sink was a caboose and in front of the tub there was a rug with a long set of other train cars. The light switch plate had a train theme too as did the shower curtain hooks above the bathtub.

His mother had found a miniature toilet like the ones at his school and that made it easy for him to use the bathroom on his own. The sink was also lowered so that it would be easier for Daniel to reach the knobs and to brush his own teeth without having to stand on a stool. His mother had thought of everything she could think of to make his room bright, cheerful and comfortable. After he used the restroom, he went over to the little sink to wash his hands. He did it instinctively because he knew that the very first thing his mother would ask him was whether he had gone to the bathroom. The second thing would be whether he had washed his hands. He always said yes, whether he had actually washed them or not, but she had gotten on to him and had started inspecting and sometimes even smelling his hands, so he knew better than to lie.

As he went back into his room, he noticed his clothes were laid out on the little chair near his desk. How could he have forgotten? It was Saturday and that's why his soccer uniform, soccer shoes and shin guard were sitting there. No wonder it was so late, he thought. It was the one day a week that he didn't have to be up before seven. Saturday also meant it was pancake day. Every other day he would just get a little yogurt for breakfast, but on Saturdays, his mom would fix him real pancakes, not the frozen kind you put in the toaster. Most of the time she added some vanilla or cinnamon to the batter and you could smell the aroma long before you made it to the kitchen. This Saturday was no different. As soon as he opened his bedroom door, he could smell the pancakes and he could hardly wait to taste them.

When Daniel got to the kitchen his dad was already eating.

"Hey lazy bones. You better come on before I eat all the pancakes," his dad teased.

"Don't eat them all Daddy," he pleaded as he always did. "I'm a growing boy." It was their little game—this silly banter back and forth that they did every week. But Daniel never got tired of it. From a very young age he had come to depend on the feeling of security and stability he got from the regular routines his family had established.

When Daniel first started preschool, Alexa had learned that establishing and maintaining a consistent routine helped a child feel safe and secure and allowed them the peace of mind to grow emotionally and intellectually without fear or concern about what to expect next. When Daniel was less than two years old, Alexa had created a nightly routine chart for him by taking pictures of everything he was supposed to do and then putting the pictures in order on a small bulletin board. It was all there for Daniel to follow and although Alexa initially had doubts about whether a baby that young could follow it, he actually did. The first picture showed Daniel having some milk, the next taking off his clothes, the next putting his clothes in a hamper, then putting his shoes away, then bathing, brushing his teeth, looking at a book, saying his prayers and going to bed. Every night he ran to the board, determined what activity he should do next, did it and then returned to the board to see what was next.

At first Alexa thought the school was kidding when they told the parents to try to give these little bitty kids a routine, but she saw very quickly how orderly and happy it made Daniel's life and theirs. Even though Daniel was older now, he still benefitted from the consistency and stability that Anderson and Alexa were able to create through their regular routines for the family.

As soon as breakfast was over they all went off to Daniel's soccer game together. It was what they did every Saturday. He played on a team of six year old boys called the Tigers. The league he played in was extremely organized. Although they were coached by a parent volunteer, the league provided training for the coaches as well as the umpires. One day a week they practiced with the parent coach but they had a second practice each week with a professional soccer coach. At this age, they still played three on three soccer. The kids were very serious about their games, but in reality they didn't even keep score for this age group and it was big fun for everyone.

When the game was over, Anderson would always go off to his office to work for a few hours and Alexa would drag Daniel along with her while she did Saturday errands. Anderson used to go with them, but over the years, he had started begging off. They would generally meet up around dinner time.

As soon as the game ended, Alexa and Anderson waited on the sidelines for Daniel. When he finally showed up this day, he had a little teammate in tow.

"Mom, Dad, can I go over to Clay's house for a play date. His mother said it was ok for me to come over if it was alright with you."

"I suppose so," said Alexa, "just let me go talk to Clay's mom first.

"Well, it's ok with me honey as long as he's home for dinner," Anderson chimed in.

"Ok, then let's go talk to her and you can leave with them. I'll pick you up from their house on my way home."

With that, Daniel was off for the day with his friend and teammate and Alexa suddenly had the afternoon to herself. Anderson walked Alexa to her car, kissed her goodbye and watched as she pulled out of the parking lot. He adored her and Daniel too, but sometimes he felt that Alexa spent too much time focusing on her role as a mother and not enough time focusing on her role as a wife. He realized that having a child had been such a focus for them for so long because of Alexa's inability to bear children, but he had hoped that once they had Daniel that they might somehow be able to get back to focusing on their life as a couple, but it had never happened. All in all though, he had to admit that they were happier than many people he knew so he decided not to focus too much on this one small shortcoming that he saw in their marriage.

Alexa decided to take advantage of her free afternoon to start planning for their spring and summer vacations. Like most of the families that they socialized with, all vacation plans centered around school vacations. Every year they went skiing for the Martin Luther King holiday weekend in January, and when they returned, Alexa knew that was her cue to start looking for summer camp for Daniel, finalize their plans for spring break and start planning for a summer trip for the family. Alexa usually tried to use the spring break for an educational excursion of some sort and make the summer vacation one for fun.

She had heard a lot about an excursion to Mexico to see the monarch butterflies and thought that might be a good trip for spring break. Some friends had told her that the butterflies descended on this small Mexican village in the thousands on their way back north for the summer. There were walking tours and ecological lectures all about their migration. It seemed like a good choice for spring break for them, even though it was sometimes difficult for her and Anderson to juggle their schedules to go on vacation. But the thought of not going on a spring break vacation was almost out of the question among Daniel and his peers. The year before when Alexa asked Daniel what he had done at school the first day after spring break, he had told her that they had gone around the room and each child had described where they went for their spring break vacation. The trips ranged from spring skiing in Vail to Sea World in San Diego and the beach in Florida. But absolutely nobody said that they hadn't been anywhere on spring break.

She really wanted to plan something special for their summer vacation this year. As a child, she had often heard her mother say that she aspired to use the word summer as a verb like many of the easterners who talked about summering in Martha's Vineyard or the Hamptons. Alexa vowed she would "summer" too, but for folks living in Texas, the summers meant a chance to escape to someplace cooler and that usually meant Colorado or Montana or Wyoming. Lately though, a number of their friends had been raving about going out to west Texas to a little town named Marfa. At 5000 feet, the high desert climate was just cool enough to give them a break from the Houston heat. Alexa had managed to find a wonderful ranch in the Ft. Davis mountains where there was horseback riding and hiking. It was also close to the McDonald observatory where they housed several high powered telescopes for use by the scientists who worked there and that the public could also use for the weekly stargazing parties. She had read about the star parties they held there every weekend where you could actually use the research quality telescopes that allowed you to see the rings around Saturn and the craters on the moon. Daniel had long been interested in the solar system so she thought this might be a wonderful chance for him to see the planets up close. She stopped at the office of their travel agent that very afternoon. Without Daniel in tow, she was able to concentrate and get their plans finalized and booked including airfare to the closest city, a rental car, a two week stay at a dude ranch and reservations at the McDonald Observatory.

Once she had completed that task, she ran a few more errands before picking up a wonderful dinner and heading home. She scooped up Daniel on the way and by the time they got to their house, Anderson was standing in the front yard watering the grass just as he always did. Alexa smiled when she saw him. She couldn't help thinking how safe and blessed she felt here with her family. As they climbed out of the car, she looked forward to another pleasant Saturday evening with her two favorite guys.

On Monday, they were back to their workday routine. Alexa usually had early rounds, so Anderson always took Daniel to school in the mornings. Anderson was very methodical about how to manage the car pool line. He knew that if he left the house at exactly twenty minutes after seven he would get to the school at 7:28, just before the security guards went on duty. That way he could whiz right into the parking lot and drop Daniel off before the big rush started at 7:30. He usually didn't pick Daniel up because he was always at work in the afternoons and left it for the nanny to take care of. But today, he was going to surprise Daniel and pick him up himself so they could take care of a couple of errands. When Daniel heard his name called out in car pool line, he was confused at first because he didn't see Maria's car. His dad had to roll down the window and yell to him before he realized his dad had come to pick him up.

"Hey Daddy. What are you doing here?" Daniel asked.

"I decided to pick you up myself because I have a couple of errands we need to take care of."

"But Dad, Jack was going to come home with me today."

"Jack, did your mother say you could come home with us?"

"Yes, Judge Pierce."

"What's your mom's number, I'm going to call her right now to be sure."

After confirming that Jack was indeed scheduled to have a play date with Daniel that day, Anderson took the boys off to do the first of two errands on his list that afternoon—getting library cards at their local neighborhood public library.

"What are we doing here, Dad?" Daniel asked.

"Going to get a library card."

"What is it?" Jack asked.

A card that allows you to check out books anytime you want. You're big boys now so you need to have your own cards."

"How do we get one?", Daniel asked.

"Well, we go inside and fill out a form and then they give you a card—kind of like a credit card, that you can use later to borrow books."

"You mean kind of like when we go on vacation and we rent a car?" Daniel asked.

"Yes, something like that, except you don't have to pay for it."

The boys came out a few minutes later, excitedly clutching their new cards.

"Now can we go get ice cream, Daddy?"

"In a few minutes. I have one more errand to do. I'm going to get a surprise for your mom."

"What is it?"

"You'll see in a few minutes."

They drove to a nearby park and got out. Anderson hurried the boys along to a picnic table that sat back from the road. In a few minutes, Daniel noticed his Aunt Jackie approaching them carrying a large case.

"Aunt Jackie! What are you doing here? What is that in your hand?" Daniel asked excitedly.

"Hello to you too, Daniel. It's a violin case and the violin your mother used to play when we were growing up."

"Why did you bring it?"

"Because you and your mom are going to take violin lessons."

"No, she's not, just me," Daniel replied.

"Daniel, the school that we picked won't allow you to take violin lessons unless one of your parents takes lessons too. So I volunteered your mother since she played the violin before. Your Aunt Jackie was nice enough to bring me her old violin."

Jackie handed the violin to Anderson and he hugged her gently before taking the boys to get ice cream. They dropped Jack off at home and then went to the house. When they got there, Alexa was already preparing dinner. Daniel couldn't wait to see his mother's face when she saw her surprise. Anderson held the violin behind his back as he came in.

"Honey, I have a surprise for you," he cooed.

"I love surprises," Alexa said excited. "What is it? Some jewelry."

Anderson and Daniel both started laughing and Anderson pulled the violin case from behind his back.

"My old violin?" Alexa exclaimed.

"Since one of us has to take violin with Daniel, I volunteered you. I thought the least I could do was to get you your old violin."

"Thank you, I think," Alexa said laughing.

And with that, they sat down for dinner as a family.

Chapter 8A

Birth Mother

Andre had worked as an auto mechanic in his uncle's shop for as long as D'Andre could remember. D'Andre loved it on the days that they didn't have school because of a teacher work day or bad weather. On those days, he got to go to work with his dad. Sometimes he even got to go to work with his dad on weekdays after school or on Saturday afternoons. D'Andre was a quick learner and by the time he was seven he was already able to identify a carburetor and other parts of the engine. His dad gave him the job of tool boy. That meant he had to stand in the shop while the workers yelled out what tools they needed and then he had to retrieve them and make sure they got them. He knew what every wrench looked like, how to identify every type of pliers, and what to do with lug nuts, bolts and spark plugs. His dad had taught him how to measure the tread on a tire to see if it needed replacement and how to check tire pressure.

When business was slow, he and his dad would work on old engines that were in the shop. His dad showed him how to break an engine down and take it apart. By the time he was eight years old, he knew more about cars than most grown men did.

Late one Saturday afternoon a boy came into the shop with his father. His dad said that the air conditioner wasn't getting cold enough. D'Andre knew that meant that the freon must be leaking. That was a small job that his dad could usually finish in under an hour. Andre suggested that they wait for the repairs to be finished and told them that it wouldn't take that long. The boy eagerly jumped out of the hot car, but he insisted that his dad open the trunk for him. To D'Andre's great surprise, the boy pulled out a large scooter that had an electric motor on it. He flipped a switch on the bottom of the scooter and D'Andre watched in amazement as the boy took off around the parking lot looking like he was hanging onto the handlebars of the scooter for dear life. The boy swerved around the parked cars and carefully avoided a set of old tires that had just been replaced. He came to a sudden stop just a few feet from where D'Andre was standing.

"Wow," D'Andre exclaimed. "I really like your scooter."

"I got it for my birthday. You're supposed to be eight to ride it and I'm only seven, but I talked my dad into buying it for me anyway," the boy said.

"I wonder how much it costs," D'Andre said, mostly to himself.

"I can ask my daddy," the boy replied as he used his scooter to make his way over to where his dad was standing. He was back a few moments later with an answer. "My dad said it costs eighty-five dollars."

"That's a lot of money," D'Andre exclaimed.

The boy just kind of shrugged and whizzed off on his scooter. As Andre observed this whole exchange between his son and the boy, he began to think that if this guy could afford to buy an eighty-five dollar scooter, then he should be able to afford a battery too.

"Come on over here D'Andre and help your daddy with this job."

"Ok, Daddy. But did you see that scooter the boy had?"

"Yeah, I saw it—so what."

"Nothin'."

"All that says to me is that if he can afford something like that then maybe he needs a little more work on his car than what I originally thought. You have to remember son. There are two kinds of people in life. Suckers and people who take advantage of suckers and it is always better to be one of the people that takes advantage of a sucker. You just remember that."

When they finally got home, they were both covered in grease. All they wanted to do was to get into a hot bath and shower. But when they opened the door Erica was sitting at the kitchen table with her head in her hands.

"What's the matter?", Andre asked without even saying hello.

"The hot water heater is broken and we don't have any hot water."

"What?!"

"I already called the home repair store down the street to see how much a new water heater might cost."

"And . . . ?"

"And, it's between $300 and $500 plus installation charges of about another $150 to install a new one and take the old one away."

"Damn. So a minimum of about five hundred bucks, huh?"

"Yeah, something like that."

"Shit. We can't never get ahead. I ain't got it baby. We gon' have to pawn your ring again. Then I'ma hav' to go get a payday advance to get the rest."

D'Andre listened intently. One thing he had always understood was how hard money was to come by. What he hadn't quite figured out until now was what you did about it when you really needed some money for something.

"Ok, baby. Well go over to Muriel's and take a shower first. I already told her you would be coming. I heated up some water on the stove so

I could wash D'Andre up in the sink. When you come back, I'll have dinner ready and then we can go and get the money."

"Awright. Lemme get some clothes then."

"D'Andre, go take off your clothes and come on back in here so I can wash you up."

"Momma, why can't I wash myself up? I'm eight years old."

"Because I didn't heat up enough water to fill the bathtub, so come on here boy and stop acting silly."

After dinner, they piled into Andre's old car and headed for the pawn shop. Erica's ring wasn't fancy, but the thick gold band had gotten them through some tough spots before when they pawned it. Tonight they needed to put it to use again. As they drove to the pawn shop, D'Andre sat with his face pressed against the car window. The area where the pawn shop was located was a seedy, run down part of town that looked as if nobody had bothered to cut the grass on the island in months. As a result, it had turned into the perfect place to throw trash and so that's what people had done. There were beer cans, paper and even old broken pieces of furniture strewn in the island in front of the pawn shop. The strip center where the pawn shop was located contained a liquor store, an auto parts store and an adult novelty store. They parked in the only free spot which was in front of the adult novelty store and D'Andre's eyes grew wide as he looked at the mannequin wearing the bra top with the nipples cut out and a matching set of black and red panties.

As they were getting out of the car, D'Andre asked, "How do you get money from a pawn shop, daddy?"

"Well, you take something valuable, like your momma's ring, and you let the people hold it for a little while. They give you some money for it—how much depends on how valuable the thing is that you give them. If you don't pay the people back by the time the loan is due, then they can sell your stuff."

"Is that what all this stuff is that is for sale—people's stuff that they didn't come get back," D'Andre asked wide eyed as they entered the store.

"Yep, that's what all this stuff is. Stuff that belonged to somebody else at some point, that they had to give up to get some money.

"Are you gonna give up my momma's wedding ring."

"Naw man, we gon' come get it back just as soon as your old daddy finds a few more suckers who need their cars worked on.

D'Andre remembered coming to a pawn shop with his dad before, but this was the first time that he understood how all this stuff got in here. There were rows and rows of other peoples stuff. Musical instruments, televisions, microwaves, bicycles and lots and lots of cases of jewelry. D'Andre looked around and saw one family with a young son in tow examining the saxophones. He wondered whether the dad or the little boy played the instrument. At one of the counters where watches were on display, D'Andre observed a very well dressed business man looking intently into the case. What struck D'Andre as funny, however, was the fact that he already had a watch on each of his wrists. As they approached the back counter, D'Andre could see a man standing behind a caged sort of area. When they got to the counter, the man shouted out in a gruff voice, "Can I help you?"

"Yeah, " Andre said, "I want to pawn this ring."

"Is it stolen," the man asked?

"No, it's my wedding ring," Erica replied.

Then the man took out a little scale and put the ring on it. After he weighed it, he said, "I can give you seventy-five dollars for it."

"Is that all?", Andre demanded.

"That's the price for gold this week. Take it or leave it."

"We'll take it."

They got seventy-five dollars for the ring and then left to go to the payday advance store.

As they pulled up to the payday advance store, D'Andre saw that it sat right next to a store that had lots of brightly colored machines in it with arms that people were pulling. He asked his daddy what kind of store it was and he told him it was a gambling place. D'Andre noticed that people were leaving the payday advance store and walking right into the little gambling store.

As they walked into the payday advance store, D'Andre asked, "How does this place work, daddy?"

"Well, you show these people some pay stubs that show how much money you make and then you write them a check for how much you want to borrow and tell them what day they can cash the check. Except that if you want to borrow two hundred and fifty dollars, you have to write them a check for three hundred dollars. That's how they make their money, by lending you money now that you pay them back on your pay day."

"So do you have a pay stub."

"Yeah, but because it's my uncle's business, I can make my pay stubs say whatever I want them to say. You got to know how to get over son."

Once again they encountered a person standing behind a caged in area. Once again the person dealt with them in a sort of take-it-or leave-it kind of attitude. D'Andre didn't like these places and he found himself wishing that they didn't have to come here and put up with these mean people.

After they left the payday advance place, they rode by the bank to get the rest of the money they needed out of the automatic teller machine.

As D'Andre watched, he couldn't help but wonder why his parents had gone through all the trouble of pawning the ring and getting the payday advance when all they had to do was come here and get money out of the bank with the little card. Finally, he decided to ask them just that. After a moment of stunned silence, they just laughed and said, "If only it were that easy, honey."

By the time they got to the home improvement store, it was nearly ten o'clock, but the store was open twenty-four hours a day and even at this late hour it was still bustling with customers. Most of the people looked like workmen in the construction business, picking up supplies for a job somewhere. There were a few families looking at paint samples and others who were examining carpet swatches. The area where the hot water heaters were located was way in the back. By the time they got there D'Andre was exhausted, Erica was antsy and Andre was just plain irritated.

"Why they gotta have this stuff way back here in the back of the store," Andre complained.

"I don't know, baby. Can we just pick one out and get it so we can get home and put D'Andre to bed, please?"

"Stop rushing me. I want to make sure we get a good deal."

The futility of his words was lost on Andre. This was a national chain, with set prices for the products and for the installation. There was no such thing as getting a good deal. They would get to pay the ticketed price for one of the four hot water heaters on display and then pay whatever these people said they had to pay to get it installed. Erica couldn't see the point in trying to argue about the price and Andre couldn't see why she wouldn't let him be the man and take care of this thing for them. Andre argued with the salesman for nearly thirty minutes about merits and demerits of each of the hot water heaters on display and then picked the cheapest one. In the meantime, Erica and D'Andre had found a chair against the back wall and Erica had sat down and let D'Andre curl up in her lap and go to sleep. By the time Andre came back to find them, Erica had dozed off too and she awoke with a start trying to remember where she was and why she was there.

"Come on, let's go," Andre said in a slightly surly voice.

"What happened?"

"I got us a hot water heater," Andre said, " and they're delivering it tomorrow."

"Thank you baby."

"You're welcome," Andre said, almost smiling to himself.

The next morning while they were eating breakfast, D'Andre couldn't help but think of the boy from the day before with the electric scooter. He decided he would mention it to his mother.

"Momma, I saw this boy yesterday who had an electric scooter."

"Oh yeah?"

"Yeah, and he was riding it all over the place at the shop."

"That's nice."

"Well, momma. I was wondering, do you think I could ever get an electric scooter?"

"Nope."

"Why not, momma? I been real good."

"D'Andre, that's got nothin' to do with it. Did you see me and your daddy struggling last night to come up with enough money to replace the hot water heater. We ain't got no savings for the stuff we need let alone the stuff you just want. And I don't want to hear no more about it because if your daddy hears you he might get mad. Do you understand me?"

"Yes, ma'am."

At that moment, Andre opened the bedroom door.

"Good morning, baby," Erica smiled. " Thank you again for getting the hot water heater taken care of for us," she said as she lifted her lips to receive his kiss.

"I told you that your man would take care of it and I did, didn't I," he replied after smacking her on the lips and rubbing D'Andre's head.

Erica gave him a cheesing sort of "you're the man" look, but D'Andre didn't lift his head from his cereal bowl. He just stirred his cereal and wished there was a way he could get the scooter.

Chapter 8B

Earth Mother

Alexa and Anderson loved Daniel's school, but one of the things that drove them crazy was how many holidays they had. Even though they had a full time nanny, they always felt that one of them should be with Daniel on any day that school was not in session. Unfortunately, the Monday after Easter was one that neither one of them could afford to miss from work. Anderson had several sentencings to handle that morning and Alexa had to go to the hospital after taking Easter Sunday off. In the end, they decided that it would be easier to have Daniel go to work with Anderson. He had been going to his dad's chambers to visit since before he could walk.

As they sat down to breakfast together that morning, Daniel leaned across and gently touched his mother's arm. At the age of seven, he already thought he was the master charmer.

"Mommy, I want an electric scooter."

"Why."

"My friend, Alex, has one and I used it at his house when we had a play date last week."

"Really? Well how much does it cost?"

"I don't know. Let's go look it up on the internet."

"Ok, but your birthday isn't coming up, so if you really want the scooter, you're going to have to use your own money."

"What if I don't have enough?"

"Then you'll have to save your money until you have enough."

"Can I use money from my savings jar and my spending jar?"

"Yes, since this will probably be a big purchase that you'll need to save for. It also means that you'll have to stop spending for a while as well. But you won't be able to spend all the money in your savings for this one purchase. You know you always have to have some money saved for a rainy day."

"What's a rainy day."

"You know, a day when you have an emergency and need some money. Like last week when our hot water heater broke. If we hadn't already had money saved up for that rainy day, who knows how we might have gotten the water heater fixed."

"Oh yeah. So if my bike chain breaks, I will have some money saved up to get it fixed."

"Exactly."

Daniel was already thinking about how much money he had in each of his jars. When he was about three years old , his parents began to talk with him about managing money. He had a wooden crate with four big jars inside it. One was labeled money for spending, one was labeled money for sharing, one said money for saving and the last one said money for college. Every time Daniel got some money he understood that he needed to divide it up among the four jars. When he was young, he would indiscriminately put money in whatever jar his hand touched first. But in recent months he had asked his dad to help him come up with a plan on how to divide his money between the jars. So one Saturday, his father gave him his ten-dollar allowance in quarters. Then they sat down together and came up with a plan on how to divide the money among the four jars. Their plan provided for one dollar out of every ten dollars to go in the share jar, one dollar for the college jar, two dollars for the savings jar and six dollars for the spending jar. Daniel was allowed to spend his money in the spending jar on anything he wanted. If he wanted to play video games or buy a small toy, he would use the money from the spending jar. If he wanted a big item and it wasn't Christmas or his birthday, then he would have to save for it. It usually also meant he would have to stop spending for a little while too.

Daniel got a ten-dollar allowance each week, but he was also resourceful about finding other ways to earn or get money. He would regularly offer to wash his parent's cars for money. Although he couldn't really do a very good job yet, his effort was usually good for five dollars. He also knew how to turn on the charm for his godparents and grandparents. He had learned early on how to bat his enormous eyes and gorgeous eyelashes and that was usually good for at least twenty dollars.

But the reality was, Daniel had become a very good manager of money. He paid attention to his parents when they talked about money. He knew they saved for his college education and for the things his family wanted and needed. As a result, he regularly counted the money in his jars and periodically rolled it in coin wrappers. When he felt that enough had accumulated, he would ask to put his money in his savings account at the bank. Daniel and his dad would make a Saturday morning trip to the bank a special occasion. Anderson taught him how to fill out a deposit slip and take it to the counter and how to record the deposit in his bank book. Daniel was not just interested in knowing about the money he was saving, he also wanted to know about the money his parents were saving for him to go to college. Whenever the statement came in the mail for his college account, his dad would sit down with him and show him how much money was in the account and talk to him about how much he still needed to be able to go to college. Daniel understood that saving for college required planning and sacrifice by his parents. He also understood that he had to sacrifice for the things he wanted.

"Come on mom, let's get on the internet and see how much the scooters cost."

"Ok, ok," said Alexa.

She knew that after she logged on, Daniel would quickly take over, easily maneuvering his way around the search engine. It didn't take them long to find what they were looking for. Alexa was shocked, however, to see that the scooter he wanted was almost ninety dollars.

"There it is mama! That's the one."

"My goodness, that's expensive."

"But, I'll spend my own money."

"Do you have ninety dollars in your savings? And before you answer, you know I am not going to let you spend all the money you have."

"No, mama, not yet, but if I save all my spending money for the next three weeks, and I earn a little bit more, I'll have enough to buy it . . . and without spending everything I have either," he added quickly.

"Are you willing to do all that to have a scooter?"

"Yes, mommy, I am."

"And how are you going to earn some additional money?"

"Well, I'm going to work with dad today and I am sure that they have some work around there for me to do to allow me to earn some money."

"Ok. Well, here comes daddy, why don't you talk to him about what you can do."

"What are you two talking about?" Anderson asked sensing a conspiracy was afoot.

"I need to earn some money, Daddy. So I would like to do some work for you today at your office."

"Oh, really? Well, we do have some books that need shelving, do you think you can do that. And there may be some other work around there you can do as well. But if I let you work for me, you have to remember what I told you before about what I expect of you. Do you recall?"

"Yes, daddy. Strive for perfection and settle for excellence."

"That's right. Ok, then let's go."

When they got to Anderson's chambers that morning, he got Daniel settled in the library shelving books before he went into court. Daniel worked hard at his task, using a step ladder to reach the shelves that were too high for him. He had the job completed in no time at all and decided that he needed some more work to do. He asked Jennifer, his father's secretary, if he could go ask anybody else if they had some work he could do and she said yes. So he set off down the hall to talk to some of the other judges.

When Anderson finished court that morning, Daniel wasn't in his chambers. He wasn't worried, but he decided to go out and find him to see what he was up to. Just as he opened the door to the hallway, Daniel walked in the door grinning from ear to ear.

"Well hello there," Anderson said. "I was just about to come looking for you. Where have you been?"

"Oh, I was doing some work for some other people up here today. I told them I was trying to earn money for my scooter so they all gave me something to do. Daddy, everybody up here is nice to me. They all know my name and they paid me for my work too!"

"Well, Daniel, your dad is a judge," Anderson said laughing.

"No, daddy. They liked me!" he said emphatically, as if Anderson had nothing to do with it.

It was not lost on Anderson what intangible benefits would flow to Daniel because he was a judge and Alexa was a doctor, but for now, he was happy that it translated into more self confidence and happiness for Daniel.

Chapter 9A

Birth Mother

It was a day that started out like any other. Erica awoke to a cold house and an even colder life. She wondered what in the world she and D'Andre would do for food that day. The night before she had used the last of the beans they had for dinner. D'Andre complained because beans often gave him terrible gas. When Andre came home and saw what they were eating, he went into a tirade. It was as if they were insulting his manhood by eating beans for dinner.

"I know you are not feeding us this crap again. Don't you know how to cook? And where is all the money that I gave you for groceries? You must be spending it on crap. Or maybe you got a man and you givin' all my money to him?"

Erica had tried to hold her tongue but finally she couldn't take it anymore.

"We wouldn't have to eat beans for dinner if you would go out and get a job."

"I had a job, but I got laid off," he said defensively.

The reality was that his uncle had closed his auto repair shop when his diabetes made it too hard for him to work. Andre had been used to the lax schedule he was able to work at his uncle's shop—coming and going when he got ready, and thought that he could continue the same bad habits at the new garage. But the new owner didn't appreciate

Andre showing up late and when work got a little slow, Andre was the first to be let go. Erica was sick and tired of hearing Andre making excuses for his own poor decisions. She knew she should keep her thoughts to herself, but tonight she had just had enough of his whiny little pity party.

"Well what did you think would happen when you kept showing up late," Erica asked? Before the words were fully out of her mouth, she knew that she had crossed the line that would make Andre want to hit her. She tried to get up from the table to avoid the blows she was expecting, but she was too late. By the time she was halfway out of her chair, he was all over her, hitting her at first with his open hand and then with his fists. D'Andre screamed for his daddy to stop, but Andre just pushed him out of the way and kept going after her all the while cussing her for making him feel like he was less than a man. It ended like it always did, when he got tired.

"Why do you make me hit you?" he screamed.

She thought about saying something ridiculous like, "Because I like it when you give me a black eye. It gives me something to talk about with my friends." But instead, she just looked at him and said,

"How do you think you would feel if the love of your life beat you on a regular basis. The person you had built your life with, raised your child with, shared all your dreams with. How would you feel if you had to tell your eight year old son that he should still love his father when he watches him slap his mother around. Really, I'd like to know how you would feel?"

"I'm sorry," he said, retreating for the door.

Erica thought of picking up something to throw at the door after he closed it, but she knew that she should be the parent to their child who was standing in the middle of the floor with his head hung down.

Of all the regrets she had about Andre's behavior as it related to her, the worst was the impact she believed it was having on their son. She knew it was not good for D'Andre to see his father hit her so often. She feared that he would believe that battering women was perfectly acceptable. She hoped and prayed that Andre wasn't creating a batterer in D'Andre, but she knew that there was a good possibility that he was. Her other concern was just how depressed D'Andre got after an episode between them. Often after his father stormed out, D'Andre would rock back and forth like he was in a trance. Sometimes when he was already in bed, he would rock so hard that he would bang his head on the headboard. On those nights Erica would put a pillow against the headboard to try to soften the blow and then rub D'Andre's back until he calmed himself down. But even she knew that putting a pillow on a headboard to keep her child from hurting himself was an unsatisfactory and temporary solution for what she knew had to be deep pain that her child was experiencing over the situation.

Andre was in deep pain too. In his heart he knew that the rage he was feeling shouldn't be directed at Erica and D'Andre. He loved them both, but he felt so much pressure trying to be a man and provide for them. When money was good, and he could make sure that they had not only everything they needed but some of what they wanted too, they were happy and he felt good. He knew that he had done that. He had been the provider and taken care of his family like a man should. But when he couldn't provide for them, he didn't feel like a man and even the slightest sarcasm or cross-eyed look from Erica was enough to set him off and make him go into a rage. On those days, he hated her and D'Andre. He hated them for needing so much, for wanting so much and for expecting him to get it for them. And his hatred took the form of violence—violence toward the very family that he professed to love.

As he slammed the door and walked out of the house, he knew what he had to do. At the end of the day he knew he and Erica had to be responsible for their choice to have a child and D'Andre didn't ask to be here. He had to provide for his family and he had to do it any way he could. Without a high school education his job choices were limited. He would never make enough money legitimately to pull them above the poverty line. Even when he made a little extra money here and there, there was always some emergency, an illness a broken appliance that sucked that money up. Taking care of his family was his responsibility and he had to do it by any means necessary. As he thought about what would be necessary, he stopped and said a silent prayer before he backed out of the driveway.

As Erica moved to get out of bed the next morning, she winced from the pain she felt. She was just glad that Andre wasn't there. He had managed to bruise the entire left side of her face. She grimaced as she looked at herself in the mirror. As she was contemplating how she was going to cover the bruise she was snapped out of her own thoughts by the sound of the doorbell. Who could that be this early in the morning, she thought?

"I'll get it Mommy," D'Andre yelled from the living room where he was sleeping on the couch.

"Just a minute honey," she yelled, pulling on her robe and running her fingers through her hair as she stumbled toward the door. Standing at her door were two uniformed officers. She made D'Andre go into the bedroom and then opened the door tentatively.

"Hello, Mrs. Parker?" one of the officers asked.

"Yes?" Erica answered tentatively. "Do you need something?"

"Well, ma'am, we're here because your name and phone number were listed on the emergency contact card in Andre Parker's wallet. I assume you were his wife," the officer said.

Emergency contact card, she thought, her mind racing. Did he say "were his wife"? She was afraid to ask what kind of emergency there had been. She swallowed hard and then asked, "Exactly why is it that you're here?"

"Well, we regret to inform you that Andre Parker is dead. He was killed last night in a robbery."

"Why would anybody rob Andre?" she screamed through her tears.

"No ma'am, you don't understand. He was killed while he was trying to rob somebody."

"Oh, my God!" she screamed. "Why would he be involved in a robbery?"

But before she could finish the words, she already knew the answer to her question. Andre had been upset that he hadn't been able to be the man and bring home enough money for their family. She felt like she was going to pass out. She turned to grab the door handle to hold onto and as she did, she saw D'Andre coming out of the bedroom. But before she could move or say another word, she saw reporters with cameras approaching the front door. She tried to push D'Andre back inside, but it was too late.

"How do you feel knowing your husband was killed in a robbery?"

"Mama, mama," D'Andre yelled. "Is my daddy dead?"

"Please stop it," Erica screamed. "Can't you see you're upsetting my son?" She tried to push the door closed, but a reporter had jammed his body inside the door.

She looked at the police officer for help, but he just turned his head. The cameraman focused on her bruised face while the reporter continued to pepper her with questions.

"Were you having domestic problems? Is that what led him to rob that store?"

She ran into her bedroom, grabbing D'Andre by the hand. Once she had the door closed she felt momentarily relieved. A few minutes later she heard the front door close. Only then did she realize that the officer was gone too and she had no idea where to go to try to find Andre's body. As she moved toward the front door to peek out, she realized that nothing in her life had prepared her for this moment. She had no skills, no diploma, no husband and an eight-year old child to take care of by herself. And to top it off, she had no life insurance on Andre. Andre had not taken care of her in life and now, he wouldn't take care of her in death either.

As she approached the door, it flew open. She jumped back, fearing that the reporters had returned, but to her great relief, it was Andre's Aunt Muriel.

"What happened, Erica?"

"Andre is dead," she moaned, falling into Muriel's arms.

"Oh, my God! What happened?"

"He was killed in a robbery. There were reporters here and I was so scared. I didn't even get a chance to ask the police how to get Andre's body. What am I going to do?"

"Calm down, calm down, honey. Auntie M will take care of everything. Just go sit down."

Erica was exhausted and ready to let Muriel take over as she suggested. After all, she didn't have any idea what to do. She had never dealt with anyone's death before and didn't have a clue what to do first.

As she sat down, she watched Muriel move into action. She picked up a phone book that was on the kitchen counter and flipped it open.

"Hi, James? This is Muriel Parker. Well, it isn't good news if I'm calling you. My nephew has been killed—yeah, Andre."

Erica listened to Muriel's side of the conversation. She seemed to have such a sense of ease. Erica wouldn't have even known who to call or what to ask. She heard Muriel calmly explain the situation.

"Can y'all go down and pick up his body? What time can we meet you at the funeral home. Ok, we'll wait for your call and then we'll be right down. Thanks, goodbye."

"What happened?" Erica asked.

"They'll go right down and pick up his body and then we can go down to the funeral home and make all the arrangements for the service."

"But Aunt Muriel, I don't have any money. How will I pay for a funeral."

"Don't worry girl. Folks around here take care of each other. You'll see. People will be around here starting this evening and we just put a bowl on the table for the funeral expenses. Everybody will bring something and then we'll figure out how much money we have to work with. It will be fine, we'll have enough."

Erica had been so caught up in her conversation with Aunt Muriel that she had forgotten to check on D'Andre. When she opened the bedroom door, her breath froze in her chest. D'Andre was curled up on her bed in a fetal position rocking back and forth.

"Oh my God, D'Andre," she yelled!

"What happened?" Muriel screamed."

"He's just rocking. It's like he's in a trance."

"Has he done this before?"

"Yes, sometimes."

"Well, what do you do when it happens?"

"Just rub his back and try to calm him down. He usually feels better in a little while."

"Well, start rubbin' then, girl. You got to calm him down some."

"Come on baby," Erica crooned, "come on. Mommy's right here. Come back to me baby," she said as she rubbed his back. He didn't stop rocking, but he moved a little closer to her, pressing his small body against her hip. She kept rubbing and talking and eventually he started straightening his legs out, but he didn't stop rocking. So she laid down next to him and put her arms around him and began to rock too. At first she let him control the rocking back and forth. After a while, she took over and began to slow the rhythm down. She moved in tandem with him, but they went slower and slower and slower until finally, she stopped the rocking all together, but she held onto him tightly. His breathing slowed down and became more even and his small body melted into hers. Then he closed his eyes and drifted off to sleep.

Later that evening, just as Muriel had predicted, people started coming by her house. Erica and Muriel had been to the funeral home earlier that day and had gotten an idea how much money they needed for the funeral. It was clearly more than Erica had and she was scared. But Muriel had calmed her down and told her not to worry because this was the kind of community that took care of its own. That evening, people started coming by, bringing food and drinks and money. The little basket they had placed on the table for donations filled up and then they emptied it. It filled again and then again. By the end of the evening when they counted the money, there was almost three thousand dollars, which was more than enough to get the funeral package they wanted.

Erica kept D'Andre close to her for the next couple of days. She knew that his emotional state was very fragile and getting him through the funeral would be an ordeal. Not only was his father dead, but D'andre knew that his father had died as a thief. She felt like she should talk to somebody about how to get D'Andre through the trauma of his father's death, but she didn't really know anyone to turn to. At the end of the day, she knew it was her job to take care of D'Andre and her job alone.

Chapter 9B

Earth Mother

It was a day that started out like any other day. Alexa could smell the coffee that Anderson always left brewing for her. The night before they had ordered in a wonderful meal from their favorite Chinese restaurant and then the three of them had played a game of Scrabble. They had started playing Scrabble as a family right after Daniel started kindergarten. Alexa had read somewhere how much it could help Daniel with his spelling and she had always loved playing herself. He had taken to it right away and they played as often as they could.

Even though they both had said they were tired, when they got to bed, Alexa and Anderson couldn't keep their hands off of each other. Alexa knew that as hard as Anderson worked, he always seemed to save his best for her. It was just one of the things that made her love him. That night their lovemaking had been especially passionate. She had found a new massage cream that had phermones in it and she had been anxious to use it with Anderson. They bathed together in their big whirlpool tub with only candlelight in the room. Anderson had brought home some new wine and they sipped it as they bathed. When they got out of the tub, Anderson wrapped a towel around her and then gently began to dry her legs and feet. He picked up the cream she had bought and slowly began to massage it into her feet. When he finished, he worked his way up her legs, starting with her calves and then moving to her thighs. When he reached her thighs, he massaged them with both hands until her back arched back in delight. He gently picked her up carried her into their bedroom. She tried to roll on top of him so she could massage him for a while, but he pushed her back down and said, "Next time. Tonight is going to be about you." And it was. There didn't seem to be an inch of her body that Anderson left untouched. His mouth covered hers hungrily and he sucked her tongue as if it was the sweetest thing he had ever tasted. When she thought she just couldn't take it any longer, he gently entered her, rocking in rhythm with her gyrating hips. Everything seemed to be in tandem that night. Alexa felt like she was in heaven with Anderson. He reached beneath her and pulled her into him harder and harder until they both exploded in ecstasy. Spent and exhausted, they fell asleep in each other's arms.

The next morning as she turned over, she winced at the pleasant pain she felt between her legs. Anderson had been so passionate in their love making the night before that he had actually left little bruises on her thighs. She was lulled out of her pleasant day dream about the night before when the doorbell rang. Who could that be this early in the morning she thought.

She grabbed a robe and ran her fingers through her hair as she stumbled toward the door. As she looked out the peephole, her heart stopped. Standing at her door were two uniformed officers. She opened the door tentatively.

"Hello officers."

"Mornin' Mrs. Pierce . . . uh, Dr. Pierce. May we come in?"

Yes she said, " an icy feeling creeping over her.

"Without asking, they moved toward the living room and motioned for her to sit down. She shook her head, but held onto the edge of the sofa in front of the Scrabble board, still set up from the game they had played the night before.

"Dr. Pierce, we regret to inform you that your husband was killed in a robbery."

"No," she screamed, "why would somebody rob Anderson?"

"No, he walked in on a store clerk being robbed early this morning. He tried to talk the guy down. He actually saved the clerk's life."

"Did they catch the guy?"

"He was killed also. While he was distracted by your husband, the clerk was able to get his own gun. He shot the robber, but not before he had already killed your husband."

She stood there swaying back and forth in stunned silence. How could this be? She and Anderson loved each other. They had a child who needed his Daddy that they were supposed to raise together. They were young, they had faith and believed in God. How could He do this to them? She felt herself swaying the way she did when she was trying to do the standing tree pose in her yoga class but just couldn't keep her balance, and then she fainted.

When Alexa was awakened by the smelling salts, she was on a paramedic's stretcher. She glanced around frantically. Her first thoughts were of Daniel. When she couldn't see him, she became frantic.

"Daniel, Daniel!"

"Calm down Dr. Pierce. We have your son in the kitchen."

"What happened?"

"You fainted and fell and hit your head on the side of the table. You have a nasty gash."

She looked down for the first time and saw blood all over the front of her white robe. A couple of Scrabble tiles were pasted to her robe in the sticky blood. She looked around the room and realized she must have hit the Scrabble board when she fell. The board was upended and there were Scrabble pieces everywhere. There were blood stains on the new berber carpet that they had just gotten to replace the outdated shag carpet. She tried to steady her voice so they would let her see Daniel.

"Can you bring my son in here please?"

"Ma'am, we need to get you to the hospital right away."

"I know. But my son must be frightened. He's only eight. Let me just tell him what happened."

"Alright ma'am. Just a minute."

Nothing in her life had prepared her for this moment. How was she going to tell Daniel his father was gone? He had already been abandoned by one set of parents. Now the only dad he had ever known had left him too. As she was composing her thoughts, Daniel ran into the living room, his eyes wide with fear.

"Mommy! What happened? Why are these people here. What happened to your head? Where did all that blood come from?"

She sat up painfully and wrapped her arms around his skinny body. He was trembling. Inside she was trembling too, but she needed to remain calm right now.

"Daniel, you know God loves us, right?"

"Yes mommy, " he said a little tentatively.

"He loves us the way mommy and daddy love you—with all His heart. And God is with us every day because he lives inside you. We ask God to protect us and watch over us and He does. But all He really owes us is a beautiful life in heaven. That is our reward for our faith. Today He gave that reward to your Daddy. He gave him a place in heaven. Daddy didn't want to leave us, but he had to go. Do you understand?

"Daddy went to heaven today?"

"Yes, baby."

"But I didn't get to tell him goodbye."

"We can talk to him together later when we say our prayers," she said, trying to console him. But in reality, she felt the same way Daniel did. There was so much that had been left unsaid. So much more they needed to talk about. Where would they send Daniel to college? Where would they live in

retirement? Were they ready to file their taxes yet? How could he just leave them? The thought of it was overwhelming.

"In the meantime, you can see mommy hit her head and I need to go to the doctor, so bring me the phone so I can call Saundria and see if she can watch you for a little while."

"No! You can't leave me too! What if you don't come back either?" he wailed.

At that point he began to cry inconsolably and she realized she hadn't thought about how frightening it would be for Daniel if she left him too—especially all covered in blood and looking as she did. Through her own pain, both physical and emotional she regrouped and came up with an alternate plan.

"Honey, bring mommy the phone and I'll call and see if Aunt Saundria can ride with us to the hospital."

But before he could answer her, Saundria was standing by her side.

"What do you need honey?" Saundria asked.

It was the voice of an angel. Saundria and Jack had lived next door to them forever. They were both lawyers and they had a little girl who was just a couple months older than Daniel. The four of them had often joked about how they would marry their kids off to each other. Saundria was a good and dependable friend. They often left their kids at each other's house so they could run errands or sometimes when either of them didn't have a sitter.

"Can you ride with me and Daniel to the hospital, please?"

"Sure honey, but where's Anderson?"

Anderson she thought. Had it only been a few minutes since the officers had told her he was dead. It seemed like a dream from some earlier time. She remembered hearing the words of the officers and then nothing. For the first time she had to really focus on the fact that her husband was dead and she began to weep. The sorrow in her eyes must have said it all because Saundria didn't say another word. She just squeezed her shoulders and kissed her cheek then turned and picked up Daniel.

"Come on honey. We're going to ride with your mommy to go get her head fixed."

Alexa saw Saundria walking briskly toward the front door, grabbing Alexa's purse and keys with one hand and holding Daniel firmly with the other. Alexa allowed herself to feel momentarily relieved by that kind gesture. Shortly after that the paramedics were pushing her toward the same door. She realized it would be the first time she left this house as a widow. Alexa, Saundria and Daniel all got into the back of the ambulance with one paramedic for the short ride to the hospital. In the ambulance, the paramedic sat on one side and Saundria sat on the other side of her holding her hand while she balanced Daniel on her lap.

"Honey, we're here for you. Whatever you need. We'll get you situated and we'll look after Daniel."

Alexa was really just too tired to respond, so she just nodded her head. When the ambulance arrived at the emergency room entrance, Alexa could see through the windows that there were television cameras everywhere. Although it was easy for Alexa to forget about his celebrity, Anderson was a well-known judge who had tried many high profile cases in his years on the bench. She realized she wasn't going to be able to shield Daniel from the reporters when they started questioning her about the robbery. Momentary panic set in, but Saundria squeezed her hand reassuringly and said, "I'm right here with you honey."

Alexa sat up and moved closer to Daniel and grabbed his little hands in hers.

"Would you sit my stretcher up please?", she asked the paramedic.

"Come on baby, mommy's right here."

The reporters were on them as son as the doors to the ambulance opened, snapping pictures and asking questions.

"Dr. Pierce, what was your reaction when you heard your husband was dead?"

What a stupid question she thought. Maybe she should say something ridiculous like, "Oh it didn't bother me as much as getting the wrong order from the take out restaurant last night." Instead, she looked directly at the reporter and said,

"How do you think you would feel if the love of your life was killed suddenly in a robbery? The man you have built your life with, raised a child with, shared all your dreams with. How would you feel if you had to tell your eight-year old son that he was never going to see his father again, that God had taken him to heaven? Really, I'd like to know how you would feel?"

The stunned reporter answered her, "I would be devastated."

"And how would your children feel if they suddenly lost a parent and then moments later reporters with cameras were surrounding them, taking their picture," she continued

He replied, "They would be horribly upset and scared."

"And what would you do to someone who bombarded your scared child with stupid questions about how they felt about the fact that their dad had died unexpectedly?"

As she finished this last question, she glared at the other reporters who where already shrinking away.

"We're sorry for your loss ma'am, " he replied, also retreating.

With that Alexa Pierce, head held high was rolled into the emergency room holding her son's hand. Nobody bothered them again. But it was clear to Alexa that Daniel was terribly bothered and upset by what had happened both to his dad and to her. She knew she needed to deal with his concerns right away and she knew just how to do that.

"Saundria," she said turning to her friend, "can I ask you one more favor please?"

"Of course, honey, what do you need?"

"Would you call Jasmine and get her to come over right away to see Daniel?"

"I'll call her right now."

Jasmine was a friend of theirs that was a child psychologist. Alexa knew from their conversations that Jasmine had done a lot of work with children who had faced trauma in the lives, including the death of a loved one. Even though Daniel would eventually have the comfort of knowing that his father had died a hero, she needed to deal with how he felt today. She didn't know how Daniel might deal with his father's death, but she knew she didn't want to wait until he was having problems before she took some action. In this case, she wanted to be proactive not reactive. Right now that meant having him talk to a psychologist as quickly as possible.

Chapter 10A

Birth Mother

Thanks to the generosity of their friends and neighbors Erica was able to collect enough money to have a small service at the neighborhood church. After counting out what they needed there was still a little money left over. Erica thought they should probably save it for necessities, but Muriel insisted that she take some of the money to go get her hair fixed for the funeral. She told Erica that it was important that she look good even if she wasn't feeling so good. Erica got D'Andre dressed and carried him downstairs to Muriel's house.

"Hey, Aunt Muriel. It's us," Erica called out as she went through the kitchen door.

"Come on in baby. I was wondering what was taking you so long. You better get on to your hair appointment. You were lucky she agreed to take you at the last minute like this."

"Yeah, I know. And you were right. I really do need to get my hair done before the service. I know it will make me feel a lot better. Thanks for keeping an eye on D'Andre. I brought some toys that he likes in case he gets upset. And I put a few snacks in this bag."

"Erica. Get outta here please. I was raising children before you were even being thought about. D'Andre and I are going to be just fine. Now go," she said as she pushed Erica toward the door.

Erica smiled as she waved over her shoulder. She quickly walked to the corner and arrived just in time to catch the bus she needed. When she got to the beauty shop, it was packed. On Fridays, there was usually a big crowd of ladies getting ready for their weekend dates. Today was no different.

"Hey Erica," Vonna said cheerfully as Erica walked in.

"Hey Vonna. Thanks for taking me on such short notice."

"No problem girl. It's the least I could do. We got to have you looking nice for that service tomorrow. I'm so sorry about Andre, girl. And there's no charge for your service today either."

"Really? Thank you so much," Erica said trying to hold back the tears that were welling behind her eyelids. Everybody really was being so good to them, and right now she really appreciated living in a community where people reached out to take care of each other in their times of need.

"Come on, let's get you started."

Vonna usually had a shampoo girl take care of shampooing her clients so she could just take care of styling her clients' hair. But everyone knew she was famous for her shampoos and today she decided to shampoo Erica's hair herself. Erica leaned back into the shampoo bowl and Vonna raised the footrest so she could relax. Then Vonna reached in the back of the cabinet for some of her special shampoo. As she worked up a lather and began to rub Erica's head, she could feel the tension leaving her neck. All she could think was that this woman had magic fingers. She started out slow, rubbing the nape of her neck, then her temples and then finally ending with a vigorous rub of her scalp. It was heavenly. After the first shampoo, Erica lost count. She didn't exactly fall asleep, but she felt that she was as close to it as she could get.

After Vonna conditioned her hair and rolled it up, she placed Erica under a hot dryer. Although she handed her a couple of magazines to read, Erica nodded off almost as soon as the dryer started. When she woke up, she was initially disoriented. She couldn't remember where she was or why she was there. Going to the hairdresser was a luxury that she could only afford a couple of times a year. The rest of the time she just bought the products she needed at the beauty supply store and did her hair herself. She straightened herself up and looked around. Vonna was nowhere to be seen. Erica knew that by now she was up front working on another client. Every dryer in the place was occupied. The women in the two dryers right next to her were engrossed in conversation. Even though the way they were turned toward each other seemed conspiratorial, they had to talk loud to hear each other over the noise of their dryers. At first Erica wasn't paying much attention to them, but then she heard a snippet of their conversation that made even her ears perk up.

" . . . . and Andre said he wouldn't have even been with her except that she tricked him by getting pregnant," the woman closest to Erica said.

Who were they talking about? It couldn't be her Andre. She wanted to hear the rest of their conversation, so she lifted her own dryer hood, but picked up one of the magazines in her lap and pretended to bury her head in it.

"I know girl. And it was probably her demanding, whiny ass that got him killed. Didn't you tell me she was always pressuring him to bring home more money for that baby," the other one almost screamed back.

"Yeah. He was supposed to be going over to my girl's house that night he was killed, but she called me later to say he didn't show. I think his baby momma had done something to get him upset again like she always did. He said she would never fix him any decent food. Half the time, he had to go to my girl's house just so he could get something to eat."

Just as the other one was about to answer, Vonna came back into the room. It was clear from the look on her face that she had heard the tale end of the conversation as she came in. She shot the women an icy stare and then rushed over to Erica.

"C'mon girl, let's get you out of here," she said as she grabbed her hand. But Erica's hand was trembling and she could barely move. At this point, the woman whose back had been to Erica turned around. Instead of shock at seeing Erica, her face registered pure contempt and she just sucked her teeth. Erica was speechless, but she allowed herself to be lifted from the chair and guided into the other room.

"Vonna, who is that woman that was sitting next to me?"

"Girl, that's nobody. Don't even worry about it."

"But I know she was talking about Andre and about me—and I don't even know her."

"And you don't want to either. She's just a little tramp who works down at the diner at the truck stop."

"I think she was talking about somebody who was seeing Andre. It sounded like they were lovers from what she was saying. Is that true?"

"Why do you want to know? What difference does it make now? You can't miss what you can't measure. Your job now is to take care of your son and take care of yourself. And you can't do either worrying about something that you can't do nothin' about. Let it go and give up the idea of ever having a better past."

"You're right Vonna. It's just that I want to at least hold on to the memory of what we had together."

"You can girl. Nobody but you knows what you really had. People always think they know what's going on in somebody else's house. But they on the outside lookin' in. Only you know for sure what you and Andre had. Hold onto that girl."

Erica thought about what Vonna said. In a way she was right. Nobody could really ever know what was going on in someone else's house. But now, she was beginning to wonder if she even knew what was really going on in her own house. Had Andre been cheating on her? And if so, with who and for how long? It didn't seem like it really even mattered anymore now that he was dead. She was going to take Vonna's advice and just try to hold onto the memories of the good times and let the rest go.

On the day of the funeral, Erica decided she would put her best face forward. Her hair was freshly done and she had also been able to get a new dress for the service. She dressed D'Andre in his nicest outfit and they rode to the small church in their neighborhood with Andre's aunt and uncle. When they arrived, people were already starting to enter the church. She could see that many of Andre's friends and D'Andre's classmates had showed up. It made Erica happy that her son could see how many people had liked his dad. This was especially so since there was so much negative talk about the way Andre had been killed.

They walked toward their seats at the front of the church. Before sitting down, they stopped at the casket together. Erica had already seen Andre at the funeral home, but this would be the first time that D'Andre had seen him and she was worried about what his reaction would be. The funeral home had done a good job and he really looked natural as the old folks would say. When D'Andre approached, Erica could see that he had a puzzled look on his face more than anything else. She looked at him expectedly and he turned to her and said," Mommy is my daddy sleeping?"

"No baby, he's not. He is dead. You know that."

"But he doesn't look dead. He looks like he is sleeping. Are you sure he can't get up?"

With that, the first big tear rolled down Erica's face. The last two days it had been hard for her to cry. She had been so angry at Andre for everything, for mistreating her, for leaving them like this and maybe even for cheating on her. But now, her son's innocence had overwhelmed her emotionally and she just let the tears flow.

"Come on baby. Let's sit down."

They took their seats in the front row. Immediately afterwards, people began to come forward to view the body. As they did so, they would turn and come and offer their condolences to Erica and Andre and his other family members who were sitting with them. There was a parade of familiar faces. Andre's coach from high school and his favorite teacher. Some of the guys from the auto shop came up next. Then Erica saw a face, that made her heart stop. It was the woman from the beauty shop and she was walking down the aisle holding onto another young woman who looked like she was so overcome by grief that she could barely walk. Erica began to fume. Was this the woman that Andre was seeing? How dare she show her face in here at her husband's funeral? Erica didn't know whether she should confront her or just let it go.

Just as she was sorting through her feelings, the two women approached the casket. The woman from the beauty shop shot a sideways glance at Erica and then turned her attention back to her friend. Everybody who had come up so far had respectfully viewed the body, nodded and moved on. But Erica could see that this woman had no intention of moving on. She placed her hands on the side of the casket and began to weep uncontrollably. Then without any warning, she reached into the casket and began to hold onto Andre's body. Her friend tried to pull her back, but she shook her off and started wailing, "why baby, why did you leave me?"

Erica was on her feet before she even realized it. She pushed the woman from the beauty shop out of the way and then grabbed the woman who had obviously been having an affair with her husband and slapped her across the face. She hadn't intended to do that, but it just happened. A collective gasp went through the church. The woman, who had only moments before been wracked with grief turned into the bitch from hell.

"Oh no you didn't just slap me, bitch," the woman yelled at Erica. "I'm gonna kick your ass up in here in front of God and everybody."

Erica tried to step back, but the woman pushed her with both hands before she could get away. Instinctively, Erica pushed her back, but the woman was standing too close to the casket. The force of Erica's push forced the woman against the casket and caused it to be knocked off the pedestal. Before anyone could even react, Andre's body tumbled out of the casket and onto the floor. Aunt Muriel screamed and promptly fainted. The woman from the Beauty shop helped her girlfriend up and they quickly scurried away. Erica was standing there in shock not knowing what to do. The funeral director and his staff moved quickly to the front to pick up Andre's body and put it back into the casket. Other people rushed up too in an effort to be of help. Suddenly, the entire place was filled with commotion and noise. Everything and everyone was moving quickly, but to Erica it seemed like it was happening in slow motion. And then she turned to look at her son. What she saw caused her heart to leap into her throat. D'Andre was curled up in the front pew of the church rocking back and forth and hitting his head on the back of the pew.

CHAPTER 10B

Earth Mother

Alexa knew that she had to start planning Anderson's funeral as soon as she got out of the hospital. Unfortunately, that meant that she had to go downtown to his office where he kept their important papers. They had both decided long ago that with the ever present possibility of hurricanes and other natural disasters in Houston, that they would keep their emergency files in Anderson's office at the courthouse. The building had been built in the early 50's at the height of the cold war and it was the only official bomb shelter in town. They had placed their insurance policies, will and some other documents related to the house and basic information about all of their financial advisors in a fireproof metal box and Anderson had taken it all downtown. It had been years since she had seen any of that stuff.

When she got to the courthouse, the court security officers escorted her to Anderson's chambers immediately. His secretary jumped up from her desk as soon as she walked in.

"Alexa, oh, my God, oh my God. What will we ever do without the judge."

"I know she said," hugging the woman who had been Anderson's secretary almost as long as she had been his wife. "It's going to be hard for all of us. Right now I need to get our insurance papers and start planning his funeral."

"I think he still keeps that metal box on the shelf in his closet. Go on in. Let me know if I can help you with anything."

"Thanks Jennifer. I appreciate it."

Alexa went into the office and closed the door behind her. She had been in this office many times over the years, but she was always struck by how beautiful it was with the paneled walls and bookshelves and the cordovan leather desk and chairs. She went straight to the closet where she knew their fire proof box would be. As she opened the door, she was overcome by Anderson's smell. He kept two of his robes hanging there that were still thick with the smell of his cologne. Just standing there taking in his scent made Alexa's knees go weak.

She held onto the doorknob to steady herself and then stood on her tiptoes looking at the shelf above for the metal box. She could just barely make it out. She looked around to see if there was a chair, but the closest one which sat behind his desk had wheels on it. She decided to just stand on her tiptoes to try to reach the box. Just as her fingers touched the box, she could feel a plastic bag was underneath of it. She decided to use the bag to pull the box forward. As she did so, the bag slipped off the edge of the shelf and a handful of letters came raining down on her.

At first she just started to grab the letters and put them back into the bag, but as she gathered them in her hands, she could see that they were all in pastel colored envelopes with Anderson's name scrawled across the front. What caught her attention was the sweeping line under his name, that had a heart on the end of it for punctuation. If she didn't know better, she would think these were love letters of some sort. Her heart began to race, but she took the stack of letters and sat down at Anderson's desk. She opened the first letter and could instantly smell the faint scent of perfume. The letter was dated nearly three years ago and was addressed, "My Dearest Andy". Andy? Who would dare address Anderson as Andy? That was something that he didn't even allow her to do. Only his mother and brother had ever called him Andy. She was incensed, but she had to read on. The letter continued:

> *Today was another wonderful Saturday with you. I could hardly wait for you to get here after your son's soccer game. Even though we only have this little time together, it is comforting to know that you will be here every weekend. I know how precious your time is and I appreciate it. But just one weekend, I wish that we could actually spend the night together and not have to rush off at the end of another beautiful afternoon in each other's arms. Please try to figure out how we can spend a weekend together.*
>
> *Until then . . . . all my love,*
>
> *Denise*

Alexa's head was swirling and her heart felt as if it was going to beat out of control. She wanted to scream, but instead she bit her trembling lip and fell back into the leather desk chair for support. The questions in her mind were coming rapid fire. Who in the hell was Denise and how long had she been having an affair with Anderson? Did Anderson really spend every Saturday afternoon with her when he told them that he was working? Was Anderson in love with her too. How could he have been having an affair with somebody else when things seemed so perfect at home? She wanted to know more, and so she opened another envelope. The letter started with the same greeting, "My Dearest Andy" and read:

> *I can't begin to tell you how much it meant to me to be able to spend the weekend with you. I will never forget the time we had together. The walks on the beach, drinks in front of the fireplace and making love until dawn. You are an incredible lover and I can hardly wait to see you next weekend. I know that for you I represent a forbidden fruit, but for me you are my safe harbor. You are somebody I know I can depend on, week in and week out. It is hard to believe it has already been two years now. I*

> *almost feel guilty sometimes since we met while I sat at your table during the Links dinner, but then I realize that it must have been God's divine plan for me to sit next to you that night. My life has never been the same since then and I hope that we will be together forever.*
>
> *All my love,*
>
> *Denise*

This time Alexa had trouble suppressing a scream. Before she knew it, Jennifer had thrown the door open to check on her. She quickly covered the letters with some legal pads that were laying on the side of the desk.

"Are you alright, Alexa?" Jennifer asked.

"Yes, yes, I'm fine," she managed to say. "It's just a little bit hard getting through this."

"Can I help you?"

"No, no. Please. I really need to be alone right now. I'm sorry if I startled you in any way. If I need anything, I'll let you know. Ok?"

"Ok, then. I'll be right outside. Just call me if you need me."

Denise! That bitch. They were both members of the same social, service organization—the Links—and Denise was one of her Link sisters. Alexa remembered that dinner well. Because Denise had been recently widowed, she didn't have anyone to sit with so Alexa had graciously offered to let her sit with them. She had even insisted that she sit next to Anderson and had asked Anderson to be attentive to their guest at dinner because she was alone. Well the old adage must be true, "No good deed goes unpunished." So many things were clicking into place now. Anderson working every Saturday after the games, the weekend conferences that he wanted to attend alone, even the fact that she could never reach him on his land line when he worked on Saturdays. How could this have happened? She knew that the letters would hold some of the answers, so despite her pain she continued to read on.

What she found was that although Anderson apparently loved her, he felt that he had married too young before he had really had a chance to live. And although he loved his family, he thought that Alexa was too devoted to Daniel and that their relationship had changed after he came into their lives. He wanted the carefree life they had before they became parents and Denise was apparently willing and able to indulge him in this fantasy. It was all too much coming on the heels of Anderson's death. But even in her pain, Alexa was determined that Anderson's reputation remain intact, if not for him, then for Daniel's sake. She gathered up all the letters and put them back in the bag. She put the bag into her briefcase to take with her. After she located the insurance policy and the will, she placed the metal box back on the shelf. Then she realized that this wouldn't be Anderson's office anymore and she would have to take that box and all of his other things home too, so she retrieved the metal box, shut the door, turned off the lights and left the building.

Alexa planned a funeral to end all funerals. All of the judges were invited and were to attend in their robes. Alexa had managed to catch up with her good friend, gospel singer Yolanda Adams, who also lived in Houston, and she had agreed to sing at the funeral. And as usual, her Link sisters planned to show up in force, all dressed in white, to perform a traditional ceremony for Links or connecting Links, as they called their husbands. Alexa just prayed that Denise didn't have the nerve to show up at the services.

On the day of the service the church was packed to the brim. When Alexa and Daniel arrived there were so many cars in the parking lot that their limousine could barely get through. In addition to the funeral home and their security detail, there was a second security detail from the court. Alexa knew that at least she and Daniel would be well protected—but from what? When they walked into the sanctuary, every head turned to watch them. She was resplendent in a new black designer suit, a fresh haircut and some sexy black sling back pumps. She wore a small hat with a slight veil. She never understood why anyone wore veils until now, but today she was grateful for the cover it provided for her puffy eyes.

When they got to the front, the ceremony began. There were so many people who wanted to speak at the services that she had to choose carefully so as not to offend anyone. Then the guys from Anderson's fraternity performed a traditional farewell to their fallen brother. After that, it was time for her Link sisters to come up and perform a traditional ceremony for deceased spouses of Link members. Alexa just knew that Denise would not have the nerve to come up with the rest of the sisters, but to her great shock and amazement , she did. Alexa's breath caught in her throat and she began to clutch at her pearls. Despite her shock and outrage, however, she was able to maintain her composure and smile at her Link sisters as they performed their ceremony. At one point, Alexa caught Denise looking directly at her, but when she did, Denise quickly averted her eyes. Was that guilt or was Denise trying to figure out if she knew. In the end, Alexa realized that despite her pain, her and Anderson's reputation was important to the future happiness of her son and she was not going to do anything that might upset his world. As she gritted her teeth, she could feel the acid attacking the lining of her stomach. She thought how much better she would feel if she could just go slap Denise in her face right now. At that moment, Daniel leaned over and put his head on her lap.

Chapter 11A

Birth Mother

In the weeks that followed Andre's death, all Erica could think about was how he had ruined her life, and left her with a humiliating finale to deal with. Not only did she have to deal with Andre being a poor provider and a thief but he had also cheated with some two bit bitch who humiliated their entire family by performing at the funeral. Erica knew she should have controlled herself, but with all that she had gone through, she just wasn't able to do so. The scene at the funeral was the talk of the town. Erica and D'Andre could barely show their faces around town without people pointing and whispering about how Andre had been killed in a robbery and how D'Andre's momma was crazy too since she slapped a woman so hard that she had knocked her into the casket and made Andre's body fall out onto the floor.

Then early one morning, about three weeks after the funeral, Erica heard somebody outside messing with their car. When she opened the door, some guys were hooking Andre's car up to a tow truck.

"What are you doing?" she demanded.

"We're repossessing your car," the man said snarling at her.

"We don't owe anything on that old car. My husband paid cash for it years ago."

"That may be, but he pledged the car for a loan and gave us the title two months ago. See for yourself," he said as he handed her the paperwork.

Erica read in disbelief a loan document from an outfit called "Cash for your Car". The slogan underneath read, "You get the cash, you keep the car, we keep the title". Andre had given them his title for two hundred fifty dollars in cash and then failed to pay it back. Now they were there to take the car because they already had the title and there was nothing she could do about it.

"Look, my husband is dead. Can I give you the two hundred and fifty dollars he borrowed?"

"I'm sorry ma'am for your loss. But the amount owed now is going to based on the value of the car. You'd have to buy it back at fair market value."

"You've got to be kidding. I have to pay to get my own car back?"

"It's not your car anymore. It's owned by the guy who has the title." And with that he closed the door to the tow truck and drove off with the car in tow.

Erica just hung her head in despair. And to top it all off, Andre had never gotten her wedding ring out of the pawn shop and that was now gone too. In the confusion and crisis following Andre's death, Erica had forgotten that they had pawned her ring. She went back to the pawn shop two days after the ten day grace period she had to redeem her ring and found it for sale in a case with a price tag of five hundred and fifty dollars. She tried to argue with the owner, then reason with him, even to prevail upon his sympathy since her husband had died. All of this was to no avail. He said she could have the ring back, but she had to pay the new sales price of five hundred dollars, not the ninety-five dollars she owed on her debt. She left the shop feeling that her loss of Andre was somehow amplified by the loss of the ring.

By the time Erica had managed to get to D'Andre in the church that day of the funeral, he had banged his head on the pew so hard that he had managed to draw blood. She wasn't even able to stay for the service because D'Andre was in such acute distress, rocking back and forth while he was balled up in a fetal position. They had rushed him to the hospital, and after they bandaged up his head, they gave them a referral to MHMRA—the Mental Health Mental Retardation Authority. Erica didn't waste any time calling to get D'Andre an appointment, and she was fortunate to be assigned to a young new therapist who arranged to see them the very next week.

The therapist had an office in a small house close to where they lived. Erica immediately liked the homey atmosphere she felt when she walked in. D'Andre was with her, but she had told him very little about the purpose of their visit—only that they were going to see a doctor about everything that had happened to them. It was clear to Erica, however, that D'Andre really understood why they were there.

When the doctor came out to see them, Erica stood up nervously and extended her hand.

"Hi, I'm Dr. Peters."

"Hello, I'm Erica and this is my son, D'Andre."

"Well come on in and let's get started."

Dr. Peters lead them down a small hall and stopped at a brightly colored room that was filled with toys and games. A young woman came to the door and Dr. Peters introduced her and asked her to take D'Andre in to allow him to play with the toys.

Erica followed Dr. Peters into an adjoining office that had a glass wall in it that allowed them to look in on D'Andre while they spoke. The office wasn't very large, but it was filled to the brim with furniture. There was a soft couch with lots of pillows on it and another chair on the side of it. A coffee table sat in front of them that contained a pretty container of flowers. A large armoire sat in the corner that was filled with all sorts of gifts and knick knacks and a large bookshelf was placed on another wall that was filled with books. It almost seemed like there was too much furniture in the room, but instead of feeling crowded it gave one the sense of being in a cocoon and it felt safe and comfortable. Erica immediately began to tell her story. The words seemed to tumble from her lips like she had been holding them in for too long. For a long time, Dr. Peters just listened and nodded her head. Then she began to ask a few questions. Erica told her how D'Andre would ball himself up and start rocking back and forth and how he had banged his head at the funeral until it bled.

Dr. Peters explained to Erica how D'Andre's actions were in response to the stress and trauma that had been created in the home atmosphere from the abusive behavior of his father. It was his own way of retreating from the unpleasantness of the conflict between his parents. She explained that D'Andre needed a safe place to express his feelings not only about what happened with the death of his father, but also other things in his home that had caused him so much pain and anxiety. They made a plan to begin sessions that would be held both for Erica and D'Andre individually and some that would be held together. For the first time in a long time, Erica felt like she could feel hopeful that things would be ok for her and D'Andre.

As soon as Erica walked in the door of her house the phone was ringing. She was half afraid to answer it. These days it was either a bill collector or some friend calling to ask more questions than she really felt like answering. But today her talk with the therapist had given her a little more courage than usual so she picked up the phone on the fourth ring.

"Hello," Erica said hesitantly.

"Hey Erica, it's me, Peaches. Girl, I been trying to call you for a few days.

"Oh yeah, what's up," Erica said, half expecting to hear the same series of questions that she had been getting lately from all of her old high school buddies. "What you gonna do now that Andre's gone?" "Who was that crazy bitch at the funeral?" "How you and little D'Andre gonna make it girl—his people gonna throw you out?" Some days it was just all she could do to say she didn't want to discuss any of that. In reality, she felt like saying, mind your own business, but she never did. She waited for Peaches to continue.

"Well, look girl, me and some of the girls been thinkin' about you and hoping you ok. So we wanted to see if you could come over for dinner on Friday night, maybe play some cards, have a few drinks and take your mind off things for a minute."

"Uh, yeah," Erica said, a little stunned. She had been so ready to have to defend herself again that Peaches' small act of kindness had left her speechless. "I would like that Peaches."

"Ok, then. Well come over about 7:30. And bring D'Andre with you. He can play with my kids while we have dinner."

"Ok, thanks girl. I really appreciate it. I'll see you then."

Erica hung up the phone feeling more light hearted than she had in weeks. She was so happy to have something fun to look forward to. It had been so long since she had seen a lot of the girls she used to be so close to in high school. After D'Andre was born she made an effort to keep in touch. Although many of her girlfriends had babies early too, not one of their boyfriends had stuck with them. Whenever Erica had talked about trying to get together with them over the years, Andre had as much as forbidden it. He had told her he didn't want her hanging around those women because he was sure that all they did was man bash all day and he wasn't having that kind of attitude come into his house. Eventually, it had caused Erica and her girlfriends to drift apart, so she was really surprised that they had reached out to her now when she needed them most.

When Friday night came, she and D'Andre took the bus over to Peaches' house. It was a small shotgun house on the edge of town on a street filled with similar houses. As they walked down the street, people waved at them from their front porches. Most of the houses were painted white, but almost all of them looked as if they hadn't seen paint in more than twenty years. The porches were filled with an assortment of odd furniture—old couches, broken rocking chairs and cheap lawn chairs. Most of them also had barbeque pits on them and as they walked down the street, they noticed that several people had their grills fired up and were cooking on them getting ready for a night of partying.

Finally they arrived at the house that Peaches lived in at the end of a dead end street. The yard looked like it must have had grass at some time, but was now just a dusty brown patch of dirt. There were children's toys strewn across the front of the house and a big wooden swing hung from the porch. The front door was open, but a dilapidated screen door was in place in a vain attempt to keep the bugs out. Erica approached the house and knocked on the screen door, yelling out for Peaches.

"Hello, we're here."

Erica could see straight through the house to the back yard from the front door, but she didn't see anybody.

"We're in the back," she heard a voice yell out.

Erica climbed down off the steps and she and D'Andre made their way to the back of the house. When she got there, she saw that several of her friends were already there, sitting around at card tables that had been set up in the back yard. Peaches got up and greeted her warmly with a big hug. Then she went around the tables and hugged and kissed all her girlfriends. D'Andre had already run off to play with the other kids who were happily involved in a game of football.

"Girl, we are so glad to see you," Peaches said.

"It's good to be seen," Erica replied. "Thank you so much for getting me out of the house. It has been really hard lately."

"I know, I know. But you with your sisters now, so just relax."

"Yeah, now that your man is gone, maybe you can hang out with us sometime," said her girlfriend Cristal.

"Sure. I'd like that."

"To be honest," Cristal continued, "we was all hatin' on you when you and Andre was together. All of us got babies and that brotha was the only one stuck around to at least try to take care of his own. And then to top that off, he died at least tryin' to provide for his family. Whatever you wanna say, you got to at least give him credit for that."

"That's right," Peaches chimed in. "The rest of our no good men are on crack or running around with some other woman."

"At least two or three other women," Cristal said.

Erica just listened as the women continued to talk about how men were no good and didn't do what they were supposed to do. She finally realized why Andre had been so reluctant to let her hang with her girls. She also realized for the first time that they actually admired the fact that Andre was trying to rob somebody to provide for them. She hadn't ever really thought about it that way. But despite the sometimes negative tone of the conversation, Erica felt happy and relaxed and glad to be in the company of these women. They laughed and talked, ate and played cards. When she and D'Andre finally headed home later that evening, she felt more content than she had in ages.

The euphoria she felt when she hung out with her girlfriends quickly dissipated over the coming weeks as she realized how difficult it was going to be for her to raise D'Andre alone. Her job at the grocery store paid minimum wage and she mostly only worked part time so it just wasn't enough for them to live on. Were it not for the kindness of Aunt Muriel, she and little D'Andre would probably have been homeless. Finally, one of her girlfriends turned her onto a job at a daycare center downtown. It was a fancy place that a lot of women executives who worked downtown took their children. When she went for the interview, she was immediately impressed by how clean and neat everything was. The parents would pull into the circular driveway in front of large plate glass windows and the children were checked in at a receiving area just inside the doors. From there, they were taken down the hall to their classrooms which were bright and airy with large windows that mostly faced the street. The back of the building had a play area with lots of bright colored playground equipment.

Just being there had lifted Erica's spirits and it must have shown in her interview. She was immediately offered the job making nearly four dollars an hour more than she was making at the grocery store. She was ecstatic. But her happiness soon took a turn for the worse. Day after day, she watched enviously as the mothers and fathers brought in their obviously pampered children. The children were always neatly dressed in beautiful clothes and it was apparent that their every need was being met. Many of the parents came back at lunchtime to sit with their kids or to observe them while they played. There was even a closed circuit camera that the parents could link to from their own computers anytime they wanted to look in on their kids during the day. And while the few parents who acknowledged her existence were always pleasant to her, the majority of the parents seemed to look through her as if she were invisible. It seemed obvious that they considered her the help—there to make the lives of their children pleasant and happy. It never occurred to most of the parents who were there that she might have her own child that she wanted to make happy too. But instead of being able to pick up her child at the end of every day, he was left to walk home from school alone and let himself into an empty house while his mother was across town putting these children into the backs of fancy suv's to be taken home by their parents. It was a great job, but Erica began to feel a growing resentment that these people and their children seemed to have life so easy. Despite the great pay, one day Erica felt on the verge of quitting, but then something happened that changed her mind.

One of the mothers came in to observe at lunchtime and sat down at a table next to Erica. As she watched her daughter play, she turned to Erica and asked, "Do you have children of your own?"

The question really caught her off guard because it was the first time that somebody had acknowledged that she had a role besides being the caretaker for their children. Erica stammered, but managed to answer, "Yes, I do. A son who is nine. He's in the fourth grade."

" I bet he's a handsome boy."

"Yes, I think he is, but then I'm his mother."

Both of them laughed.

Then the mom continued. "Listen, I hope I am not out of place here, but I have a ten-year old son who seems to be growing like a weed. He has some great clothes that he hardly got to wear and I was just about to pack them up to give away. Do you think you might want some of them for your handsome son?"

Erica was moved. For the first time one of the parents had actually spoken to her mother to mother instead of just treating her like she was there to be their helper and had no life of her own to get back to.

"Yes, that would be nice. Thank you," Erica finally managed to say.

"Well great, I'll bring them in tomorrow. I'm glad that somebody I know can get some more use out of them. I guess I better get back to work. Thank you so much for looking out for my little darling."

Erica just nodded as she watched the woman leave, but she finally felt acknowledged as a real person with a real life of her own that existed outside of her role as a caretaker of their children. It was just the lift she needed to go on.

Even with this new job, however, Erica still needed to work weekends at the grocery store to make ends meet. Every Friday night, she would take her check from the day care center to the local check cashing business next to the grocery store. Andre had overdrawn their checking account before he died and the bank had closed it. Now, without a checking account, this was the only way for her to get her money. One Friday evening not long after Andre had died, Erica went in to cash her check. The check was for two hundred and seventy-five dollars, so after the 3 percent check cashing fee, she was expecting two hundred sixty-six dollars. Instead, the cashier handed her a one hundred dollar bill.

"What is this?" Erica demanded.

"It's a hundred dollar bill. What I owe you."

"Oh no it isn't. I gave you a check for two hundred seventy-five dollars. Where is the rest of my money?" Erica said, now raising her voice.

"Well, your husband got a payday advance for one hundred dollars that he failed to pay back and now with interest, it is up to one hundred sixty-six dollars, so you're only getting one hundred dollars today, honey."

Erica was furious, but there wasn't anything she could do about it. Andre had come here and done what so many people of limited means do. He had written a check on their checking account and gotten a one-hundred dollar advance. The check was post dated to be cashed on some date after he had died. By the time the check cashing place had deposited the check, there was no money left in their account. The check had bounced and the account was now closed. But interest and penalties had continued to accrue on the debt at an exorbitant rate. Now that one-hundred dollar advance had cost her one hundred and sixty-six dollars—money she really didn't have to lose. She started to open her mouth to say something, but felt a large lump forming in her throat. She turned quickly to leave so the woman wouldn't see her crying.

When she got home, she called the grocery store immediately to ask if she could work the late shift on Friday night unpacking and stocking. Usually she only worked Saturdays and Sundays, but this weekend she needed the extra money. As she hung up the phone, D'Andre came running in from outside.

"Hi momma," he said grinning.

"Hi baby," she said, trying to manage a smile.

"Can you read to me tonight?"

"No, honey. Mommy has to go to work tonight. I'm going to fix you a quick dinner while you take a bath. Then I want you to get in Mommy's bed and watch t.v. I'll ask Aunt Muriel to come check on you later. Ok?"

"Ok," D'Andre replied, as he dragged himself into the bathroom.

Erica could tell he was clearly disappointed that they weren't going to get to spend Friday night together like they always did, but she didn't have a choice. She quickly threw together some spaghetti noodles and a hot dog and put them on the table for D'Andre. She changed her own clothes and grabbed a muffin and stuck it in her purse. After she made sure D'Andre was ready for bed, she called Muriel and asked her to check in on him later that evening and then ran out the door for work. As she turned to look back at the house, she could see D'Andre watching her from the window with tears in his eyes. She wished she cold make spending time with D'Andre a priority, but this extra job was the only thing that would assure their survival.

Chapter 11B

Earth Mother

In the months following Anderson's death, all Alexa could think about was what she needed to do to make sure that Daniel came through this as whole as he possibly could. Although it was humiliating to learn that Anderson had been having an affair, she couldn't see what good it would do to raise a big stink about it now. It would only serve to humiliate her and Daniel and smudge Anderson's name and hers in the process. No, that was water under the bridge. In the end, she decided to hang onto her own memories of their time together and her view of what their life had been. She believed it would be good for Daniel to believe that his father had died a hero and that's all.

Still, it wasn't easy for either of them. She missed him terribly and some nights she was angry with him. Not for the affair, but for having to be the hero. Why did he think that it was his responsibility to take care of the world. His responsibility was to take care of them. She had never bargained to be a single adoptive mother. Now she would have to be both mother and father to their son. And while his death did not leave them wanting for anything financially, it did leave a big hole in both of their hearts.

Alexa had done what she could to address Daniel's emotional needs related to his father's death by getting him into therapy as quickly as possible. Although her friend Jasmine had seen Daniel immediately after Anderson died to deal with the crisis, she told Alexa that she would rather not see him long term because they were too close of friends. Jasmine had been good enough to refer them to another therapist and Alexa had made arrangements for Daniel to see him immediately. The first time that they went to Dr. Clarkson's office they met as a family, but the next session was for Daniel alone. As they sat in the waiting room, Daniel clung tightly to Alexa's hand.

"Are you sure I have to go in by myself, mommy?"

"Yes, honey, Dr. Clarkson said he wants to talk to you alone."

When Dr. Clarkson finally came out to get Daniel, Alexa almost had to pry his fingers from around her wrist. Alexa stood up, but Dr. Clarkson dropped to his knees to address Daniel at eye level. Alexa realized that it was Daniel who was the patient and she appreciated what Dr. Clarkson was doing to ease his anxiety. With that simple gesture she could feel Daniel's grip on her arm loosening up and then he let go and took Dr. Clarkson's hand as he led him into his office.

Alexa waited nervously counting the minutes until they finally reemerged from the doctor's office. Dr. Clarkson asked Alexa to come in for a few minutes to talk. And although he was very reassuring, he told Alexa that Daniel would need a lot of care and attention from her if he was to have a healthy mental attitude about life without his father. Alexa assured Dr. Clarkson that she was determined that she would do everything she could to help Daniel get through this.

Getting back to work was hard for Alexa but after she got Daniel resettled back in school she needed to go back to work so she could stop thinking about everything that had happened. On her very first day back she was greeted warmly by everyone she knew, but in the weeks she had been gone the new crop of interns had started and there were several faces she didn't recognize. She had lunch with a couple of her colleagues who convinced her to help them work on a new case for a child named Sheila Sanders. The case was challenging and interesting and for the next couple of weeks until they got her condition stabilized, Alexa spent most of her time working on it.

One day as she was getting out of her car for work, she spilled a cup of coffee on her white coat and had to take it off. She knew she had another coat in her office, so she walked into the building wearing only her scrubs. As she got into the elevator that morning, two young interns got in after her. They looked in her direction, but didn't really look at her as much as they seemed to look through her. And then, as if she was invisible, they began to talk about the Sanders case, berating the work of the team of doctors that had worked tirelessly to save the girl's life. She was incensed and opened her mouth to respond to their criticism. At that very moment, however, the door to the elevator opened and John Kerrigan, the Chief of Staff of the hospital got on. He nodded to the two young interns who had suddenly perked up, but he looked right past them to speak to Alexa.

"Dr. Pierce, great work on the Sanders case."

"Thanks John. I think our young colleagues here were just discussing our case."

She shot a nasty glance at them as she watched the color drain out of their faces.

"Well good. You two could learn a lot from Dr. Pierce," he replied touching her arm.

"I'm always willing to help the young and uninformed," Alexa replied.

She and Dr. Kerrigan laughed at her joke and she noticed the young doctors' faces go from pale white to red.

With that, she thought to herself, my work is done here, and she got off the elevator when the doors opened even though it wasn't her floor. As she walked down the hall she thought to herself, this is only a job. Taking care of Daniel is my priority now. I can't let these ignorant people upset me and make me have a stroke when I have a child to raise.

Alexa was also determined not to become the kind of lonely widow that she had guessed Denise had been. Always afraid to go somewhere because she didn't have a date. She and Anderson had a busy social schedule while he was alive and she saw no reason, after an appropriate period of mourning, to change any of that. About a month after the funeral, Alexa saw that she and Anderson had previously rsvp'd to a dinner party with several of their friends. She decided that enough time had elapsed and that she was going to go. She picked up the phone to call her hostess to reconfirm, but before she could dial the number, the telephone rang.

"Hello," Alexa answered.

"Alexa, hello darling. It's Penny Baker."

"Wow. Hello Penny. It is so funny you would call. I was just getting ready to call and reconfirm that I would still be coming to the dinner party on Saturday."

"Oh dear. Well, that's what I was calling about. You see, we assumed that you wouldn't be able to come and then without Anderson we had an odd number, so we invited another couple to take your place. I'm so sorry. That's why I was calling."

"Oh, I see. Well certainly. I understand. You couldn't have known I would still want to come and of course you can't have an odd number can you?"

"You're upset, aren't you?"

"No, no," Alexa lied. "I understand perfectly. We'll do it another time."

"Oh yes. Please let's do. I'm sure we'll see each other soon. Let's do lunch sometime."

"Well lunch is kind of hard for me with my schedule at the hospital, but we'll get together."

"Okay, then, goodbye."

"Goodbye," Alexa said, but then she realized that Penny had already hung up the phone.

The receiver was still in her hand, so instead of hanging up, she pressed the button and dialed the number of her good friend, Andrea. She needed some perspective on what had just happened and Andrea was a worldly woman and right now, Alexa needed some perspective on her feelings. The phone call with Penny had left her feeling hurt, humiliated and angry . She needed Andrea to help her figure out if she was being over sensitive about feeling snubbed.

"Hello."

"Hey girl, I need to talk to you. You always seem to have the answer to all the social do's and don'ts. I was supposed to go to a dinner party at Penny Baker's house and if I am not mistaken, I think I just got uninvited. Am I being over sensitive or am I justified in having my feelings a little hurt right now?"

"Well, honey, I hate to tell you, but this is going to be your life from now on."

"What do you mean?" , Alexa asked genuinely perplexed. "We've always been good friends with the Bakers."

"You are no longer a 'we', you are an 'I'. And nobody wants a single woman at their dinner party."

"Are you serious? But these are my friends," she protested.

"It doesn't matter, girl. All is fair in love and war and you are single now—even if it was not by choice. First you get uninvited, then you'll start noticing that the invitations just don't come anymore. Finally, they will stop calling you so they don't have to risk the possibility of having to ask you to a social affair where you would be coming alone. They're all afraid you are going to be after their husbands just like that hussy Denise. Oops, did I say that?"

Alexa's heart caught in her throat. "So you knew?"

"Yeah, girl. I knew. And I swore I would never say anything to you about it."

"But why?" Alexa pleaded.

"Because the messenger always gets shot. If I had said something to you about your husband running around, he would have denied it and then you would have been mad at me for trying to break up your happy home. No, it's just better to stay out of other people's business."

"Yeah, I guess you're right. But still, I wish I had known. It was so humiliating to watch her stand there at Anderson's funeral like she was any other friend paying her respects. I wish I would have snatched that fake hair right off her head."

"And then what? You know you would never have done anything like that."

"I know. But I can have a fantasy can't I?"

"Yeah, I guess you're entitled."

"But why would Anderson cheat on me. Unlike a lot of our friends, I at least worked hard to keep myself looking good."

"Girl please. Show me a pretty woman, and I'll show you a man who's tired of fucking her."

"Andrea, you are so crazy! But what do you think happened to us?"

"Well this is how I see it. Now this is just my opinion, but I think Anderson kind of saw himself as a rough, uncut diamond and that he was looking for a setting that would show him off. You're a whole ring all by yourself."

"And Denise?"

"She's a setting. But that is water under the bridge. You have to give up the idea of ever having a better past and move on. But if you think that life is going to go on as usual now that you are single, think again. Your best bet is to find a new man just as quick as you can or throw yourself full time into raising your son. And believe me when I tell you that the pickings out here are slim, so you'd be better off working to be the best soccer mom possible."

"Well, I'm not ready to think about dating anytime soon, so I guess I'll sign up to be team mom again. I'm really enjoying it and besides, Daniel really needs me right now."

And with that Alexa had chosen her course. She came home from the hospital early every evening to help Daniel with his homework. It wasn't long though before they got frustrated with each other over the math homework. Alexa kept trying to show Daniel how to do math problems the way she had learned to do math. But under the Everyday Mathematics program that they were now teaching at Daniel's school, the children were actually learning how to problem solve instead of just memorizing a bunch of tables. Alexa tried to figure out how to work with this new program, but eventually decided that she and Daniel would be better off if she got him a tutor.

Alexa still came home early to be with Daniel, but mostly just to monitor the work that the tutor was doing. She decided to use that time to cook them wonderful meals like she used to do when she and Anderson had first gotten married. Cooking had been something that Alexa had always enjoyed, but when she and Anderson had gotten busy in their careers, she had gotten away from it. Now that she was coming home early again to be with Daniel, she felt that cooking a meal and sitting down at the table with him every night was a good way for them to stay connected and keep the lines of communication open. She was determined to do everything that she could to make this transition easier for both of them.

Alexa also decided that she needed to do a little cleansing for her own spirit. She still held onto the memory of the good times she had shared with Anderson, but some part of her needed to feel like she could wash away the unpleasantness of the recent discovery. At lunchtime one day she passed a new linen store that had just opened in her neighborhood. She went inside and before she knew it, she had purchased five thousand dollars of new linens. Feeling like she had taken the first step toward cleansing her bedroom of the essence of another woman, she got on the phone and called her decorator and instructed her to bring her some plans for completely refurbishing her bedroom including a new bed, mattress and box spring. When she got home that evening, Daniel was sitting in the window looking at her with a big grin on his face. It always made her happy to see him waiting for her when she got home.

Just as she stepped inside the door the phone started ringing. Alexa picked up the phone sounding slightly exasperated at having been caught before she could even put her purse down.

"Hello," she snapped.

"Well hello yourself," Andrea said laughing slightly.

"Hey girl. I'm sorry. It's just that I was just walking in the door and I assumed it was some telemarketer trying to sell me something. You know they're the only ones who call you at six o'clock just as you are getting home."

"Yeah, I know. I usually ask them to give me their home number and tell me what time they get off so I can call them back just as soon as they walk in the door from work."

"Andrea, you are ridiculous. Those people are just trying to do their jobs. But what's up? I need to go hug my son."

"Oh, I was going to try to talk you into going to church with me tonight. Bishop Jackson is coming in from Fort Worth and I thought you might want to hear him preach."

"No girl, I want to fix dinner for my son and then sit and talk with him about his homework. I'm probably not going back to Anderson's church anymore."

"Anderson's church? But you've been going there since you two got married. What's up?"

"I went there because of him, but I can't say that it has been the most spiritually fulfilling thing for me. I've been going to my old church recently

and I have found that I have a lot more time to think about what God wants for me when I don't have to deal with all the phony people in our church."

"What do you mean?"

" I mean that it just seems to me that the faith community has adopted a lot of adjectives and titles to unnecessarily elevate church people in recent years and it is both annoying and distracting. We don't just have pastors or preachers anymore, we have anointed pastors, and what's the other new term . . . oh yeah, prophetess. And everybody who has two people listening to them is a bishop. Where did all this self aggrandizement come from in recent years? It sounds so vain and to me, it takes away from the entire church experience. No, you go ahead. I'll catch up with you another time. I think my son needs me here with him right now and I'm trying to be here as much as I can. But thanks for asking."

"Ok, girl, but we've got to continue this conversation later on. You can't let a few crazy church people keep you from going to church."

"Oh , I won't. Trust me on that one. My faith is the only thing that is getting me through all this right now. It's just that I need my relationship with God more than ever right now, and I don't want church people to interfere with that."

"Ok, talk to you soon."

"Bye."

As Alexa walked back into the family room, she picked up the mail. One of the items that came in the mail that day included some documents from her lawyer about Daniel's trust. She and Anderson had set up a trust for Daniel to make sure that he would be well taken care of in the event that anything happened to them. But Anderson's death had triggered a portion of the trust and it was now going to be paid to Daniel. At nine years old, of course she would still manage his money as the guardian of his trust, but she still thought that it might be a good idea to start explaining how the trust worked to him so he could have some assurance that he would be well taken care of no matter what happened. And so, after dinner that night, Daniel and Alexa sat down at the table together and she started explaining his trust to him.

Chapter 12A

Birth Mother

As far back as D'Andre could remember, his parents always fought about the fact that his dad didn't like going to church. Every week his mother would start on his dad on Saturday, trying to convince him to go to church with them on Sunday. His mother had belonged to the same southern Baptist church since she was a little girl. His grandmother belonged to the same church and even sang in the choir. His mother had told him that the people from the church had always been there for her. Whenever she needed help with money or other things for her family, she knew that she could depend on the good people from her church.

D'Andre liked going there too. Every Sunday while his mother attended church, the children would attend Sunday school. Most of his friends from the neighborhood would be there and he always had a good time with them making art projects and singing songs about God and talking about how Jesus was going to save them. He wasn't always sure what Jesus was going to save them from, but he knew it was supposed to be something good. They learned bible verses and played games and they always got some donuts and orange juice at the end of Sunday school.

His father always said he wouldn't have minded going to church as long as he didn't have to deal with church people. He didn't like the fact that people were always calling and asking questions about how you were doing and if you needed anything. He said they were pretending to be concerned about you, but really just wanted to get all in your business so they could tell everybody else about it. One time his dad had even called one of the ladies from the church who had called to check on them a nosy old biddie and told her to mind her own business. D'Andre had even tried to get his father to get involved with the church boy scout troop, but his dad had refused. Because his church was old fashioned and didn't allow mothers to be involved in scouting, D'Andre had never been able to join the troop.

After his father died, the people from the church had been very nice to them. He remembered how they had brought food over to their house for several weeks after his father's funeral. During those first weeks, he had stopped going to Sunday school and had started going to church with his mother. He just didn't like being away from her during that time. D'Andre remembered feeling like all eyes were on him whenever he walked into the sanctuary. He knew it wasn't his imagination since he often saw people point at him and whisper.

One Sunday, a few weeks after his father died, the minister began a sermon about sin and redemption. It started out like any other sermon, but then the pastor started talking about how young men who go out and commit crimes destroy themselves and their communities, and bring disgrace to their families. He talked about how God would forgive even these horrible people, but not if they didn't ask for God's forgiveness. At that moment D'Andre felt like the minister was talking about his dad and calling him a horrible person. He knew that his dad had been killed in a robbery and that meant, of course, that he had never been able to ask God for forgiveness for his sins before he died. He thought the pastor was trying to tell him that his dad was in hell and had not been forgiven of his sins. From that day forward D'Andre never felt the same about going to church again. Not long after that he told his mother that he didn't want to go to church anymore. When she asked him why, he wouldn't tell her, and for the next year they argued about it constantly. But after a while she got tired of arguing with him and just went alone. He felt bad about it, but he didn't know how to explain to his mother that he didn't want to go to a place where the people thought his father was a horrible, unforgiven sinner.

Even though they didn't attend church together much anymore, D'Andre and his mom still found ways to spend time together on the weekends. They would often go to the park on Saturday afternoon after his mom came home from work. In the summer, the swimming pool at the community center was open and his mom would take him there sometimes to watch him swim.

D'Andre's mom also always made his birthday a special treat and he really looked forward to it every year. For as long as he could remember they would start the day by going to the big mega store in their neighborhood where he would get ten dollars to buy himself a gift. After that they would go to the park and he was allowed to ride the little ponies. After that they would go over to the zoo and ride the paddle boats and the little train. It was a special time for him. It wasn't quite the same after his dad died, but when he was turning ten years old, his mother told him that she was going to give him fifteen dollars instead of the usual ten dollars. He already knew what he wanted too—a racing car track. He had priced it when they were in the store last and it was just fourteen dollars and ninety-nine cents. He knew exactly how much it would be after tax was added and he had enough money in his bank to cover the difference. He could barely wait for Saturday to get there.

When the big day came, he got up bright and early and closed his sofa bed in the living room and straightened up. He went to the kitchen and fixed himself a bowl of cereal so he would be ready to go as soon as his mother got up. Every time he heard a sound, he turned his head toward her bedroom door hoping she was ready to go. He knew she was tired, but he really wanted her to get up. When he finished his cereal, he couldn't stand it anymore. He tiptoed over to the door and cracked it slightly. Even in the gloom he could see that his mother was still asleep. He closed the door gently and went back to the kitchen. The one thing that he knew would wake her up right away was the smell of bacon cooking. So he quietly pulled out a frying pan and set it on the stove before he went to the refrigerator to get out the bacon. Soon he had the bacon sizzling. He eased back over to his mother's bedroom door and cracked it slightly to make sure that the aroma would fill her room. Then he got out some bread and put it in the toaster and poured a glass of milk and put it on the placemat on the small corner table. Just as he predicted, it wasn't long before his mother came stumbling to the door.

"Hi baby," she said still wiping the sleep from her eyes.

"Good morning, mama. I'm making you breakfast."

"Thank you baby. Mommy was just so tired from working yesterday. But, I haven't forgotten it is your big day. Happy Birthday baby."

"Thanks mom. Go get dressed so we can get ready to go as soon as you finish eating!"

"Ok, ok. I'll be right back."

After breakfast, they went downstairs and stopped at Aunt Muriel's house. D'Andre knew she would probably give him some birthday money too and he wanted to make sure that she didn't forget it was his birthday.

"Hey Auntie," D'Andre chirped happily as he opened the back door to her house.

"Who is that coming in my house this early on a Saturday?" Aunt Muriel said grinning.

"It's me, D'Andre. I just wanted to come see you, just in case you were looking for me today for any reason," D'Andre said hopefully. This was their small game. He would hint around about his birthday and she would act like she had no idea what he was talking about.

"No, I wasn't looking for you today. Is there some reason that I should have been looking for you?"

"Well, just in case you needed to tell me something. Maybe something special?" he asked grinning.

"Oh, it seems like there was something. Oh, yeah, congratulations on your good report card last week."

"No, that's not it," D'Andre said grinning.

"No. Well, let's see. Hmm?"

"Auntie!" D'Andre said exasperated.

"Ok, ok I think I know a little boy who is going to be ten today. Could that be you?"

"Yes, it's me!"

"Well, happy birthday then honey. And I think I have something for you right here ," she said as she reached for a card on the counter.

D'Andre excitedly opened the card and then read the words out loud slowly.

"To . . . my . . . . nephew. The most hand . . . some and intel.."

"That says intelligent, honey."

" . . . intelligent boy I know. Happy Birthday. And look mama, ten dollars!"

"What are you going to do with your birthday money, baby?" Aunt Muriel asked.

"I'm going to spend it on a new car and racing track. Me and mommy are going to the store right now."

"Oh, you are? Well have a good time then."

D'Andre almost felt like skipping as they went to the bus stop. It was his birthday and he had twenty-seven dollars in his pocket. As they walked down the street, the only thing that dampened his spirits was the sight of some boys from the neighborhood who had beat him up once before and taken his lunch money. He gripped his mother's hand tightly and thrust his other hand deep into his pocket around his money. They snickered at him as he passed, but he knew that they wouldn't do anything with his mother there. He was relieved when they only had to wait a couple of minutes for the bus to arrive. He didn't take his hand out of his pocket until his street and those boys were out of sight.

As soon as they saw the store in the distance D'Andre's mood lightened again. He practically dragged his mother off the bus when it stopped.

"Come on mama!" He said excitedly.

"I'm coming baby. Just slow down a little."

D'Andre went right to the toy aisle as soon as they got in the store. He was scanning the aisle looking for the car and racetrack he wanted. When he couldn't find them, he stopped a store clerk to ask for help.

"Hello. Can you help me?"

"Yeah, buddy, what you looking for?" the clerk asked.

"That new pop wheel car and the track that goes with it. It's my birthday and I'm going to buy it with my birthday money," he said proudly patting his pocket.

"Well, how about that. Hey did you know that on your birthday, you get to pick a special balloon from the front that has a prize inside it. Come on, I'll take you and your mom up there right now."

"Can we go mama and get the prize for my birthday?"

"Yes, baby."

They made their way to the front of the store. Behind the store manager's desk was a display of balloons with a sign that read birthday balloons. The clerk told the manager that it was D'Andre's birthday and the store manager grinned and waved them over.

"Good morning young man. I understand it is your birthday."

"Yes, and I am going to spend my birthday money today to get the new pop wheel car and race track."

"Well good for you. We also have another prize for you inside of one of these balloons so just pick one out and let's see what it is."

D'Andre grabbed a purple balloon and the manager gave him a small pin to pop it. A piece of paper floated to the ground. D'Andre picked it up and opened it to read it.

"It says I won twenty dollars mama!" he yelled excitedly.

"Actually, son, it says you won a twenty dollar savings bond."

"What's a savings bond mama?"

"Uh, I don't know honey."

"It's money that you keep until later to use to help pay for college."

"College?" his mother asked incredulously. "D'Andre ain't going to college."

"I'm not going to college, mama?"

"No. Who you think is going to pay for you to go to college? Do you have any other prize you can give him? Something he can use right now?"

"Well, uh, yeah, sure we do," the manager said somewhat taken aback. "How about this gift certificate for a free train ride at the zoo?"

"Yes, yes, yes!" D'Andre screamed. "We always ride the train for my birthday. It goes around and around and around the park. It doesn't really take you anywhere, but I like it."

"Ok, then, instead of the savings bond you get a free ride on the train to nowhere," the manager said, barely hiding his sarcasm.

But neither D'Andre nor his mother even noticed. D'Andre was as happy as he could be. To him, this was a perfect birthday.

The euphoria of that day was short lived. Not long after they got home, Muriel came over to see them and D'Andre could tell from the look on her face that it wasn't going to be good news.

"Hey auntie. Look what I got—free train tickets."

"That's great, honey" Muriel said, thinking how ironic that they would have gotten some free train tickets given the news she was about to drop on them. "Go outside, so I can talk to your mom."

Muriel waited until the door closed behind, D'Andre and Erica nervously pulled up a chair beside her.

"What's going on Aunt Muriel? Is something wrong?"

"Yeah, honey, something's wrong. We bought this house almost twenty years ago from old man Jackson. But when we bought it, we didn't have enough money to make the 15 percent down payment, so he let us buy it on a contract for deed."

"What's a contract for deed?" Erica asked.

"Well, it is a way of buying a house without having to make a down payment. Under a contract for deed you pay a monthly payment that goes toward the purchase price, but the seller keeps the deed to the property. Mr. Jackson agreed under our contract to let us pay as much as we could afford at the time and then he gave us ten years to convert it to a regular mortgage so he could get the rest of his money."

"Well, what happened?"

"Well, at the end of the ten years, we still couldn't afford to get a regular mortgage, so he just let us keep livin' here and paying the same amount, but technically our contract for deed had expired. Now after twenty years, we have paid a good amount toward the original purchase price, but old man Jackson died last year and his son owns the house now. Since he still had the deed, he took out a loan and allowed the bank he borrowed the money from to put a lien on the property. Now he has defaulted on his loan and the bank is taking this house."

"What? But that's not fair. You've been paying for this house for twenty years!"

"You're right. But in the eyes of the law, we never got title to the house because the Jacksons still had the deed. We are looked at as little more than renters."

"So you have to forfeit all the money you paid toward the purchase price for the last twenty years?"

"Yes, that's what it means. Even though we were paying with the idea that we would eventually own the house, under a contract for deed, the owner keeps the title until all the payments are made. We should have gotten the loan financed while Mr. Jackson was still alive, but we didn't and now it's too late."

"So what happens now?"

"Well, we've been given two weeks to move out."

"No, Aunt Muriel. What are we going to do?"

"Well, we're going to move in with my sister for a while and I guess you're going to have to move back in with your mother."

Erica just put her head down on the table and wept. The last thing that Erica wanted to do was move back in with her mother, but she really didn't have any choice. She knew it meant she would have to listen to her mother's "I told you so" and she just didn't know how much of that she was going to be able to take. She finally got the nerve to call her mother and Ricky made her sorry almost as soon as she did.

"So what happened, his family put you out?" Ricky asked.

"No, mamma, they lost their house."

"Sure they did. They only been livin' there for twenty years. Well, I knew that it would eventually come to this. I'm just surprised it took you this long to come crawling back home."

It was all Erica could do to hold her tongue and not tell her mother off, but she didn't have the luxury of doing that because she needed somewhere to live. So she swallowed her pride and she and D'Andre moved back in with Ricky. When she got there, she was surprised to find out that Ricky had a live in boyfriend who made it clear right from the start that he didn't like children and didn't want to see any more of D'Andre than was absolutely necessary. Erica had hoped that Ricky would stand up for her, but she just sat and listened to her boyfriend lay down the ground rules for them living in her house without saying a word. When she finally did speak, it was only to ask Erica about something she had been trying to forget.

"What happened to your wedding ring? I can't believe you already stopped wearing it."

"My daddy took it to the pawn shop to get us some money," D'Andre blurted out before Erica had a chance to stop him.

"Oh, no he didn't," Ricky said laughing. "You mean he couldn't take care of you after all. Didn't I tell you he wouldn't amount to anything? Well I hope he at least traded the ring in to buy you something nice."

"He bought us a new water heater," D'Andre said almost proudly.

Oh, God, thought Erica, here it comes now.

"A new water heater for the house that you just got kicked out of?"

"But we didn't get kicked out," D'Andre protested. He looked at his mother trying to get her to tell his grandmother what had really happened, but she just hung her head in a defeated way. More than anything right now, D'Andre wanted to be able to hold on to his belief that his daddy was doing all that he could to take care of them when he was alive and that he really loved them. Being here with his grandmother made him feel that she was trying to take all that away from him.

He had never been very close to his grandmother and now he understood why. As he watched the exchange between his mother and grandmother he felt small and helpless. He wanted to run up to his mother and throw his arms around her and tell his grandmother to leave her alone. His daddy was gone and it was his responsibility to take care of his mother now. But he couldn't do it with that mean grandmother and her boyfriend bossing him around and telling him what to do. That night when his mother quietly slipped into the room they were sharing, he called out to her from the darkness.

"Mommy, I don't want to stay here."

"Me either, baby."

"Mommy, whatever you have to do, let's just move as fast as we can."

Erica knew that she had to do what D'Andre asked, but to do so meant they would have to live in a horrible part of town because that was all she could afford. Erica managed to find a small two bedroom apartment in a decaying 1950's housing project on the edge of town. The buildings were two story brick structures clustered in groups of four around a central courtyard that looked like it must have had beautiful landscaping at one time, but now only had dirt in the flower beds and a few patches of grass. The buildings themselves had dark narrow stairways that smelled of urine and had graffiti on most of the walls. Inside, their apartment was one large room for living and dining, but they were lucky to have gotten two bedrooms. They would have to share a bath, but at least D'Andre would finally have his own room. When Erica finally took D'Andre to see the apartment she had rented for them, he did his best to hide the disappointment in his eyes, and he threw his arms around her and squeezed her tight and said, "Mama, I knew you could do it. We're going to be alright now. Thank you."

Chapter 12B

Earth Mother

When his dad was alive there was always a debate in their house about two things—where they should go to church and where they should go on vacation. As far as church went, Daniel had understood that when his parents got married his father had more or less decreed that his wife would attend his home church. He had grown up in a strong southern Baptist church where everybody knew everybody else and everybody knew everybody else's business. His grandfather had been a deacon there and his father was a deacon there too before his death. His dad had wanted his mom to become a deaconess but Daniel knew that she had resisted because although she accepted that it was her obligation to join her husband's home church, she had never been really comfortable there. She went out of a sense of loyalty and because she loved him. She knew that since his dad was in politics, it was even more important that he had a strong church to support him. Like most progressive churches in the black community, their church believed in encouraging their congregants to vote and in openly supporting candidates from the pulpit. Anderson had, consequently, enjoyed very vocal support from their congregation.

On the rare occasions when his dad didn't go to church, however, because he was sick or out of town, he and his mom would sneak off to another church that his mom had attended before she married his dad. It was a Unity church of Christianity. And although it was a Christian church, and published the Daily Word that his father read every day, whenever his parents discussed it, his father would always refer to it as "church light" because he thought that they didn't put enough emphasis on sin and redemption. What his mother liked about it was the fact that it emphasized the Christ in all people and the fact that God was all around us all the time. It encouraged its members to see the good in everyone and the ability of everyone to be more Christlike. His mother liked it better than the church she attended with his dad and over the years, Daniel had come to enjoy it also. Many of his friends from school attended the Unity church and he enjoyed talking with them about the principals that they learned there. But ultimately, he enjoyed going to his dad's church more. Something about that place moved his spirit in a way that his mom's church had never been able to do.

After his father died, his mother started going to Unity full time. Daniel asked his mom if they could go back to his dad's church again, but she didn't want to. At a time when he needed to feel that he hadn't lost everything associated with his father, he wanted to go to his dad's church. When his mother refused, he felt that she had taken that part of his connection to his dad away from him too and it only intensified his loss. A small part of him resented her for that.

As far as vacations went, his father having been raised in Texas was never into the whole east coast tradition of summering in Martha's Vineyard, a small island off the coast of Massachusetts that was accessible by ferry or by air. He thought that it was pretentious and stuck up sounding and that it would not be a boost for his political career so they had never been there as a family even though Alexa's parents still owned a small cottage there. About a year after his dad died, Daniel's mom declared that they would spend the summer in "the Vineyard" as she called it.

That first summer, it was like a whole new world for Daniel. There were lots of other kids his age and he had more freedom than he had ever dreamed of. Even though he was barely ten years old, he and his new friends would get on their bikes each morning and ride all over the island exploring the beaches and forests. When they got tired, they would ride into town for lunch or ice cream. There were no locks on the doors and everyone was free to wander from house to house visiting and socializing with their friends. Daniel had never met so many affluent black people before having spent his entire life in Bayou Oaks and he loved knowing that there were so many other kids just like him at east coast prep and boarding schools. He was also glad to see his mother so happy and taking advantage of the numerous invitations she received to cocktail and dinner parties on the island. He was so glad that his mother had decided they should come there. It made him feel that eventually they were going to be alright.

His mother promised that they would still use their spring break vacations to explore new places, and use long weekends to ski, but it was clear that from now on they would be spending their summers in Martha's Vineyard.

When they got home from vacation at the end of the summer, Alexa settled into a comfortable chair with a stack of mail and a cup of tea. While she was opening her mail, she began playing the phone messages on her machine. The first couple of messages were from solicitors trying to raise funds for charities. The next message, however, was more interesting. It was a developer calling to ask whether they had any interest in selling their home. He explained that he had just purchased the homes on either side of them and that he was interested in acquiring their property as well so that he would have a large contiguous tract of land. Alexa was shocked. She knew that one of her neighbors had been interested in selling her house, but not the other. She didn't know that either one of them had actually put their houses on the market. She decided to take a break and go talk to her neighbors to catch up on everything that had happened since they had been gone. She learned that developers had discovered their little street over the summer and wanted to build a number of giant McMansions as they called them. Not one sale on the street had been to someone who wanted to renovate one of these beautiful old homes. When she went back inside, she told Daniel what was going on in the neighborhood, but before she could finish, he stood up and walked over to her.

"Mom, this is our home. It is where we lived with Dad. We're not going to sell it."

Alexa was shocked by the authoritative sound of his voice and by his quick and clear response. But he was right, this was their home and they were there to stay.

Chapter 13A

Birth Mother

By the time D'Andre got to middle school, life was pretty much broken up into days when he had school and days when he didn't. Whether he had school or not, his mom was always working, so either way he was pretty much on his own. When they lived in the apartment behind Aunt Muriel's house that had not been such a big deal. He had become adept at taking the bus across town to get to school. Every day when he came home he stopped in to let Aunt Muriel know he was home and to get a snack before he went up to his own house. Although Aunt Muriel respected his privacy, she did check up on him from time and time and it was comforting to know that somebody so close by was looking out for you.

All that changed when Aunt Muriel lost her house. After they moved out of his grandmother's house into the apartment in the projects, life became a lot more dangerous for D'Andre. There were constantly drug dealers around trying to talk you into doing drugs or working for them selling drugs. The temptation was hard to resist because they always had big money and nice cars in a neighborhood that was short on both.

When school was in session, he had to get up early to ride the bus to school. His mother always left him some breakfast, which generally consisted of some sugary cereal, and made him something to take for lunch, which more times than not was peanut butter and jelly. He knew he was lucky to always have food to eat. There were some kids he knew that didn't. At the beginning of the school year some older kids tried to take his lunch from him one day, but he knew two things. One was, he didn't want to be known as a punk and the other was that if they took his food, he would be hungry all day. So he had no choice but to fight. By now he was nearly thirteen and also nearly six feet tall. He gave as good as he got, and at the end of it all, the big kids decided it was easier to pick on somebody who wasn't going to fight back, so he left with his pride and his lunch intact.

During the week D'Andre's mom worked at a child care center that she had worked for as long as he could remember. On Saturdays she worked at the grocery store. Not only did it bring in extra money, but it also brought in extra food. They would let the employees take home the day old bread and the prepared foods from the deli case that hadn't been sold. His mother's coworker had also shown her how to take the dented cans from the back trash bins at the end of the night. D'Andre often wondered how anybody could throw away perfectly good food just because the cans didn't look good. Most weekends his mother brought home corn, green beans, tuna fish, tomato paste and some canned meat. They always had enough to make it through the week and it also meant they didn't have to rely on food stamps like many of their neighbors did.

On Saturdays when his mom went to work, it was always D'Andre's job to take their clothes to the laundromat and wash them. One Saturday as he was waiting for the clothes to dry, he sat down on a folding chair in front of the store. Even though the store had air conditioning, it only half worked and with the dryers running the place was always unbearably hot. As D'Andre sat there flipping through a sports magazine, he noticed two well-dressed white men walking down the sidewalk on the other side of the street. He leaned over to his friend Tommy who was sitting nearby to find out who they were.

"Tommy, what you think they doin' over there."

"My momma said white folks getting' ready to move back up in here and put us all out."

"What you mean?"

"I mean, they been buying up a lotta these old places around here and tearing 'em down. My momma said they gon' build some new stuff that we ain't gonna be able to afford."

"Well, then I guess it's a good thing we live in the projects. At least ain't nothin' over there they want."

When summer came, it was more of the same, except D'Andre didn't have school to break up the monotony of his day. His mom went to work and when he got up, he went to the park and played basketball until it got too hot. Then he would go home, eat lunch and take a nap. When it got cooler in the afternoon, he usually went back out and played basketball some more. He wasn't doing anything to keep his reading up during the summer months, but his basketball game improved tremendously. By the end of the summer, kids from the neighborhood would come and watch just to see him play. Even at thirteen years old, there was no doubt that at his height and with his skills and the heart he put into the game, he was destined to be a great ball player.

There were some organized leagues in the neighborhood, but every time he asked his mom about playing in one of them, she said she did not have the money for him to play in a league. D'Andre started to sign up for the team at his middle school, but he was so much bigger than most of the kids and they played so sorry, he decided he wouldn't waste his time. Instead he continued to hone his skills on the neighborhood courts against boys as much as five years older than he was. They didn't mind him playing, but they made it clear that he wasn't getting any slack just because he was younger than they were.

D'Andre's mother wished that he would spend more time studying when she wasn't home, but she was just happy that he had found something wholesome to occupy his time and keep him out of trouble. Every time she saw him coming home tired from a great game of basketball, all she could do was smile.

Chapter 13B

Earth Mother

Alexa had a busy and important job at the hospital, but she always made sure she was available to participate in as many of Daniel's school activities as possible. At the beginning of middle school when they had the first open house, they put out sign up sheets so the parents could volunteer to work at the fair or go on field trips or read to the class. Alexa would pull out her electronic calendar and sign up for as many things as she could manage with her schedule. Sometimes she would get a smart ass comment from one of the perpetually thin moms who spent her days working out or getting the first spot in car pool line. Invariably, one of them would notice how many activities she was signing up for and feel compelled to comment.

"Alexa, I just don't know how you do it. You work, take care of Daniel by yourself and still have time to sign up for school activities. How do you do it?" a woman named Stacy asked her at one such event.

At first Alexa was offended by these sanctimonious women, but then she realized that they just needed to feel better than her somehow since they had given up their careers to stay at home. Finally, she had come up with a retort that generally stopped them in their tracks and got used to saying it without batting an eye.

Alexa looked straight at Stacy and responded, "Well, I don't have to waste a lot of time trying to impress someone who got tired of me years ago." And then for effect, she glanced over at the woman's husband. The woman opened her mouth to speak, but was clearly shocked and speechless. Before she could say another word, Alexa turned and walked away.

Alexa felt blessed that Daniel's teachers were so attentive to his needs. If they sensed that he was falling behind in the least bit, they would call her immediately and suggest that he get tutoring in that subject or offer to tutor him themselves. Daniel was polite and very mannerable so his teachers were often happy to tutor him and save her the fifty-five dollars an hour that it generally cost to get a tutor in a specific subject. As a result, Alexa was never faced with a situation where she would show up for a parent teacher conference only to be caught off guard by a report that Daniel had failed to exceed expectations in some subject. By the time Daniel finished middle school, he was well prepared to take the PSAT—the preliminary scholastic aptitude test for college.

Additionally, as she had done all the years that Daniel had been in school, Alexa began researching available summer camps by early January. Most of the best camps had their summer schedules available by then and she knew that spots in the best camps were usually full by early March. Daniel had expressed a desire to work on his violin studies in the summer after he finished eighth grade as well as his golf game and his chess game. She and Daniel also discussed whether they should work on Spanish as well. So she decided that she wold work on finding camps or activities in each of these four areas for that last summer before high school started.

Although Alexa couldn't imagine giving up any of their time in Martha's Vineyard, she had learned about an intensive language immersion program in Cuernavaca, Mexico that seemed like it would be an ideal way for both she and Daniel to brush up on their Spanish. She found the program on line with little effort. It provided an opportunity for them to stay with a family for total immersion or in a small hotel near the campus of the school. Classes generally ran for about six hours a day with students divided by skill level.

There were also evening and weekend cultural excursions. She decided to sign up for that program for the first two weeks of August, then save the last two weeks of the month for their trip to Martha's Vineyard.

Finding a good chess camp was easy. St Matthews had a strong chess program and they offered a camp with chess masters each summer. Alexa also had no difficulty getting a golf camp arranged. The club to which they belonged had a great golf school and offered a wonderful program for juniors during the summer. Alexa arranged some private instruction time and signed Daniel up for golf camp as well. She was particularly excited that Daniel wanted to play golf. She had been quite a golfer before he was born, but those early years of parenting had left her little time to indulge in such a time consuming sport. She looked forward to being able to spend more time playing golf with Daniel.

Finding a music camp was quite a bit more challenging, however. They didn't have any personal experience with violin camp so Alexa asked Daniel's violin instructor for some suggestions. He sent home brochures for about four different camps. One offered camp only in August so she eliminated them because it conflicted with their plans to go to Cuernavaca and Martha's Vineyard. Another one seemed interesting except for the fact that the camp was just too far away from where they lived.

The last two camps were offered during June and July and each offered both individual and group instruction. They were both in close proximity to their house and they both offered the opportunity for recitals at the end of the program. So it really came down to the experience of the instructors and the recommendation of other students. Alexa encouraged Daniel to ask his friends who had attended the camps last summer what they liked about the camp they attended. For her part, she got on the internet and did some research on the instructors. Then she and Daniel sat down like they often did and compared notes before they finally agreed on which camp to choose.

The only other thing that Daniel wanted was to have someone other than Maria carry him to his camps that summer. He felt he was too old to have a real nanny driving him everywhere. Alexa had heard of something that she thought might be a solution to that problem—hiring a manny. A manny was a young male babysitter, usually a college student, that would act more like a big brother than a babysitter and could drive Daniel to all his camps that summer. Daniel agreed that was the perfect solution and with that, their summer was set. Alexa was so happy about how mature and thoughtful Daniel was in his choices. All she could do was smile.

Chapter 14A

Birth Mother

At fourteen years old, D'Andre was already six feet two inches tall and it was clear that he had not yet finished growing. Without much to do after school, he spent a lot of time on the playground playing basketball. A lot of people said he was a natural, but he knew if he hadn't put the hours into practice that he did that he would just be another average player. Instead, he was a star. The basketball court was someplace where he could get respect. Even though he was a lot younger than most of the boys who showed up at the neighborhood park for pick up games, when he got there they always let him play and he was a sight to behold.

D'Andre wasn't tall and willowy. He was solid. He had great offensive moves but he was equally good on defense. When players came toward him, he was able to contort his body and twist away from them in ways that made him seem like a ghost. And when he went up for a jump shot, the full length of his body and extended arm seemed to reach into the heavens. He was quick, he was agile and above all he was fearless.

When D'Andre got to high school, the basketball coach called him to his office the very first day. He knew better than anyone how to find the best players by just asking who the star was at the local neighborhood park. Coach Johnson had been hearing about D'Andre for over a year and now that he was eligible to play high school basketball, he intended to bring him into his fold as quickly as possible. Jimmy Johnson didn't just want the raw talent he could always find in these young players. He also knew that if he started working with them early, he could use basketball as a means to keep them in school until graduation. He used basketball as a carrot—no studying, no ball. He knew that so many of the young guys that showed up here to play ball didn't have fathers in the home and he saw his role not only as coach and teacher, but also as mentor and father figure. It was a responsibility that he took seriously and willingly.

D'Andre knocked even though the door was open because he was a little nervous about just walking in without permission.

"Coach Johnson?" he asked hesitantly.

"Come on in, who is it" the coach bellowed in a loud baritone voice.

"It's me sir, D'Andre Parker. You sent for me."

"Oh, yeah, yeah, D'Andre. Come on in here son and let me get a look at you. I've been hearing about you for over a year now. I hear you got game."

"Yes, sir. Thank you sir. Yeah, I play a little bit."

"A little bit? One thing you don't need more of is false modesty. If you can play, you can play. No sense being ashamed of it."

"I guess you right, sir."

"You guess? No, I am right. Now what I want to know is if you think you got enough game to play ball on my team. If you do, I want to see you at tryouts tomorrow afternoon at three forty five so I can see what you got."

"Oh, I'll be here sir. No doubt."

"But I need to explain something to you boy, right here, right now. This ain't no fun and games. It will be hard work. And even if you are the best player I have, I will bench you if you don't keep your grades up. You need to spend as much time after school studying as you spend playing ball. Do you understand me?"

"Yes, sir."

"And if you need some help, you better ask for it and not wait for anybody to ask you if you need help. Do you understand me?"

"Yes, sir."

"Now get on out of here and be back tomorrow at three forty-five sharp."

"Yes, sir."

"Can you say anything else besides, yes sir."

"Yes, sir, I mean no, sir. I mean yes, I can, yes, I can, ... sir."

He had done it again. But the coach had to know how nervous he was. He backed out of Coach Johnson's office without saying another word and the coach was laughing to himself. He could hardly believe it. The coach had called him in to give him a chance to play high school ball. He knew better than anyone how many pro ballers Coach Johnson had turned out. He had a reputation of working you hard, but he knew that if he worked hard for coach, he really had a chance of playing college ball and then who knows what might happen. Maybe basketball could really be his ticket out of this life—and he could finally do something to help support his mother.

The next day D'Andre showed up at the gym as soon as his last class was finished at three fifteen. He didn't want to be late. At first coach had him work out with some of the other freshman players, but it wasn't long before he asked him to play against one of the best seniors on the team, Andrew Briscoe. Briscoe was fast, but D'Andre was faster. By the end of practice he was running circles around him. Coach Johnson pulled him aside at the end of practice and told him he had a spot on the team.

In the following weeks coach made him practice hard. He had skills before, but Coach Johnson helped him develop technique. The coach noticed his right ankle was a little week when he turned it one day and got him special ankle braces to make sure he wouldn't be injured. The coach also found out that his grades in math and science were suffering and he arranged for a tutor to work with him after school. By the time of the first game, he had good enough grades to play. And even though coach didn't put him in until the last quarter, he played spectacularly. The rest of the year he was able to make a real contribution to the team and show them that he had real potential to play college ball.

The same couldn't be said for his grades, however. He made it through his freshman year, but early in his sophomore year, they began to slip again. By this point he had shown that he was an invaluable asset to the team so coach Johnson went to see D'Andre's english teacher to see if there was anything else he could do to help his player.

"I wish I could suggest something to you coach," said Mrs. Scott, his english teacher, "but he just doesn't seem like he is paying attention half of the time. Even when I call on him he doesn't always respond. I'm afraid he may fail english this semester."

"Mrs. Scott, why don't you let me work with him. I promise you if you give him a C this semester, I'll make sure he brings his grade up by next semester."

True to his word, coach Johnson began working with D'Andre himself after school and he was a hard task master. D'Andre appreciated everything that coach was trying to do for him, but he had never been any good in school and he didn't think that was going to change just because coach Johnson was working with him. Day after day they worked together, but coach became as frustrated with D'Andre as D'Andre was with him. Finally, one day, coach just threw his pencil down on the desk and started to yell at D'Andre.

"You're not even trying, D'Andre!"

"Yes, I am coach, really I am. It's just that I don't hear so well and I never wanted to wear hearing aids."

"What?"

"Yeah. I had a real bad ear infection as a baby and I lost some of the hearing in both of my ears. School has always been hard for me. I'm trying coach, but I can't always hear what everyone is saying that well."

"Why didn't you tell me that before? You know they have made advances in hearing aids since you were a kid. I can probably help you get something that is not so noticeable. Come back here tomorrow and we can talk about it some more."

That night as D'Andre walked home he thought about how much coach was trying to do to help him. He wanted to show him he appreciated it so he decided he would get the hearing aids so he could do better in school. As he walked past the neighborhood courts, he saw some of the guys he used to play with. He was so deep in thought that he walked right past them without even speaking to them and that was something that they considered unacceptable.

"Oh you can't speak now that you playin' high school ball? We ain't good enough for you no more?"

"Naw man, I just got a lot on my mind."

"He got a lot on his mind," one of the guys said mocking him. "Well think about this," he said as he threw the ball right at D'Andre.

"Man, I don't have my ankle braces and I need to be careful playing out here on this asphalt."

"Oh, he done gone soft on us now. I don't have my ankle braces."

"Awright, awright, but you made me mad now—I'ma have to whip you like you stole something," D'Andre said laughing.

The truth was, D'Andre loved these pick up games. These old guys could play and they had heart, even if they were a little rough with the elbows and other fouls. They had never seen a shot they didn't want to block. But these courts were a place where D'Andre could forget about the troubles of the day. D'Andre' s teammate was waving at him to pass the ball, but he wasn't really open. Instead, D'Andre cut around another guy and went for a lay up. It was poetry in motion, except that one of his opponents thought that they were playing football. D'Andre was halfway finished completing his lay up when an opposing player hit him with his full body weight. D'Andre fell and as he did so, his right ankle buckled underneath him and he heard a loud snap. The pain was so excruciating that for a moment all he saw was white light before his body crumpled to the ground.

D'Andre knew long before anybody told him that his ankle was gone. Everybody expected that he would be a professional athlete and in one stupid move he had ruined that dream for all of them.

CHAPTER 14B

Earth Mother

Ever since his dad had died, Daniel's mother was devoted to his every need. He knew he could count on his mom to volunteer to be the room mother almost every year. When she wasn't doing that, he knew she would make the time to volunteer at the mother's help desk at his school. He knew she meant well, but it still didn't ease the pain of not having his dad around. There were things that both Daniel and his mom recognized a dad was just going to be better at teaching him.

One of the things his mother was determined to instill in Daniel, however, was the responsibility of helping others less fortunate than he was. Even though Daniel understood he was adopted because his birth mother was unable to care for him, Alexa thought that far too often Daniel behaved as if he was "to the manor born". When it was her turn to organize the Jack and Jill activity for the kids, she planned a clothing drive where she had all the kids collect their clothes and clothes from their friends to give to children at one of the local housing projects in town. To her surprise, the kids had expressed genuine enthusiasm about the project and in a very short period of time her garage was filled with all kinds of really nice clothing. The day before the event, the kids came over to organize the clothing by size and separated the girls clothing from the boys. After that, they rented a big van to help them take all of the clothing to the community center in the housing project and set things up for the next morning.

On the day of the project the kids showed up bright and early, eager to work.

"Dr. P—what are we supposed to do when people get here?" one of the girls asked.

"Well, you are the salespeople. Do what you would expect any salesperson in a store to do for you. Ask people what they are looking for and then help them find something that they need. Then help them as they try things on and bring them other things that you think might work for them."

"Just like the people do for us at Nieman's?"

"Uh, yeah, just like at Nieman's, except when they find what they want, they won't have to pay anything for it. They'll be able to shop 'til they drop without spending a dime."

"This is kinda neat," one of the other kids said.

"Well then, let's get ready for our customers," Alexa said enthusiastically.

As soon as the doors opened an eager group of teens rushed in. They were wide eyed with expectation and began running from rack to rack looking for clothing. The kids fanned out as they had been instructed to do, and began to assist their customers. As she watched, she couldn't help but smile.

She saw Daniel helping a young man who said he was looking for a winter coat.

"Well do you want a wool coat or do you want a parka?" Daniel asked.

"I think I want a parka—that's one of those big puffy jackets, right?"

"Yeah, here's one of my old jackets in fact. Why don't you try this on. I think it would fit you."

"Thanks man. Yeah, that's cool. I like the colors too," he said as he slipped the jacket on.

"Looks good on you too," Daniel said grinning. "Come over here and look in the mirror, man."

"Nice, nice," the young man replied. "But what are all these tags hanging on the front zipper?"

"Oh, those are just lift tickets," Daniel replied nonchalantly. "You leave 'em on there so people know where you skied last season."

"What you talkin' about? Skied last season! Man you bougie brothers are all the same. I thought you were cool," the boy said as he took off the jacket and let it drop to the floor.

"What'd I say?" Daniel said, looking shocked. "Hey man, I'm sorry. I didn't mean anything by it."

But by then the boy had walked away shaking his head in disgust. Daniel looked toward his mother.

"Mom, what just happened?"

"Daniel, you have to be more sensitive to other people's feelings."

"But how do you know how to be more sensitive to other people's feelings when you have no idea what they might take offense to. It's not like I deliberately tried to say something to hurt that boy's feelings—I just didn't know that talking about skiing would upset him so much. I mean everybody I know goes skiing at least once or twice a year. It just didn't occur to me that everybody doesn't get to go ski."

"I know honey. The problem is that all of us work and play and go to school and church in such a narrow segment of society. After a while, we start thinking that whatever life we are living is the norm and not the exception. That's why it is so important for us to get out and interact with all kinds of people, so you don't start thinking that everybody lives the way you and your friends from St. Matthews live. Your dad was a judge and I'm a doctor. We're in the top five percent of income earners in the country. That is not the norm. Try to imagine life where every school vacation means which grandparent you are going to stay with and not which ski resort you are going to check out. Think about who you are talking to before you open your mouth to speak and

then try to put yourself in that person's place. Would you be offended by the statement if you were them. At the end of the day Daniel, we are our brother's keeper."

"Thanks mom. I think I understand. I'm going to do better."

At that moment, Daniel caught sight of the young man he had offended on the other side of the room. He was talking to some boys and pointing at Daniel. Daniel turned to look at his mom for support and she nodded approvingly.

"Well here goes," he said taking a deep breath as he started across the room toward the boys.

Alexa just watched smiling. This was not a lesson she could have taught him without this experience and she said a little silent prayer thanking God for giving Daniel this experience.

As soon as they finished up at the community center, they rushed over to the school to get ready for Daniel's lacrosse practice. He had been playing lacrosse since he was nine and this was going to be his first season playing high school lacrosse. Until he started playing lacrosse, he had been devoted to soccer. He had started playing soccer at the Y when he was only three years old and he had played in one of the best organized leagues in the city since he was five. Everybody had said he was a natural and he really enjoyed the sport. He had really thought that he would play soccer through middle school and then maybe switch to football in high school. Then one day his mom showed him an article about some twins from New York who had become world class lacrosse players. Like him, they had had the option of playing many sports, but they had picked lacrosse and were transforming the game.

Daniel was immediately intrigued by their story and decided to give lacrosse a try. He too was a natural, but he added moves to the game that caught everyone by surprise. Sometimes Daniel was so fast, he would have to wait for his teammates to catch up with him. But he knew how to be a team player and his teammates appreciated that about him. Before long, he had developed quite a reputation as a lacrosse player. Lacrosse had also been a godsend in another way. For years after his father died Daniel dreaded the beginning of soccer season every year. All the other boys would have their dads there and invariably the question was always asked about whose dad was going to volunteer to be the assistant coach or referee. While his mother was always there to support him, he felt bad that he didn't have a dad who could help the coach or referee like the other kids did. Whenever he was asked, he would have to say again, "my dad is dead". Then everyone would stare, some would gasp and then they all acted like they felt sorry for him. He had no dad in a world where everybody had a dad. He hated it and at times like that he hated his dad for not being there for him. But once he started playing lacrosse, they only used professional coaches and referees because most of the dads were unable or unwilling to coach lacrosse. As a result, Daniel didn't have to worry about being the only kid without a dad to help.

There were other times too when not having a dad in a world where most of his peers did have a dad was really hard for him. When he first started cub scouts, his dad had been around, but by the time he really needed help with his scouting activities, his dad was gone. He felt awkward always having to ask a friend if he could team up with him and his dad to complete a project, but he did it anyway. The one thing that he was truly grateful for was his godfather, Uncle Brandon. He didn't really like boy scouts, but he supported him in so many ways and gave him a positive male role model to emulate. When he first started considering what college he might want to attend, Uncle Brandon took him to see his own boys at college. Daniel had always enjoyed spending time with Uncle Brandon's sons when they were home and after they both went off to college it was a thrill to go and visit them.

His mother had made it clear to him from the beginning that lacrosse was just another way to get into the college of his choice, but that they didn't need the money and if he wanted to he could quit once he got there. For years his mother went over his college savings account with him whenever the statement came in so that Daniel could see what money had been set aside for his education. Daniel was a good student, but it felt good to have the backup of lacrosse for the college admissions people to consider. It really rounded out his resume.

At the beginning of each season for as long as he could remember, all the parents would come to the first practice so they could talk about dividing up duties and responsibilities for supporting the team throughout the season. One mother would volunteer to be the team mom and coordinate all their activities including assigning responsibility to various families for the numerous parties and gatherings they held throughout the season. One mom would be the fund raising chair and plan all the fund raising activities for the extra things the team might want or need. Other parents would volunteer to chaperone for away games and still others volunteered to organize the booster club to support the team at every game. Daniel's mom and another kid's father were the unofficial team doctors and were prepared to assist with medical needs at every game. This year was no different and it seemed like the parents were as excited to see each other as the kids were to get back to playing again.

After practice, Daniel and his mom went to the Lacrosse Store in the neighborhood to see what the latest equipment was for that year. The school provided all the basics, of course, but if they wanted some fancy new equipment, that usually meant purchasing it yourself. When they got to the store, it was already crowded with students and parents from teams from all over the city. Daniel saw a lot of kids that he had played against in years past but he was more interested in looking at equipment than socializing. His mother on the other hand was busy talking to other parents, mostly about the same thing they always talked about. What colleges had the best lacrosse squads and which high school had been the most successful getting their players into ivy league schools. Everybody was using lacrosse to help their kids get into the ivy leagues, but nobody expected them to play long term or have any career aspirations that involved sports. It was just a means to an end. Daniel and all of his friends understood that and in many ways, it made playing that much more enjoyable.

Of course playing high school sports also had other social advantages. Most of the lacrosse players had their pick of just about any girl they wanted to date. They were fast like basketball players and rough like football players. But unlike the athletes that played those sports, their practice schedules weren't nearly as grueling because nobody had any expectation that they would ever be professional athletes. Mostly they got respect from their peers because they were serious athletes who still knew how to have fun.

Chapter 15A

Birth Mother

D'Andre had gotten to high school on a wing and a prayer. Since he had always had trouble hearing, he had never been a very good student. He had been passed from year to year all the way through middle school. Then basketball had helped him get over for the first couple of years of high school, but now that he couldn't play anymore, he didn't have that crutch to lean on. He had essentially gotten a free ride all the way through the tenth grade and he knew now that he wasn't going to make it through his junior year unless somebody helped him.

Among the guys he hung out with there were only two ways to get over—sports or hook up with a smart girl. Since sports was over for him, he had decided that for now he would move on to plan b—a smart girl. There was a girl in D'Andre's class that he had known since kindergarten. Her name was LaTasha Washington and everybody knew what a good student she was. They used to go to Sunday school together at the church in their neighborhood. She had been one of those girls who started out as an ugly duckling, but by the time they got to high school she was beautiful. She had a smooth caramel complexion and light brown hair. At five feet eight inches tall, she had long gorgeous legs that she was proud to show off. Lots of boys had tried to talk to LaTasha, but she was not interested. She was smart and for the most part just couldn't be bothered. But D'Andre was her boy from way back and he knew better than to approach her the way the other boys had. He knew he had the advantage of already being friends with LaTasha.

LaTasha Washington was one of those girls who was determined to make something of herself in spite of her circumstances. She was the fourth child in a family of four girls all of whom had gotten pregnant and dropped out of high school—except for LaTasha. That fact that LaTasha had managed to get to the eleventh grade without getting pregnant was an accomplishment in itself in her family. Her mother just seemed tired, like she had given up on the idea of any of her girls making something of their lives long time ago. She didn't discourage LaTasha from doing well in school but she did nothing to encourage her either. After working twelve hour shifts as a custodian in the local hospital during the week to provide for her children, she just didn't have the energy to really parent her children. On the weekend, she was busy working her second job, parenting the children of a local doctor that she had cared for almost every weekend since the time they were born.

Two of LaTasha's sisters still lived at home. One of them had a five month old baby and the other one had an eighteen month old baby. The four of them shared the larger of the two bedrooms in their small house. That meant that LaTasha shared the smaller bedroom with her mother. That was ok with LaTasha though because at least it meant that she had privacy most of the time since her mother was always working. LaTasha had made the most of her safe haven and studied hard because she dreamed of being the first person in her family to make it to college. She had dreamed of going to college ever since she saw a story on television that featured a beautiful black woman lawyer. The woman dressed nicely and wore her hair in a pretty style. She spoke well and didn't have on too much makeup either. For LaTasha, this was her ideal.

One day soon after they started their junior year, D'Andre saw LaTasha walking home from school alone.

"Hey Tasha, wait up," he yelled.

"Oh, hey, D. What's going on?"

"Nothing much. Just need to get home to hit these books. What about you?"

"Oh, I need to study too. I'm going to get ahead on my reading for history so I can spend more time studying for the SAT test."

"Oh, yeah?" he asked, barely understanding what she was talking about. "You wanna stop and get something to eat on the way home?"

"I don't have any money."

"Don't worry about it. I got you. Let's stop and get a burger. They got a ninety-nine cent special around the corner."

LaTasha was actually happy that D'Andre had suggested they get burgers because she was starving. They ordered their food and then sat near the window to eat. They had been friends for so long that they fell easily into conversation. LaTasha had wondered for a long time how D'Andre was doing since he'd broken his ankle and couldn't play ball anymore, but they'd never had a chance to really sit down and talk. Some kids they knew were sitting at the next table making up lyrics for a rap song. D'Andre and LaTasha laughed as they listened to these guys trying to outdo each other. After they finished eating, D'Andre walked LaTasha the rest of the way home.

"Hey Tasha, I was wondering," D'Andre began, "if you might want to study together sometime?"

"That'd be great," LaTasha said, not realizing that he was really looking for a tutor, not a study partner. "What class should we work on together?"

"Well, how about history?" he said, remembering that she was going to study history that evening.

"I have history homework to do tonight. You want to study together this evening? We could go to the library."

"Yeah, sure."

"Let me just run inside and put some of these other books down and I'll be right back," she said as she ran into her house.

After that, D'Andre and LaTasha began studying together on a regular basis. D'Andre was getting more out of it than she was, but LaTasha enjoyed his company. Pretty soon, they were spending almost all of their free time together. D'Andre was nice to her and he even had a car that his uncle had given him. It wasn't new, but it was his. LaTasha felt so proud when he picked her up to go to the football games on the weekend. What started out as studying together soon developed into a real relationship. Even so, she was determined that she wasn't going to let him distract her from her goal of getting into college.

Even though LaTasha hadn't had anyone to guide her, she knew that there were a lot of things she probably needed to be doing by eleventh grade if she was going to get into college like taking the SAT test. She had made up her mind that she was going to figure out what they were so as soon as the school year began, she made an appointment to see her counselor. Her high school was huge. There were more than eighteen hundred students enrolled. The building had been built back in the fifties so it had a flat roof that leaked all the time and paint was peeling off the wall in several places. The classrooms themselves weren't built to house classes that now averaged fifty students for most subjects and the teachers didn't get paid enough to try to teach fifty students at a time. Nonetheless, the administration tried as best they could to keep up with their growing population of students that still included many students who did not speak english very well.

The students were assigned to counselors by last name. If your last name began with a W, like LaTasha's, then you were assigned to Mr. Brown. It didn't matter what you needed. All of the counselors were supposed to be able to help with whatever problem you had. Because there were so few counselors and so many students, LaTasha made an appointment to talk to her counselor just as soon as she could in the school year.

"Hi I'm LaTasha Washington, " she offered timidly to the secretary in the counselor's waiting area in the suite of offices that were shared by the school counselors.

"Sign in here on Mr. Banks list and have a seat," the woman said without ever looking up. LaTasha did what she was told because she was the kind of girl who was afraid of authority. After she signed in, she sat down on a worn and cracked leather couch that had seen better days. The room was stark and uninteresting and the walls were covered with posters. There was a poster about HIV and aids. Then there was a poster for a rape crisis center. Next to that was a poster about the dangers of alcohol and drugs and finally there was a poster about teen pregnancy with some hotline numbers on it. That pretty much seemed to sum up the issues that were of concern in this school. Outside of each counselor's door was a revolving rack with various brochures on them.

LaTasha got up to go over to one of the racks. The secretary eyed her suspiciously for the first time. She spun the rack around looking for something interesting. There was a brochure with information about the SAT. She already knew that was the scholastic aptitude test she needed to take to get into college, but she didn't know much else about it since nobody in her family had ever gone to college. She picked up the brochure and put it in her purse. There were some brochures for the local community college, and one or two other colleges. She took those too. There was also information about some summer academic programs including some programs about studying abroad. She thought that sounded interesting so she picked those up as well. As she flipped through the rack, she was startled by the door opening behind her.

"Ms. Washington?"

"Yes, LaTasha replied nervously."

"Please come in. I'm Mr. Brown"

LaTasha followed him into the cramped office. It had one narrow window with bars on the outside. The small desk and credenza were stacked with so many brochures that you could barely make out Mr. Brown's face above them. There were two chairs facing his little desk, but one of them was filled with magazines. Yellowing newspapers lay in big piles all over the floor. LaTasha was still trying to take in this scene when Mr. Brown brought her back to reality and the reason she was there.

"Well Ms. Washington, what can I do for you? Are you having problems at home? Are you in any trouble?"

LaTasha was shocked by his presumptiveness. Why did the counselors at this school automatically assume that if you were here you had a problem at home or school. She just wanted to talk to somebody who would help her focus on making plans for college. She couldn't talk to her friends about it because none of them were interested in college. Her mother worked hard and wanted the best for her, but she hadn't gone to college and really couldn't help her figure out what to do. Besides, her mother worked hard to make sure that they had a decent place to live. The last thing that LaTasha wanted to do when her mother dragged in from work was bother her about something as trivial as which course selections would enhance her chances of getting into college.

"No, I just wanted some information on the SAT . . ." she began. But before she could finish her thought and explain that she also wanted some guidance about her course work, Mr. Brown interrupted her.

"There are brochures out there on the rack about the SAT," he said almost impatiently.

" . . . but I also wanted some advice about college."

"Well, what do you want to know?" he asked almost dismissively.

"I don't know. Maybe some suggestions about the courses I should take, and some ideas about where I should go, what I should be doing now to get ready for the application process, how to apply and how to get money for school. I know how expensive college is and my mom doesn't have that kind of money."

"Well, we have worked very hard to gather information about the schools and programs that would best suit the students here and that information is right outside organized alphabetically. There is also some information on how to apply for scholarships. Now if there's nothing else, " he said almost daring her to ask another question.

LaTasha got the hint. That was all the help she was going to get from Mr. Brown today. She took her cue and got up to leave. She knew she should thank him for his time, except he hadn't really done anything to help her, so she just left. When she came out of the counselor's office, D'Andre was waiting for her in the hallway.

"Hey baby. What were you doin' in there?"

"Just trying to get some information on college."

"College? We ain't going to no college."

"Well, maybe you're not interested in going to college," she snapped, "but I am going to go."

"Baby the only thing I'm interested in is getting together with you Friday night after the football game for a little one on one," D'Andre purred as he stroked her back.

"Stop it D!" she yelled even more frustrated with him than she usually was after her unsuccessful meeting with Mr. Brown.

"That's not what you said last week, LaTasha."

"Well that was then and this is now. I'm tired of you always making fun of what I want to do to improve myself," she said tersely.

"Awright, awright. Sorry, baby. You know I didn't mean it. C'mon. Let me take you to the game Friday night. We can go out for burgers after and you can tell me about anything you want."

Even as he said the words, LaTasha knew he didn't really mean it. He just wanted to get with her and he would say anything to make that happen. Friday night would end like it always did. She and D'Andre would end up in the back seat of his car drinking malt liquor out of a forty-ounce bottle while he groped her trying to get her to give in. He wasn't everything she wanted, but he was dependable and she knew he cared about her. Feeling defeated, she finally just said, "Ok D. I'll go with you."

"That's what I'm talking about baby. And look here, I have a little surprise for you." He reached in his backpack and pulled out a brown paper bag with three of her favorite magazines, a soap opera digest, a teen fashion magazine and a magazine about the stars. At least reading these magazines gave her a chance to dream. She wasn't stupid. She knew that D'Andre was just being nice to her because he wanted something. But at least he acted like he was trying to pay attention to her and she had to admit that she enjoyed his attention and company.

When Friday night came, she waited at home for D'Andre to pick her up. When his car stopped in front of her house, she was surprised to see that there were other people in the car with him. When she stepped out on the porch, she could see that it was D'Andre's cousin James and his girlfriend, Juanita. She hadn't known that there were coming, but she was glad they were with D'Andre because if they were double dating that night, then it meant that she wasn't going to have to fight D'Andre off of her again.

The football game was great fun. They had a winning team that year and the energy was always high in the stands. They ate popcorn and drank soda and screamed to the top of their lungs along with all their other friends. They were still feeling the high from winning when they made it back to Andre's car after the game.

"Let's go somewhere and get our party on," Juanita said as they climbed into the car.

LaTasha didn't know exactly what she had in mind, but she didn't like the sound of it. But she felt that if she said anything, she might spoil everybody's good mood. So she quietly slid into the seat beside D'Andre and waited to see what was going to happen.

"I got an idea," D'Andre finally said. "Let's get us something to drink and drive down to the beach."

"That sounds good to me," Juanita squealed from the back seat.

They went to a local corner store and the guys jumped out while LaTasha and Juanita sat in the car waiting. LaTasha's mind was racing because she was trying to determine if she should talk to Juanita as an ally to help prevent anything from happening that she didn't want to happen that night. Just as LaTasha was about to say something, Juanita spoke first.

"Oooh, I can't wait to get to the Beach. I just got off my period and I'ma tear Jimmy up!"

"But . . . I think we're just going to go for a ride." LaTasha said hopefully.

"I don't think so. Not the way I heard them talking before we picked you up tonight," Juanita said laughing. "Just relax or you'll spoil it for all of us."

Relax? That was the last thing that LaTasha felt like doing right now. She was determined that she wasn't going to end up pregnant like all of her sisters but she was constantly having to fight D'Andre off of her. She thought, wrongfully it now seemed, that there was safety in numbers and that with D'Andre's cousin and his girlfriend there, that she wouldn't feel pressured to have sex with D'Andre. In fact, she was feeling the exact opposite now because it seemed that everyone was on the same program except her. When the boys got back into the car, each of them was holding a forty-ounce bottle of liquor in a brown paper bag. LaTasha knew that they had probably used fake id's to buy the booze or that they knew the store clerk since neither of them was old enough to buy liquor legally.

"Come here and give me a kiss baby," D'Andre crooned as he leaned across the seat toward LaTasha.

She gave him a little peck and then backed away.

"Oh, I know I'm gonna get a better kiss than that," D'Andre said teasingly. Then to LaTasha's surprise, he leaned against her, grabbed her breast and then forced his tongue so far into her mouth that she thought she was going to choke.

"Stop it D!" She yelled.

"Hey, that's what I'm talking about," James said grinning.

Then he turned to Juanita and started fondling her breasts and kissing her too. But Juanita started moaning and gyrating her hips in a way that let Jimmy know he could have what he wanted. As D'Andre pulled out of the parking lot, LaTasha felt trapped. She wanted to ask D'Andre to take her home, but she just didn't feel she could do that in front of his cousin. She just hoped that D'Andre respected her enough to understand that no meant no.

As they drove toward the Beach, LaTasha could hear James' and Juanita's loud, sloppy kissing in the back seat. She tried to ignore them and reached over to turn up the music. When she did, D'Andre grabbed her hand. D'Andre was getting excited listening to James and Juanita in the back seat and he thought it was about time that LaTasha stopped playing games with him and give him some. They had been going out for months and he had been really nice to her so he couldn't see what the problem was. He was probably the only guy he knew that had put this much effort into a relationship where the girl wasn't having sex with him. As far as he was concerned, that ended tonight. When LaTasha reached over to turn up the radio, he grabbed her hand with his free hand and started gently stroking her arm. Then he let her arm go and started gently rubbing her thigh. He could feel that she was a little nervous but figured that she would feel more relaxed if she had a drink. He reached behind the seat and picked up his bottle of malt liquor and handed it to LaTasha.

"Here, have a drink. It will loosen you up a little bit."

LaTasha didn't think she wanted to be loosened up, but she took the bottle anyway and took a little sip. It was a sickly sweet taste that lingered in her mouth after she swallowed. She was sure she didn't want anymore. She was also sure she didn't want to have sex with D'Andre. She liked him and she knew he had been very nice to her, but she didn't want to risk getting pregnant. They hadn't even had a chance to have a conversation about sex yet so she had no idea if he understood the need for them to make sure they were protected. She also didn't want to lose her virginity on the beach. As these thoughts continued to swirl in her head, D'Andre was pulling up to a secluded beach area.

D'Andre looked over at LaTasha and he could tell that she was thinking the same thing that he was. Finally they were going to make up for all the time that they had been waiting. He knew she was probably a little nervous but he figured that would be over soon. He couldn't wait to get his hands on her and from the looks of it, she couldn't wait either. When the car stopped D'Andre reached over and pulled LaTasha toward him and kissed her gently this time, but she pulled away.

"What's wrong?" D'Andre asked, surprised.

"D, I don't want to."

"You kiddin', right? I know you been waitin' for this just as long as I have and tonight is the night."

"Well, you're wrong. I haven't been waitin' and I don't want to. We don't have any protection and I'm scared."

"Come on, baby. You know I'm not going to let anything happen to you."

"What y'all up there yacking about? It's time to get busy," James said from the back seat.

"I told you she thought she was better than all of us, always talking about how she's goin' off to college and everything," Juanita chimed in.

"Well, while y'all sittin' here talkin' about it, me and Juanita gon' go and get busy. See ya'". And with that, James grabbed a blanket that was on the back seat and he and Juanita tumbled out of the car laughing.

"You see what you did! You embarrassed me in front of my cousin."

"I didn't mean to," LaTasha pleaded. "D'Andre you know I care about you," LaTasha said as she reached for his arm.

"Well you got a funny way of showing it," he said snatching his arm away.

"Please D, don't be mad at me," LaTasha said this time with tears in her eyes.

"Don't cry baby, don't cry," Andre said as he turned to face her and began kissing her tears. He kissed her face until all the tears were gone, and then he started kissing her neck. At first it tickled LaTasha but then the tickling sensation gave way to a more pleasant feeling. Before she knew it, D'Andre was kissing the top of her breasts and pushing the nipple up toward his mouth. She wanted to resist him, but it was starting to feel so good. He squeezed her nipples between his fingers and then gently licked them with his tongue. She let out an involuntary gasp. Before she knew it, D'Andre had let the seat all the way back and he was laying down on top of her. She could feel his hardness pressing against her and she tried to push him off of her, but when she pushed him up, he used the opportunity to pull her pants down and he was right back on top of her again.

Part of her wanted to resist and part of her wanted him to go on. She turned her head, but he turned it back toward him and began kissing her harder. She wanted to speak, but he smothered her words with his kisses. She knew she shouldn't but she didn't want to make him mad. Her head was spinning from the sensory overload she was experiencing—fear, lust, panic and passion all at the same time. But by not speaking up for herself, the decision was made for her. In her heart she knew she wasn't ready for sex, but when D'Andre parted her legs, she did nothing to resist.

After they dropped off Jimmy and Juanita, they rode home in silence. D'Andre felt a little guilty because he could tell that LaTasha didn't really want to have sex but felt pressured by the situation. He kept stealing sideways glances at her trying to see if she was mad or sad, but she had her head turned looking out the window. He reached over and touched her shoulder but she flinched so he pulled his hand back. When they pulled up to her house, he stopped the car and then turned to face her, but she was already getting out of the car.

"LaTasha, wait."

"What?" she said irritated.

"I'm sorry, I didn't mean to hurt you. I thought we both wanted the same thing."

"And what was that? Sex on the front seat of the car? No, you wanted what you wanted and you got it. I hope you're happy now."

"But I wanted us both to be happy."

"Well, that's not going to happen today," she said as she slammed the door behind her.

D'Andre tried to call LaTasha the next day, but she wouldn't take his calls. When he got to school on Monday, he looked for her in the cafeteria where she usually sat in the mornings, but she wasn't there. By the time the day ended, he was frantic to find her and to apologize again. He just didn't want to risk losing her. He decided to wait at her locker after school. As LaTasha turned the corner and started coming toward her locker, she could see D'Andre standing there. She had been avoiding him ever since they last saw each other and she wasn't sure she was up to talking to him quite yet, but it didn't look like she was going to have any choice. As she approached her locker, D'Andre smiled at her.

"You can run, but you sure can't hide," he said teasingly.

"Why are you standing at my locker?"

"Waiting for you, and I am not leaving until you talk to me."

"I don't have time. I have to catch my bus."

"I'll drive you."

"You think I'm getting in a car with you again?"

"Please LaTasha. I'm sorry. I didn't mean to disrespect you."

"No, means no, D'Andre. I can't believe you put me in that situation."

"I know and I'm sorry. And it won't happen again until both of us feel ready. I don't want to lose you."

"Why, because then you won't have anybody to do your homework?"

"Well, uh, that too," he said laughing. "But seriously, because I think we got something special and I don't want to mess that up."

"I hope you mean that and that you're not just saying that to keep me from being mad at you."

"I mean it and I brought you something to try to make up."

"What is it?" LaTasha asked smiling.

Andre didn't say anything. He just reached into his backpack and pulled out some of her favorite magazines. LaTasha smiled involuntarily. It was hard to stay mad at D'Andre. He was so sweet.

"Ok, but next time, when I say no, I mean it."

"I got it, I got it, now can we go?"

"Yes, we can go," LaTasha said smiling.

Chapter 15B

Earth Mother

LaTasha Washington was only sixteen years old, but she felt so much older than her years. She had worked hard all her life to try to escape her existence. She lived in a broken down house in a broken down part of town with a family that had long since given up on the American dream. But she was still a dreamer and to escape her reality, she turned to books. She had been an avid reader since she was in the first grade. While her friends were outside playing, she would escape to her room and then escape from her room through her books.

She had all the books she ever wanted since her mother brought her home all the books that the kids she took care of had outgrown. Because those kids were a couple of years older than LaTasha, she was reading above her grade level very early in her life. Her intense love for reading had its benefits. Not only did it allow her to escape the dreariness of her existence, but it also got her noticed by her teachers at school. Many teachers had taken an interest in LaTasha over the years, encouraging her, working with her after school and telling her about special programs. Toward the end of her sophomore year in high school, her English teacher asked her to wait after class so she could talk to her. LaTasha didn't imagine that what her teacher was about to say to her would change her life.

"Mrs. Burke, you wanted to see me?" LaTasha asked politely.

"Yes, LaTasha, come on in. I wanted to talk to you about your grades."

"My grades?" LaTasha asked hesitantly.

"Yes, your grades and your plans for the future. You know somebody as smart as you could really go places if you could find an environment that would nurture your talent."

"That's kind of hard around here, Mrs. Burke. All they do around here it teach you how to pass the tests so they can get higher rankings that translate into more money for the school. That is so boring to me. I don't ever feel like I'm being challenged."

"I know LaTasha. And that's why I wanted to talk to you about transferring to St. Matthews. They have a great program to help kids like you get a superior private school education."

"What do you mean, 'kids like me'?"

"Well, to put it bluntly, kids that are bright, but not white, and so are without many of the advantages that would have allowed you to attend St. Matthews in the first place. It's expensive, but you would be able to go tuition free starting at the beginning of your junior year next fall. You would just need your mother to give you permission to go and I can arrange everything else."

"I don't know what to say Mrs. Burke."

"Just say thanks and then go and make us all proud."

"Thanks. And I promise you I won't let you down."

"Oh, I don't have any doubt about that."

Despite the wonderful opportunity, LaTasha found it difficult to adjust to her new school. Most of the kids at St. Matthews were lifers and had gone there since kindergarten. There was a big entry point at ninth grade where they took in more students to begin high school but she had missed that by coming in the eleventh grade. At the earlier entry points, kindergarten, first and fifth grade, mostly legacies were admitted—children whose parents had previously attended the school, but at ninth grade there was an opportunity for other kids to gain admission. By then most of the legacy children were already attending St. Matthews or had consciously chosen to attend school somewhere else. It was always exciting at the beginning of a school year, but eleventh grade was a hard time for a new student to be coming to the school. It was a time for reunions for everyone else—a time to talk about summer vacations, but LaTasha was new and she felt like an outsider in this world of neatly pressed uniforms and gleaming hallways. The school itself was a beautiful old building made of limestone that had a central courtyard in the back where all of the high school students would gather before and after school to socialize. It was a noisy crowded place, but even in that space, LaTasha felt completely alone and lonely.

Daniel had noticed LaTasha before but they had never really spoken. It was clear she wasn't from Bayou Bend because he knew the few black families who lived there. One day when he saw her catching the bus after school and he guessed that she was probably one of the lucky minority kids attending St. Matthews on scholarship. Taking the bus was a dead give away. Up to ninth grade, almost all of his classmates were picked up by their moms or their nannies. But by eleventh grade, most of the kids had cars and drove themselves to school. In recent years the school, in an effort to diversify, had started seeking out minority applicants. They were even known to show up at a black church now and then to encourage more minorities to apply for admission. He knew without knowing that LaTasha was likely a product of this new effort.

She was nice enough and pretty too, but she didn't have the self confidence of most of the black girls he had grown up with. Girls whose fathers represented the best that corporate America, law and medicine had to offer. They were well-traveled and sophisticated, well-read and frankly just well off. To an outsider, they might be viewed as arrogant, but in their world, they were simply displaying the self-assured attitude that their families' money and power had bought them.

LaTasha seemed afraid of her own shadow. She clearly had no friends here and didn't seem like she was trying to make any. While the other girls huddled at lockers between classes to dish the latest dirt or make social plans, she walked quickly to her next class, working hard to avoid eye contact with anyone. Daniel had noticed her anyway and now he felt bad that he had never bothered to offer a hand of friendship to this new stranger. Now he was being forced to pay attention to her today because Mrs. Manford had called on her. Mrs. Manford had asked a question and then called on LaTasha for the answer. Daniel had sat near her for nearly a month but had never really gotten to know her. They didn't have any other classes together and he knew she didn't live in the neighborhood like many of his other classmates.

The question posed seemed like a simple one, "What was the warning that Icarus' father gave to him and why?" They had in fact begun their study of Greek mythology in the tenth grade. In the beginning of the year, they always built on material covered the previous year. This question was one that almost any of his classmates could have answered easily without even thinking too hard.

LaTasha stuttered, and then said in voice that was barely audible, "I don't know Mrs. Manford."

There was an audible gasp among the students in the class. A couple of the girls actually snickered. Mrs. Manford glared at them and then called on the girl who seemed to be snickering the loudest.

"Well maybe you can tell us the answer Ms. Lewis."

"Of course I can Mrs. Manford." Danielle Lewis said as she rose from her seat. Icarus' father told him not to fly too close to the sun because his wax

wings would melt. Of course he did it anyway and he went plummeting into the ocean to his death. In fact a very famous painting of the scene is at the Louvre in Paris and we saw it this past summer while we were there on vacation."

"Thank you Ms. Lewis."

LaTasha hadn't realized until that moment that she was still standing. By this point every eye was on her as she shrank back into her seat and tried to make herself invisible. In a moment the class was involved in a discussion of other Greek mythology and her moment of humiliation was forgotten by all except her. She didn't know the answer to the question because she had never even heard of the story. All these other kids seemed to know this stuff off the top of their heads. At the school she had come from, they certainly had not been studying Greek mythology. For everyone else this was a refresher, but for LaTasha who had come for a school that had barely survived closing the previous year because of the bad performance of students, this was completely new material. She had been reluctant to come to St. Matthews, but her teacher had encouraged her to apply and they had given her a full scholarship. She was in the top of her class before, but compared to these kids, she was sloppy seconds. She envied the way they recited the material with ease and confidence and how often they were able to discuss some museum exhibit or even country where they had previously encountered many of the things she was hearing about for the first time. It seemed so easy for them, but for her every day was a struggle.

At her previous school, many of the kids dropped out before they even got to high school. The high school itself only had a sixty-six percent graduation rate and very few of her friends talked about going on to college. St. Matthews was a college preparatory school. It was understood that one hundred percent of the students would go on to college—many to the coveted ivy league colleges in the east.

While LaTasha had been brought up to be seen and not heard, these students were encouraged to respectfully speak their minds and express an opinion. They knew how to think on their feet and aggressively defend a position. Not only was this completely foreign to her, but she didn't even have anyone with whom she could express her angst about this new environment. Her friends back in the neighborhood could care less about her desire to fit in at St. Matthews. To them, she was just trying to act white by going to that uppity school. Her counselor at St. Matthews was nice enough, but it was difficult talking to her about her feelings of inadequacy among the other students. Mostly, the counselors here assumed everything was fine with you at home and school and primarily focused their attention on helping you prepare yourself for college. She needed a friend.

When class was finally over, LaTasha hung back a little so she would not have to walk out with the other kids. But Daniel hung back too. He had made up his mind he was going to speak to LaTasha today and formally introduce himself. LaTasha was startled when she felt a hand on her shoulder and jumped at the touch.

"Hey, I'm sorry. Did I scare you?"

"Yes. I mean, no. I mean, I just wasn't expecting you know, anyone to touch me."

"I know. I'm sorry. I just wanted to say hello and to, you know, really introduce myself to you. I'm Daniel Pierce. I know you're new to St. Matthews and I should have made an effort to say hello before now."

"Well, thank you. I'm LaTasha Washington."

"Where'd you go to school before?" Daniel asked curious.

"Well I live down in Pecos City, so you probably never heard of the school."

"Wow, that's a long way off. You come all the way up here every day on the bus?"

"Yeah, you noticed?"

"Well, I saw you standing at the bus stop one day after school. How long does that take?"

"I take a bus from here to downtown and then I transfer to a commuter bus that goes to a park and ride in my area and then I get a local bus from there to my house. All together it takes me about an hour and a half."

You must be kidding. I can't imagine traveling an hour and a half each way to get to school."

"How long does it take you ?"

At that question, Daniel lowered his head, blushing slightly. He was almost embarrassed when he answered.

"About five minutes. I live right here in Bayou Bend. I'm a lifer here at St. Matthews."

"What does that mean?" Latasha asked.

"I've gone to school here since kindergarten, actually preschool."

"So, I guess you know just about everybody here, huh?"

"Well just about. But this year there are a few new kids."

"Yeah, like me. Well, it's been nice talking to you, but I need to get to class."

"Hey, maybe I can catch up with you after school?" Daniel asked hopefully.

"No, I have to catch my bus, remember?"

"Oh yeah. Well maybe I'll see you at the game Friday night?"

"Maybe, " LaTasha yelled out over her shoulder as she made her way down the hall. But she doubted it. How in the world was she ever going to be able to go to a game? The games were always at seven on Friday nights. She didn't have a way back up here and she had no idea how she would get home. But she really thought Daniel was nice. He was the first one who had really taken the time to try to know her. She needed a friend so she had to figure out a way to go to the game somehow.

LaTasha had always been smart. Even when she was very young, she was more interested in books than she was in anything else. Her mom was often too tired after working all day to deal with her and she would invariably send her to her room to watch t.v.. But more often than not, LaTasha just curled up with a book for the evening. For LaTasha, the books were paradise. Reading allowed her to escape the dreary existence she shared with her mom and her sisters and go off to far away lands that she dreamed of in her minds eye.

By the time LaTasha got to high school, she was one of the brightest students in her class. Although nobody had ever encouraged her, she knew she wanted to go to college ever since she saw a show on t.v. where a black woman was a lawyer. She just admired how confident and self assured she looked in her business suits sitting behind a nice desk. From that point on, LaTasha was sure that she wanted the same thing for herself. She knew it was the way to escape the life she and her mother and sisters were living. She had big dreams. And now that she was here at St. Matthews, she felt she actually had a chance to make those dreams a reality.

As LaTasha took her long bus ride home that evening, she couldn't stop thinking about Daniel. He had been so nice to her even though he obviously came from a well off family that lived in the neighborhood near the school. More than anything she wanted to go to the game on Friday night. She knew it wasn't really a date or anything, but she was looking forward to seeing Daniel there. Usually she studied on the bus ride home, but after she made the transfer downtown, she just stared out of the window daydreaming. She watched the buildings of the city fade away as her bus pulled onto the freeway. As the bus moved down the road, she began to see the familiar shapes of the oil storage tanks on the grounds of the refineries near her neighborhood. The sickly, familiar smell of petroleum products assaulted her nose. The surrounding neighborhood was filled with small shingle houses interspersed with rundown apartments. Her house was at the end of a dead end street and had a small yard that was mostly full of weeds that surrounded her mother's old broken down car.

After LaTasha got home, she fixed dinner like she usually did and waited for her mother to get in. She could hardly wait to tell her about meeting Daniel. More than anything, she wanted to go to the game on Friday night and she was hoping that her mother would help her figure out a way to get there. She was sitting at their old wooden kitchen table doing her homework when she heard the front screen door creek open.

"Momma, is that you."

"Yes, it's me baby. How you doin'?"

"Momma, I'm good. Momma, I met this really nice boy at school today. He's one of the first kids that's been nice to me since I've been there. And momma, he's going to the football game on Friday night. He didn't exactly ask me out or anything, but he said he hoped he would see me there and I really want to go. Momma, do you think you can help me figure out how to go?"

"Oh, my goodness, LaTasha. Slow down. I haven't seen you this excited since you got a bicycle!"

"Ok mom, ok. But can you help me figure it out?"

"Well, what time is the game honey and where is it?"

"It's at the school and it starts at seven. I guess it would be over by ten. I've thought about it and I figure I could stay after school someplace near there and then just go to the game. You could come meet me there later if you could get a ride."

"So you've already thought this thing out, huh?"

"Yes, momma."

"And you really want to go?"

"Yes, momma."

"Ok, I'll ask your Uncle Henry to pick me up and take me up there to meet you. How will I find you once I get there."

" I'll pick a place that I can meet you before the game and I will call you before you get there to let you know where it is. Then you can tell me what time to be there."

"Ok, that sounds good. I'm happy that you are excited about your new school."

"Me too, momma, me too."

That night, LaTasha fell asleep right away and dreamed endlessly about going to the football game on Friday night.

The next day, LaTasha couldn't wait to see Daniel so she could tell him she was going to be able to go to the game on Friday night. Yesterday she had wondered how she would be able to come, but now that she had almost worked it all out, she was anxious to let him know. She spotted him in the hall before class and was trying to think of a way to approach him. Before she could get up the nerve, however, Daniel walked straight toward her.

"Hey LaTasha. Have you thought any more about coming to the game on Friday night?"

"Uh, yeah, I have, actually. My mom said I can go. I'm going to have to stay after school and she's going to come meet me at the game later. I just have to figure out something to do until the game starts."

"Really? Well that's great. But what are you going to do from 3:30 in the afternoon until 7:00 at night?"

"I don't know right now, but . . ."

"Hey, I've got an idea. You're welcome to come hang out at my house and have some dinner. I'm sure my mom wouldn't mind."

"Are you sure?"

"Of course. I know it must be hard coming to a new school where you don't know anybody."

"Well, if you think it's ok, that would be great."

"Sure it is. I'll meet you after school and you can ride home with me."

LaTasha was ecstatic. She could barely wait for Friday night. For the next two days she worried about what she should wear. She pulled out one top and then another, trying to find the right thing. She finally settled on a nubby blue sweater and her jeans with the sparkles down the side that had a matching jacket.

When Friday came, she waited after school for Daniel . LaTasha was shocked when they walked up to a brand new imported hybrid vehicle that she had seen on t.v.. She knew all the celebrities were driving it who were trying to be environmentally conscious.

"Nice car," she said.

"Thanks. My mom gave it to me for my birthday. I would have picked something a little more sporty, but it gets great gas mileage."

As she got into the car, LaTasha noticed Daniel's backpack which he had thrown into the back seat. The front of it was monogrammed with the initials DAP.

What does that stand for?" she asked pointing to the backpack.

"My initials, DAP for Daniel Anderson Pierce. Anderson was my dad's name, but he died when I was about eight. He was a judge."

"Oh, really? I'm sorry."

"It was a long time ago."

"Is your house far?" LaTasha asked trying to change the subject.

"No, just about five minutes from here."

LaTasha sat back and watched as Daniel made his way through Bayou Bend on the way to his house. The neighborhood was full of beautiful one-of-a-kind homes that dated from the 1930's to the present. There were stately old mansions and newer McMansions scattered among the old oak and magnolia trees. The houses were set back far from the curb, some with long winding driveways with porte cocheres and others with circular driveways in front. Daniel's house was a mid century modern home that had been designed by a rather famous local architect. A story about the architect and the building of the house sat on a table just inside the door and LaTasha was immediately drawn to it.

"This story about your house is fascinating."

"Oh, yeah," Daniel said nonchalantly, "this famous architect designed it. I don't know much about him, though."

"Well, I would if it was my house," LaTasha replied.

"Yeah, I really should know more about him. I guess I just take it for granted since I've lived in this house all my life. Let's go see what's for dinner."

LaTasha followed his lead into the kitchen. As they entered, they could smell the meal of tortilla soup and tacos that was being prepared. Beautiful mexican style plates and bowls were on the table next to glasses filled with a pretty pink lemonade. The woman cooking turned to greet them when they entered the kitchen.

"Well, hello Daniel. Who is your friend," Maria asked. Maria had taken care of Daniel since he was a baby and nothing that he did escaped her notice. Right now, she was trying to determine if this dinner guest deserved any special notice or if she was just a friend from school.

"Maria, this is LaTasha, a friend from school. She's new to St. Matthews this year. That's why you've never met her."

Maria could tell immediately from his tone that LaTasha was indeed just a friend and that there was no reason for her to keep her antennae up to listen to their conversation.

"Welcome honey, have a seat. I hope you are hungry."

"Well, yes I am thank you," LaTasha said a little hesitantly. She wasn't used to the idea of having people wait on her, so she wasn't quite sure what

else to say to Maria. She took her seat and then waited nervously to see what Daniel would do next. She hoped he would bring over the soup and tacos so Maria didn't have to wait on them, but he just sat down and turned to Maria and smiled as if to indicate that they were ready to be served. LaTasha was embarrassed and ill at ease, but Daniel seemed happy and comfortable as Maria began putting soup into their bowls. Just as they started eating their tacos, the back door opened and Alexa Pierce arrived. Daniel looked up and smiled when he saw his mom.

"Hey, mom. What's up? This is my friend LaTasha," he blurted out all in one breath without waiting for her to respond to anything he said. "We're grabbing something to eat before the game."

"Well, hello honey. I'm fine thank you and yes I can see you are eating. Hello LaTasha. I'm Dr. Pierce," Alexa said extending her hand.

LaTasha jumped up quickly and grabbed her hand. She had no idea that Daniel's mom was a doctor. She remembered that his father had been a judge. "Hello, Mrs., I mean, Dr. Pierce."

"Well, are you enjoying your dinner?" Alexa asked.

"Yes, ma'am. It's really good."

"I guess you must be new to St. Matthews this year. Where do you live? Do I know your parents?"

"No, ma'am. I mean yes, I'm new and no you don't know my parents. I live in Pecos City with my mom and two of my sisters and their kids."

"Oh," Alexa said shooting a quick glance at Maria. She was looking for some clue as to whether she should be worried about this newcomer to her home. Was she some little ghetto girl looking for a way out of the ghetto who saw Daniel as a good catch. Maria could clue her in with just one gesture and as she looked her way, Maria nodded her head in a way that said, this girl is just a friend, nothing more, don't worry. With that reassurance, Alexa put on

her best fake smile and said, "Well, we are so happy to have you in our home for dinner. I'm going to catch up with you guys at the game later."

"Ok, mom," Daniel said casually, never picking up on the unspoken exchange between his mother and Maria that had taken place right before his eyes.

Daniel stopped on the way to the game to pick up three other kids from the neighborhood. Two other boys and another girl climbed into Daniel's car. On the way to the game, they talked effortlessly about things that were obviously a part of their shared history with each other . . . friends who would be there, who would be with who, where they should sit, what happened at the first game of last year. LaTasha squirmed nervously in her seat, trying to figure out a way to break into the conversation without sounding like she was trying too hard. Finally, the other girl addressed her directly, "Hey, cute jacket. Where'd you find it?"

"Uh, oh thank you. Well, my mom got it at WalMart, and I put the rhinestones on it myself."

There was a short silence before the girl finally replied, "If I die at WalMart, drag my body to Nieman's." Everyone laughed uproariously except for LaTasha. She wasn't sure if they were laughing at her or not, but it didn't feel good.

When they got to the stadium, the girl, whose name was Ashton, linked her arm in LaTasha's in a conspiratorial way and they walked arm in arm into the stadium. "I hope I didn't say anything to hurt your feelings, but if I did, I apologize. I didn't mean anything by it, ok?"

"Ok," LaTasha said, feeling a little better.

The game was a typical Friday night football game, but for LaTasha it was wonderful. She was having so much fun that she almost forgot to go meet her mother at the concession stand at the end of the first quarter. She jumped up from the bleachers and told her friends she would be right back. When she got to the concession area, she could see that her mother and her uncle were already there waiting for her.

"Hi mom, sorry I'm late. I was just having so much fun."

"It's ok baby. We were enjoying the game too. So you're having a good time?"

"Yes, momma, I really am. I'm sitting with some friends. Is it ok if I stay with them and meet you back here after the game?"

"That's fine."

"Oh, look momma. There's Daniel's mother."

"Really, well why don't you introduce me to her so I can thank her for having you over for dinner. Is his dad here too?"

"No. His dad is dead. It's just him and his mom. Let's go over so you can meet her."

LaTasha and her mom pushed their way through the crowd toward Alexa Pierce. She was standing talking to a couple of other moms from the school and was startled when LaTasha touched her shoulder and called out her name.

"Oh my goodness. Yes, dear, what is it?"

"Dr. Pierce, this is my mom, Sarah Washington. I wanted her to meet you."

"Oh, well hello Mrs. Washington. Nice to meet you. Are you enjoying the game so far?"

"Well, yes, we are. And I just wanted to thank you for having LaTasha over for dinner."

"Not at all. I'm glad she was able to accept Daniel's invitation. I know how hard it is to try to juggle all these activities for our kids."

"Yes, well I'm glad you understand. I also understand that we have something in common."

"What is that?" Alexa asked, slightly taken aback by the comment.

"We're both single moms."

Alexa's heart caught in her throat and she wasn't able to respond for a moment. How dare this woman lump her into the category of single moms as if this was something she had chosen for herself. Alexa gathered that this woman had probably never had a husband and here she was trying to compare her life and her choices to the tragedy of Alexa's life that had left her to raise a child alone. Alexa was livid and her anger was only exacerbated by the looks that she was now receiving from the other mothers she had been standing there talking with.

Without skipping a beat, Alexa tossed her hair then looked directly at the woman and asked as casually as she could, "Oh, was your husband killed as well?"

"No, I've never been married. I was just thinking about the kids."

Alexa smirked to herself. Just as she thought. This woman had made a choice to have children out of wedlock and she was trying to compare her life to hers. The other mothers were now staring at the two of them and Alexa wanted to extricate herself from this uncomfortable situation as quickly as possible.

"Oh, well it was nice to meet you," Alexa said, turning her back slightly with the hope that the woman would get the hint and walk away.

"You too," Sarah said.

As LaTasha walked her mom back over to where her uncle was standing, her mother said, "Well she seems nice."

"Yes, she does," replied LaTasha.

At that same moment, one of Alexa's friend was commenting on their encounter with Sarah, " Who the hell does she think she is coming over here talking to you about being a single mother. Was she honestly trying to compare her life to yours?"

"I have no idea," Alexa said, "but I can see I need to have a conversation with my son about the company he's been keeping."

"I'll say you do," the mother replied.

When LaTasha made it back to where everyone was sitting, Daniel wasn't there. The other two boys were just getting up but Ashton was still sitting there.

"Hey LaTasha," one of the boys called out.

"Come go with us to have a little refreshment," the other one said laughing.

"Uh, ok," LaTasha replied.

"LaTasha," Ashton almost yelled. "Come sit with me instead."

"Uh, ok," LaTasha said again. "I'll see you guys when you get back."

They walked off laughing to themselves as LaTasha made her way over to where Ashton was sitting.

"What's up," LaTasha asked, feeling there was something amiss.

"I'll tell you what's up. Those two are going off behind the stadium to smoke weed. They waited until Daniel left to bring it up because they knew he wouldn't go along with it. But I'm not down with that either. We don't have to do something just because somebody else thinks we should. I didn't want you to go with them and be put in a situation where you felt you had to smoke marijuana just because everyone else was doing it."

"Thanks, I appreciate it," LaTasha said.

The rest of the evening she thought about how glad she was to be here at St. Matthews. Meeting Daniel and now Ashton had really been a blessing for her. She was now more determined than ever to make the best of this chance she had been given.

Chapter 16A

Birth Mother

By the end of his junior year, D'Andre was thinking of dropping out of school. LaTasha had really helped him a lot, but his mother was only thirty-four years old and she looked as though life had beat her down a long time ago. More than anything he wanted to make her life more comfortable. He had hoped that basketball would let him do that, but now that that dream was over, he had to work to bring more money into the house. He started working in the grocery store sacking groceries. He had started going right after school every day and he worked until ten or eleven each evening. That obviously didn't leave any time to study, but when he brought his money home and saw the smile it put on his mother's face, he knew he was doing the right thing. Since he didn't have a dad, he knew it was his job to take care of his mother and he didn't want to disappoint her.

Even with LaTasha's help, when he worked a schedule like that, it wasn't long before his grades went completely downhill and he felt like a failure. But when he brought money home to his mother, it made him feel like a man. D'Andre believed that he was doing what he had to do. LaTasha was constantly on him to quit his job, but he just didn't feel he could. In addition to that, the guys who hung out on the corner near his house each night taunted him and made fun of his job. On a typical night he would hear them say things like, "hey grocery boy, you got any nuts?". Then the others would laugh. He would try to laugh it off, but inside he felt hurt and humiliated. One night, when he walked by the guys on the corner, they offered him something to drink.

"Hey man. Come on over here and get a beer. You look like you been working hard tonight."

D'Andre hesitated. He figured they just wanted to make fun of him again for working at the grocery store. At the same time, if he took the beer, they would probably stop messing with him.

"Come on man. We don't mean no harm. We just messin' with you about your job. Come on get a drink."

"Ok," D'Andre mumbled.

"Hey, you like workin' over there at the grocery store?"

"It's awright. I gotta help my moms out, so I gotta do what I gotta do."

"Well how much you pull down working over there at the grocery store?"

"Sometimes about one-fifty a week."

"A hundred fifty dollars? Is that all?"

"That's almost six hundred a month and it helps my mom out a lot."

"Well what would you say if you could make one fifty a day?"

"Are you kiddin'?"

"Naw, we ain't kiddin'. We dead serious. You interested?"

D'Andre knew in his heart that anybody making that kind of money was doing wrong. But he dreamed of making life easier for his mom. She had always had to work so hard, especially since his father died. He knew she depended on him to bring home a little extra money for them to live on and he was happy to do that. He also knew she hoped he would play pro basketball but that dream was over. But even as he stood there talking, fear was gripping his heart. He knew he could make more money, but at what cost. He finally steadied his voice enough to respond and ask a question.

"What would I have to do?" he asked.

"Not much, man, not much. Just run a little package somewhere for me and bring me back my money—all of it—and I will give you a buck fifty."

"A buck fifty?"

"Man, I'm talking about a hundred fifty dollars."

"Oh, snap. Well, I can't do it tonight, but, uh . . . ."

"That's ok, man. We understand."

But even as D'Andre walked away, he could hear them laughing behind him.

"Man, why you fuckin' with that little punk? Leave that kid alone."

D'Andre was humiliated, but he knew he had to make more money somehow. He finally decided to go talk with his uncle about working at his auto shop. His uncle had owned an auto repair business a long time ago and he had recently reopened it. His dad used to work there when he was alive and D'Andre had fond memories of playing in the shop while his dad worked when he was a little kid. But after his father died, he had lost his interest in working on cars. Oh he could fix anything he wanted to on his own car, but he didn't think he was up to working on other people's cars. His uncle convinced him otherwise and in no time at all, he had regular customers who asked for him by name.

Not long after that, D'Andre decided to drop out of school so he could have more time to work. With his hearing problem, he had never been a really good student and now with no chance of playing college ball he couldn't see any good reason to stay in school. The only thing was that he hadn't gotten up the nerve to tell LaTasha yet and he wanted to do so before she found out from someone else. He picked her up from school like he usually did one day. As she got into the car, she noticed D'Andre was wearing a new necklace with a large jewel encrusted medallion hanging from it. The initials DAP were outlined in large rhinestones.

"Where did you get that?" LaTasha asked.

"You like it don't you?"

"I wouldn't say that. What is it?"

"My initials, DAP, D'Andre Parker."

LaTasha just rolled her eyes, but D'Andre didn't even notice. As they continued the ride home, he decided to break the news to LaTasha.

"So, I'm not going to school anymore."

"What? You dropped out!" LaTasha screamed.

"I'd say it's more like I got pushed out."

"And what do you mean by that?"

"I mean I went to see Coach Johnson, the same man who told me no grades, no ball, to ask him for some advice. He said I wasn't a very good student and I certainly wasn't college material now that I couldn't play ball, so he couldn't see the use in my staying in school when I was already making good money down at my uncle's shop. He suggested I go take the GED and get it over with."

"So are you going to take the GED?"

"Well, yeah, just as soon as I can find some time to study to get ready. I don't think I'm ready right now."

"Yeah, uh huh, sure. You gon' get a GED later, huh? Just like everybody else who leaves school with the intention of getting a GED."

"What do you mean, girl?"

"I mean it will never happen. Wake up. You start making more money and pretty soon you forget all about school and the thought of getting a GED goes out the window. Just take me home. I can't talk about this anymore right now," LaTasha said rolling her eyes again.

And just like LaTasha said, it wasn't long before D'Andre started getting used to the money he was making. It wasn't much, but to him, it was more than he had ever had and he felt his life was good.

LaTasha, on the other hand, just kept wishing that somebody would help her figure out what to do with her life. Her mother wanted to be there for her, but she was too busy working to keep a roof over their heads. For years she had worked taking care of the children of a local doctor. They had two children, a boy and a girl that were a couple of years older than LaTasha, but their lives were very different from LaTasha's. All her life she had envied how easy life had seemed for them. Whatever they wished for or dreamed about was theirs for the asking. Her mother had told her that the kids were nice enough, but they seemed to have no understanding or conception that other children had dreams too, but that most of the time there was no way to fulfill them.

LaTasha had hoped that once she got to high school that at least her dream to go to college and become a lawyer might come true. But after her counselor wouldn't even help her by giving her some guidance on how to get prepared for college, she didn't believe she had much of a chance. She went to class faithfully every day, but she didn't have any idea how she was going to make anything of her life. She still daydreamed about the beautiful woman lawyer she had seen on television, and it made her wish that she could be a lawyer someday, but she didn't know any lawyers, so she didn't really think that was a realistic possibility.

One day after school, she decided to go to the local community center to see if there was anybody there she could talk to about her desire to go to college. By the time she got there, it was close to closing time, but one of the counselors was still there. He was a man of about forty with thinning hair and a stomach that was just starting to hang over his belt, but when LaTasha walked in, he smiled a warm smile that made her feel right at ease. She walked up to him and introduced herself and asked if he might be able to provide her some information on college admissions. He told her that he could, but that he needed to clean up a little bit before the end of the day and asked LaTasha to wait in his office. For the first time in a long time, LaTasha was excited about her future.

When the man finally came into his office where LaTasha was waiting, he closed the door behind him. LaTasha didn't feel as comfortable at this late hour with the door closed, but she needed help and this man was one of the first people she had met who seemed at least willing to talk with her. Instead of sitting in the chair behind his desk, he took a chair next to LaTasha and then turned to face her directly. As she started explaining her dilemma about how she needed help with the SAT tests and information on some colleges he nodded sympathetically. Then he patted her arm in a reassuring way. Before LaTasha could finish talking, he had started rubbing her arm. The gesture was barely noticeable at first, but then he began to rub higher so that the side of his hand brushed against her breast. LaTasha backed up, but the man grabbed the arms of both of the chairs and pulled her chair closer to him.

"Stop it," LaTasha yelled.

"Calm down, calm down. Don't you want me to help you with your problems?"

"Yes, but you're making me feel uncomfortable."

"Really? I didn't mean to. I just wanted to see if I could make you feel better. You seem so tense and upset right now." And with that he reached over and began to massage her shoulders.

"Listen. I came in here to get some help and I don't want to be touched like that. Take your hands off me or else . . ."

"Or else what?"

"Or else I'm going to tell somebody what you did to me."

"Oh come on. I don't mean any harm. Besides, who's going to believe you. I've been a counselor here for ten years and I have a great reputation."

"Well, I've lived in this neighborhood all my life and I know that there are two ways to get justice—the legal way and the illegal way. And I have a crazy boyfriend who would probably love to help me get some justice if you messed with me."

"Aw baby, why you have to be like that. Ok, ok, look, I'm sorry. You're just so damn pretty. But my bad. Let me just walk you out."

When he got up, LaTasha noticed for the first time that he had to use a key to unlock the door. Her heart raced in her throat as she jumped up and ran for the door. She knew she really couldn't tell D'Andre about what had happened because he would probably kill the guy. So she went home feeling defeated and no closer to getting the help she needed to make her dreams come true.

CHAPTER 16B

Earth Mother

After going to the football game LaTasha was on cloud nine. She couldn't wait to get to school the next Monday so she could see Daniel and thank him for inviting her to the game. Even though it wasn't exactly a date since they sat with a whole crowd of people, it really had seemed like Daniel was glad that she was there. She had thought about calling him the rest of the weekend and had even looked his number up in the school directory, but she couldn't think of any excuse to call him. So she had waited anxiously for Monday to come so she could see him again.

Daniel had been really glad that LaTasha had decided to come to the game. He knew that she was new to the school and he was empathetic about how difficult it must be to try to make friends in a new setting. He hadn't realized when he suggested it how much trouble it would be for her to get to the game that evening since she lived so far away. He was really glad that he was able to help her out by letting her come hang out at his house after school until the game began. He could tell that LaTasha wasn't that comfortable around his friends at the game, but he was hoping that she would befriend some of the other girls soon and become a little more comfortable hanging out with everyone. He decided he would ask her when he saw her in English class that day whether she had talked with any of the other girls over the weekend.

The last period of the day D'Andre and LaTasha took English together. That week they were studying the use of language. Their teacher had asked each of them to bring in a favorite poem to recite to the class. LaTasha had struggled with the assignment because she hadn't ever read any poetry so she didn't have a favorite poem. When she went to the library and started looking at some of the poetry books, she really couldn't find anything that moved her. Flowery poems about love or the seasons didn't really appeal to her or match her reality and she couldn't seem to find anything else that would work.

LaTasha was glad that she wasn't going to be reached that day because she didn't have anything prepared to recite to the class. Finally, it was Daniel's turn and she wondered to herself what he would recite that day. Daniel was actually excited to have the chance to recite his poem to the class. He knew he would get a chance afterward to explain why he had picked this poem, "Dream of Freedom" by Langston Hughes. He wanted to recite this particular poem to introduce his classmates to the poetry of Langston Hughes who often wrote about how America had not provided African Americans a real chance at the American dream. Daniel had been moved by his poetry and he hoped his friends would also feel moved or at least enlightened. He had practiced it over and over in the mirror because he wanted to give a moving delivery, and he did. He recited from memory, speaking slowly at first . . .

There is a dream in the land
With its back against the wall . . .

He continued on a little louder to emphasize the next stanza

There are those who claim
This dream for theirs alone—
A sin for which we know
They must atone.

Daniel then paused dramatically. He wanted his words to sink in. He noticed some of his class mates twist uncomfortably in their seats. That was exactly the reaction he wanted. He hoped it would stir some lively discussion after he finished. He recited the next two stanzas that continued with the theme of providing the dream for everyone, equally without regard to class or race. Then he took a deep breath so he could make a dramatic finish as he got to his favorite part of the poem . . .

This dream today embattled,
With its back against the wall—
To save the dream for one
It must be saved for ALL—

When he finished, you could hear a pin drop in the room and then finally Mrs. Manford started clapping and the rest of the class followed suit. As if he had just finished a violin recital, he took his bow, grinning from ear to ear. The discussion that ensued was stimulating. Daniel talked about how Langston Hughes had lived during the Harlem Renaissance of the 1920's and had written extensively about the struggle of African Americans against racism and in celebration of black culture. His classmates were intrigued to find such an outspoken and forward thinking man had accomplished so much during his lifetime and Daniel was thrilled to have been the one to share his work with his classmates.

LaTasha had listened intently as Daniel read his poem. But it wasn't just what he said, it was how he read it. He seemed to have so much feeling for the words. She wondered how he was able to find something that moved him so much. She wondered how she would ever be able to feel that moved by reading poetry.

After class LaTasha waited for Daniel in the hallway. "I really liked the poem you recited today. I was wondering how you choose that poem?"

"I chose it because it had personal meaning for me. You really start enjoying poetry when it touches you personally in some way and that poem does that for me."

"Why?"

"Because it reminds me of something that Dr. Martin Luther King once said, 'we may have come here on different ships, but we're all in the same boat now'. And it makes that point without being defiant or militant. It just states a fact. You can't keep somebody down without staying down there with them."

"I didn't know that poetry could touch you so deeply. I don't really know anybody who reads poetry. Back in my neighborhood people think it's lame and they make fun of you if you read poetry."

"Really? That's too bad because it can really be inspiring. In fact, I'm meeting a group of friends this afternoon at the River Bend Grill to talk about music lyrics as poetry. What we realized is that music lyrics are really poetry for our generation, so we're all getting together to talk about it. Do you want to come with me?"

"Oh, I don't know," LaTasha said hesitantly. I don't even know where that is or how I would get there."

"I'll give you a ride. Come on."

"Ok, then, but can you drop me back at the bus stop later."

"Sure."

They walked to the parking lot behind the school and climbed into Daniels' car.

"I have to admit, I'm a little nervous about going to a study group. It's not something I've ever done before."

"You'll be fine. And it could actually help you figure out how to find a poet that can inspire you. I didn't used to go to study groups either, but then my mom made me go with her to a lecture by a woman named Lani Guinier. She went to law school with my dad. She talked about her new book and discussed how much African-American students had improved their grades after they began studying in a group setting. It seems that the Asian kids who had better grades already understood the value of collective thought. They weren't any smarter, it's just that they took advantage of their collective wisdom—they just studied smarter. She really made an impression on me and the next time somebody asked me to join a study group, I jumped at the chance."

"Has it made any difference in your grades?"

"I think it has."

Just then they pulled up to the Bayou Bend Grill. It was like something out of a 1950's sitcom. LaTasha could hardly believe that a place like this still existed. There was a counter with stools where they made real malts, fresh lemonade and ice cream soda's. There was a grill in the back serving wonderful looking and smelling hamburgers. The walls were lined by booths, but the center of the restaurant had several large round tables that served as community tables. Anybody could sit and join in whatever conversation happened to be going on there. The poetry group was sitting in one of the large tables near the front window. Most of the students had already ordered drinks and food as well. LaTasha's heart caught in her throat for a second as she realized she didn't have the money to buy any food. Daniel looked at her and then at the table and sensing her hesitation, leaned over and whispered, "Don't worry about the tab—just order what you want—I've got you covered."

They joined the other students at the table who were already having a lively discussion about the lyrics of a new Kanye West song. LaTasha felt right at home joining in this discussion and wondered to herself why she hadn't made the connection before between music lyrics and poetry. The discussion opened her eyes to a whole new way of looking at poetry. Daniel was happy to see that LaTasha really seemed to be enjoying the discussion. He ordered burgers and fries and thick malted shakes for both of them. They devoured their food as they continued a very heated discussion about whether hip hop had lost some of its legitimacy as message music by letting the record labels co-opt them to sell gangster rap. When it was finally time to go, LaTasha leaned over to Daniel and said, "I can pay you back later."

"Don't even worry about it. My mother keeps an account here and I just charge whatever I eat on it. She's used to me taking friends out to eat. It's really no big deal. Did you enjoy yourself?"

"More than you'll ever know. Thanks for inviting me."

After Daniel dropped LaTasha off at the bus stop she rode the bus home smiling all the way. She had no idea that students could get so excited about studying and discussing their ideas and arguing their points of view. This was a whole new world to her where learning was fun and exciting and nobody made fun of you for wanting to learn and explore new ideas. She was already thinking about how she would go about finding a poet to read so she could finish her class assignment. As the bus rolled down the highway, she daydreamed about the day until she nodded off to sleep. When the bus pulled to a stop, she woke up from her dreams to the nightmare of her own crumbling, ramshackle neighborhood, but this time, she had a little hope in her heart.

The next morning she went in to see Mrs. Manford before homeroom. She confessed right away that she didn't have a poem picked out and didn't know how to go about finding a poem that she wanted to read. But she felt different somehow. Even though she was confessing to not having been able to complete the assignment she felt excited and confident and was anxious to get the help she needed. Mrs. Manford just smiled as the words poured out of her excitedly about searching for a poem that had meaning for her.

"Well, LaTasha, you might start by picking a subject that interests you. You may recall that yesterday Daniel picked a poem about freedom and equality because it was clear that he felt passionate about that. You may want to pick something about nature, or the seasons or love."

"Or maybe how hard it is to find good love," she replied laughing.

"That's a good point," Mrs. Manford said. "Hey how about this poet," she said as she turned to take a book off her shelf. " Her name is Wendy Cope. She is a modern poet with a wry sense of humor about life. I think you would enjoy reading her work."

"Thank you Mrs. Manford. I'll take a look and bring your book back to you."

LaTasha read the book until the start of class that morning and read in between every class that day. By lunchtime she had found her poem so instead of taking lunch with the other kids, she went off in a corner and began practicing for her presentation that afternoon. By the time class began she was ready. When Mrs. Manford asked who was ready to recite, LaTasha was the first one to raise her hand. Mrs. Manford looked a little surprised, but she smiled and called on LaTasha.

LaTasha got up and turned to face the class. She was nervous, but Daniel caught her eye and gave her a little wink. That was just the reassurance she needed to begin.

"The name of the poem I have chosen to recite for you today is "Being Boring" by Wendy Cope."

She took a deep breath and began to recite. She noticed that not only did she have everyone's attention, but several of her classmates began smiling at her after she read the first stanza. The poem was about a woman who was extolling the pleasure of living a simple and drama free life in a boring but happy relationship. It went on to discuss how happy the woman was to escape from her past life full of troubled relationships. It was something that resonated with her because all she wanted was to have a normal, drama free life and drama free relationship. It was something that she had dreamed about most of her life. The feelings it inspired in her made her know she would be able to recite it well. She ended with a flourish.

Someone to stay home with was all my desire
And , now that I've found a safe mooring,
I've just one ambition in life I aspire
To go on and on being boring.

Her classmates got to their feet and clapped while they laughed aloud at the poem. LaTasha knew that they were laughing at the poem, not at her and her heart beat so fast it felt as if it was going to leave her chest. She could not stop grinning and she looked over at Mrs. Manford and saw that she was smiling broadly too. She managed to also sneak another look at Daniel and again he winked at her. She was half tempted to wink back, but decided that there was plenty of time for that later.

When they got out of class that day, Daniel came up to LaTasha and gave her a big hug. He was genuinely happy for her success, especially since he knew that studying poetry and having to recite in front of others was so new to her. He really wanted her to know how proud he was of her accomplishment and he hugged her spontaneously without even thinking about it.

LaTasha was shocked and delighted when Daniel hugged her in the hall after class. She felt sure that the hug was a sign that there was a real chance that he might like her. As they walked down the hall together they talked easily about their next homework assignment. This time, they had to select a work of art they admired and then write an essay about it. LaTasha was scared to death, but Daniel talked easily about selecting an artist for the project.

"How will you figure out what piece of art you're going to write about?" LaTasha asked.

"Well, the easiest way is just to pick an artist that your parents collect and then write about one of those pieces. That way you have all the information you need right at home."

LaTasha stared at him blankly. Suddenly, something that his mother had said to him a long time ago came back to him. "Think about who you are talking to before you open your mouth to speak and then try to put yourself in that person's place. Would you be offended by the statement if you were them. At the end of the day Daniel, we are our brother's keeper." He had done it again. He had spoken nonchalantly about using your parents art collection to complete an assignment as if everybody's parents had an art collection. How could he have been so insensitive and what could he do to recover? Suddenly it occurred to him that he had a chance to correct his faux pas.

"If you like, you can come over to my house after school today and start working on the assignment. I can show you some of the art at my house. My mom has a great collection and a book that she has compiled with information on each piece. It would really help us get started on this paper."

"I would like that," LaTasha said smiling.

"Ok, meet me at my car right after school."

"I'll see you there."

Daniel was relieved. He had accidentally spoken without thinking but he had made a good recovery. He really hadn't thought about how difficult it might be for somebody like LaTasha to come to a new school and especially one with a culture like that of St. Matthews. So many of the assignments were given because the teachers already knew that you had access to things that they were demanding of you. When they gave an assignment to write about your summer travels, they actually expected that you were going to have some summer travels. When they requested that a mother participate in some activity at school, they expected her to show up and she always did. If you were told to bring some materials to school the next day, you brought them. There was no question about whether you could afford them. That consideration never entered into anyone's consciousness.

For her part, LaTasha was ecstatic. Daniel had invited her to his house again. She was sure that this meant something special. She was so happy to be invited again so soon. Daniel waved as he saw LaTasha approach his car.

"Hey there," he said smiling, "ready to go?"

"Absolutely."

A few minutes later they arrived at Daniel's house. As he held the front door open for LaTasha, he said. "Let me show you my mom's collection."

As LaTasha went into the hose, Maria yelled out to Daniel from the kitchen.

"Danny, is that you baby?" .

"Yes, Maria it's just me and my friend LaTasha. ?Que tiene para comer? Tenemos hambre."

"Sopa y pan."

"What are you talking about," LaTasha asked nervously.

"Want some soup and rolls for a snack? Maria already has some ready."

"Sure."

"Then I can show you our art collection."

Maria served them the best tortilla soup that LaTasha had ever tasted along with some flaky, buttery rolls. It was warm and satisfying. As soon as they finished, Daniel walked her around the living room and dining room, painting to the work of various artists and explaining something about each artist and their painting. LaTasha finally saw a painting that took her breath away. Daniel explained that it was a work by William Tolliver called

"Pas deDeux". It depicted two beautiful black ballet dancers, a man and a woman dancing gracefully across the canvas. Daniel said he had always liked the piece, but had never thought much about it really. LaTasha, on the other hand was fascinated by it and decided she would write her essay about it. Daniel picked a pieced by Henry Ossawa Tanner called "The Banjo Player". They were sitting at the kitchen table discussing their choices for their essays when Daniel's mom came home.

"Hi Daniel, I didn't know you were having company today," Alexa said eyeing LaTasha.

"Oh, hey mom, you remember my friend LaTasha."

"Of course," Alexa said somewhat cooly, "what are you working on?"

"We're just studying mom. We have to write an essay for our English class about a piece of art."

"Oh how nice. LaTasha does your mother collect any artist I might know?"

Embarrassed, LaTasha just hung her head and said, "No ma'am."

Daniel was furious with his mother for this obvious slight. He recalled vividly that she was the one who told him to consider who you were talking to before you opened your mouth to speak. She obviously had to know LaTasha's mother didn't have an art collection. She was just being rude and condescending to his friend. He decided he would let his mother know how he felt. "Mother, I think it is obvious to you that LaTasha doesn't have an art collection at home. That's why we're working here. What is it you told me? We are our brother's keeper."

Touche, Alexa thought to herself, but instead she ignored his little outburst and asked innocently, "Are you almost finished?", hoping she could put a quick end to this conversation.

"We thought we could finish it up this week, but it looks like we'll have to do some work this weekend too," Daniel said, realizing even as he spoke how much this would upset his mother

"But honey, don't you remember, we're going to the beach house this weekend? It's the first weekend in forever that you haven't had a lacrosse game," Alexa protested.

"Oh, you're right mom. I completely forgot," he lied. Hey I have an idea. We've got plenty of room at the beach house and we have to pass right by the city where LaTasha lives on our way down there. We could stop and pick her up and she could go to the beach house with us this weekend so we can finish our project!"

"I don't know," LaTasha said. "I don't think your mom would want me to go to your beach house."

Daniel turned and glared at his mother, daring her to object to his suggestion.

"Of course, we would love to have you dear," Alexa said through clenched teeth. LaTasha was right. She didn't really want to have her, but the way she said it made Alexa feel like she was on the spot, so she thought the only way to keep peace in her house was to be gracious and invite her. Of all the girls that Daniel could befriend, Alexa just couldn't understand why Daniel would bring home some girl from the hood. Alexa had heard all about these kind of girls. They latched on to any well-to-do black boy they could find and then they tried to get pregnant to trap him. Alexa could see that her relaxing weekend at the beach was out the window. She was going to have to stay awake to keep an eye on LaTasha this weekend.

When they got to the beach that weekend, LaTasha felt awkard and ill at ease, but Daniel did his best to reassure her. Alexa was doing her best to keep an eye on Daniel and LaTasha, but one afternoon she had to go to the store and leave them alone. As she pulled out of the driveway, she was relieved to see that Daniel and LaTasha had decided to leave the house to go for a walk on the beach. Daniel had decided to take LaTasha to one of his favorite secluded spots on the beach. When they got there, they sat down on the sand.

The sun was beating down on them and although it was a cool day their bodies were warm. It completely caught LaTasha by surprise when Daniel leaned over and kissed her. Even though she had waited so long for him to do that, it still took her breath away. As she felt the warmth of his kiss, her head began to spin from the sensory overload she was experiencing—fear, lust, panic and passion all at the same time. But she finally got her wits about her and decided to speak up for herself. She knew she wasn't ready for sex, so she decided to tell him so before things went too far. To her surprise, Daniel was very apologetic and understanding. He squeezed her hand and then helped her up so they could make it back to the house before Daniel's mother got home.

Chapter 17A

Birth Mother

LaTasha had always been one of the best gymnasts at her school. So when she got butterflies in her stomach one day as she prepared to do the vault, even she was surprised. When the feeling didn't go away after a couple of days, she went to see the school nurse.

The very first thing the nurse asked her was the date of her last period. LaTasha opened her mouth to speak, but nothing came out. Fear gripped her chest and throat as she realized her period was in fact late. What would she do? Without saying another word, the nurse directed her to the bathroom and handed her a pregnancy testing kit.

She cried as she watched the double pink lines appear that indicated the test was positive. Pregnant! LaTasha was afraid to open the door, to the restroom, but finally the nurse opened it from the outside, took the stick from her with one hand and handed her a note to proceed directly to her school counselor with the other.

As LaTasha sat in the waiting room of the counselor's office, those same familiar posters stared down from the wall. There was a poster about HIV and aids. As she looked at it, for a moment her concern about the pregnancy gave way to an even greater fear that she could have also contracted aids from unprotected sex. Then there was the same poster for a rape crisis center. Next to that was a poster about the dangers of alcohol and drugs and finally there was a poster about teen pregnancy with some hotline numbers on it. This time she took out a pencil and paper and scribbled the hotline number down. As she did so, she noticed the secretary at the desk look at her, then back up at the poster before shaking her head. LaTasha felt small and stupid under her critical glare. She got up and crossed the room to look at the brochures on the revolving rack. As she spun the rack around she thought about how different her choices were this time than the last time she came here looking for information. This time she skipped over the brochure that contained information about the SAT and picked up the one about HIV instead. She already knew about the dangers of HIV, but had never thought it might happen to her. She put the brochure in her purse. There was a brochure from a group that talked about helping unwed mothers make the choices that were right for them and finally there was a brochure from a center that helped girls place their children for adoption. She took those too. There was also information about some summer school programs for pregnant teenage mothers . She thought she might need that so she picked it up as well. As she flipped through the brochures she was startled by the door opening behind her.

As she walked into his office, she prepared herself for the same dismissive tone she had encountered the last time she was here, but was surprised when Mr. Brown addressed her in a voice that could almost be described as kind.

"How can I help you today, Ms. Washington?"

LaTasha wondered if he knew why she was here—that the nurse had sent her. And then she realized that of course he did. From the doorway she could see her pink slip from the nurse's office was sitting in the middle of his desk. How ironic she thought—pink lines on the stick means a pink slip for pregnancy for the counselor's office. She thought about what to say to Mr. Brown for a minute and then she decided this might be her only chance to ever tell this man that she felt he hadn't done right by her the last time she was here and that if he had, she might not be here at all. With her head held high, she walked past him into his office.

"Mr. Brown," she began, "I am here because the nurse sent me to see you and I need some help. But I needed some help the last time I came in here too and you didn't even try to help me. I was really interested in college but you made me feel like I had no hope and that it was out of reach for me just because I'm poor and I'm black, I live in this neighborhood, and I go to this school. Those aren't things I can do anything about. But I thought with a little help from some people who cared that I might have a chance to save my dream of having a better life. I left here discouraged and feeling like the only person who cared about me was my boyfriend. And that's one of the reasons that I'm here today. I let him, a person with no dreams for the future, talk me into making bad choices for myself. Now I'm seventeen years old and I'm pregnant and I need to try to make some good choices for myself and for my baby. Can you help me now?"

Mr. Brown was dumbfounded. Nobody had ever talked to him like that, especially not a student. He realized that much of what LaTasha said about him was true. He had grown calloused and indifferent about most of the students here. He saw so little sincere effort to succeed that he made little effort to help even those who made the effort to come and see him on their own. Mostly he had been counting the time until he was eligible to retire and now he was being called on the carpet for it by a pregnant teenage girl whose hope he had taken away. When he opened his mouth to speak, his voice cracked at first. Surprised, he quickly closed his mouth to regain his composure.

"LaTasha," he began slowly, "I'm sorry. You're right. I didn't do enough to encourage you when you came here asking about college. And I don't want you to think that because you are now pregnant that college is out of reach for you. There is a program in our school system that would allow you to finish high school at a special school for teenage mothers. There are also some colleges that have dorm settings for young mothers. But if you really want to know what I think, I think that you are too young to raise a baby."

"But I don't want to have an abortion."

"I didn't suggest that. Have you considered adoption?"

"Well . . . no, I haven't."

"Well, it's something you should think about. Here are some brochures on the high school and college programs I mentioned for teenage mothers. And here is another brochure about adoption. Why don't you take these home and give it some thought and come back and see me as soon as you can. If I don't hear from you in a couple of days, I'm going to send for you. And I'm going to think long and hard about what you said."

"Thank you," LaTasha said as she walked toward the door wondering where his care and concern was when she really needed him.

LaTasha walked down the street kicking a can, deep in thought. She decided to break the news to D'Andre that night. When he picked her up that evening they went on one of their ususal Friday night dates that ended with him trying to grope her in the back of his car. But this time, when she pushed him away, she meant it.

"Stop it D. I don't want to."

"Why not. How you gonna treat your man, baby?"

"I'm not trying to treat you anyway, it's just that I have something to tell you."

"Can we talk later, I'm a little distracted right now."

"No, D'Andre. This is serious."

"Ok, ok, what's so important?"

"I'm pregnant, " she blurted out without even trying to think of a gentler way of putting it.

"What?" he screamed.

He screamed so loud that his reaction scared LaTasha. But what scared her even more was watching his body. He literally backed away from her, moving as far away as he could without opening the driver's door. In fact, LaTasha was sure that if the door had been open, he would be laying on the ground by now. Not exactly a show of support. He had always been so nice to her, taking her out and buying her carnations on her last birthday. That's why she was completely taken by surprise when his first reaction to her news was to start backing up from her.

"You heard me, D. I'm pregnant and we need to figure out what we're going to do"

"We. I ain't the one pregnant. You need to figure out what you gonna do. But make sure that your plans don't include me paying child support because I am not feelin' that."

"What does that mean? You don't want to be a father to your child?"

"Hold up just a minute. I don't want to be a father, because I don't want a child. You need to get rid of it or something, because I am not ready for this no way, no how."

With that, the first hot tear rolled down her cheek. She had really envisioned this going differently. She didn't know why she expected it to go differently. Nothing in her background or in D'Andre's set the stage for them to have a happy and successful life parenting a child. D'Andre had lost his father at a very young age and she had never really known her father. She knew that their chance of having a successful family life was fairly remote given their history. Still, she wanted it more than anything. But it was clear that this was not going to be the time and D'Andre certainly didn't want to be the one.

"D I know we can do this if we really want to. I don't mind working to help out."

"Help out with what. Baby, I'm a high school drop out. I fix cars by day and bag groceries at night and I still barely make enough for me and my momma to get by. I'm workin' two jobs just to barely eat. I don't have the time or the money for a kid right now. My Daddy got killed out in the streets hustlin' trying to provide for me and my momma. He never knew his Daddy because he was in jail the whole time he was growing up. You don't even really know your daddy. What kind of family is that to bring a child into? Is that the kind of family you want for your child?"

"I just thought you really cared about me."

"I do care about you baby. It's been fun. But I ain't tryin' to roll like that. And you shouldn't either. I know a lot of brothas walk around all proud with their chest stuck out when their girls turn up pregnant, but I don't see none of them really takin' care of their kids. They don't spend time with them, don't take 'em nowhere. What kind of parenting is that? Now I'll give you the money to take care of things, but that's all I got to give you. Are you feelin' me?"

LaTasha's throat was too choked with tears to respond, but the one thing she knew was that she didn't want to have an abortion.

They rode the whole way home in silence. And now, the words of her counselor kept echoing in LaTasha's ears. She wanted so much for her unborn child. She wanted her baby to have the life she had never had with a mother and a father. She wanted her baby to be safe and secure and live in a nice neighborhood. She wanted him to know that he was going to finish high school and have a chance to attend college.

She wanted him to play sports and be on the debate team and go away for real vacations. She wanted him to have his own room in his own house. But mostly, she wanted her baby to be wanted. And D'Andre had made it clear, he didn't want their child. As she climbed the steps in front of her house, she was already thinking about giving this baby up for adoption.

Chapter 17B

Earth Mother

By the end of their junior year, LaTasha was excelling in school thanks to Daniel's help. Daniel had been so happy for LaTasha when she got into the summer study abroad program in England. He had gone to the same program the previous summer and it had really opened his eyes about the study of literature in a way that had made reading so much more enjoyable for him. His mother had collected classic books for years, but he had never had much of an interest in reading them until he came back from that program. Being someplace where so many of the classics had been written gave him a different view of those works.

When they left school at the beginning of the summer, he had promised LaTasha that he would write her over the summer. They had grown close in a way that had even surprised him and more than anything, he wanted to make sure that they didn't lose touch during the summer. At first he thought that he was just interested in helping LaTasha become acclimated to a new school. His mother had always told him what a kind heart he had. When he was little, he even got awards at camp for being the most positive camper because he was always so willing to help everyone out. But much to his surprise, he had begun to see LaTasha in a different light—not as someone who needed his help, but as someone who could help him open his eyes and examine his own life more closely. After the death of his father, he had always felt that he had lost another connection to who he was. But something about the way his mother had reacted to LaTasha had drawn him to her in a way he never expected. He had never thought much about the fact that he was born in the same place that LaTasha now lived. It was almost as if that hadn't been a part of his reality until he met LaTasha.

But soon after LaTasha left for England, Daniel fell into his familiar summer routine. During the early part of the summer he spent his days at the Bayou Bend country club swimming and playing tennis with his classmates. When he wasn't there, he was working part time at the hospital for another doctor who was a friend of his moms' who was mentoring him with the hope he would become a heart surgeon one day. Daniel always spent the last full month of the summer on Martha's Vineyard with his mother. Every summer the same families would gather during that month to socialize and rejuvenate and renew their friendships. Daniel and his mom always rented a house close to the beach and within walking distance from town. That assured that they were always in the middle of all of the social activities that were happening on the island. Most of the houses were of a Victorian style with huge wrap around porches that enhanced socializing among the residents. Every day someone would come by with an invitation to this party or that or an offer to accompany you to the beach or into town for ice cream. It was an idyllic setting that his mother loved for nostalgic reasons and that Daniel loved because of the freedom he had while he was there.

One night, soon after they arrived on the island that summer, Daniel sat down at his computer to write LaTasha a message on her message page. He hadn't gotten far when some friends came knocking at the front door. He jumped up from the computer leaving the page with her profile on it showing, and went outside to see his friends. He sat on the porch talking with them for a while about where they were all going to go that evening. When he came back inside, his mother was standing over the little desk in the den reading LaTasha's profile and the message he had started to her. She looked up startled, but not embarrassed to be caught reading his message. She had always made it perfectly clear to him that he had no right of privacy in her house and she would look at anything that she wanted. He was embarrassed, however, that his mother had read his personal note to LaTasha. There was nothing risque in what he had written, but the tone was clearly warm and affectionate. He missed LaTasha and he had let her know how he felt in no uncertain terms.

"Mom, why are you reading my message to LaTasha?" he asked sounding hurt.

"Please. Why are you writing to LaTasha? With all the beautiful girls you have to choose from here in Martha's Vineyard, you pick somebody who says that they don't have a favorite book because they haven't read much and that doesn't have a relationship with her father because she hasn't seen him since she was two. She seems to have no real aspirations for the future and from her background that doesn't seem surprising."

"Mom, you don't know her. You don't know anything!" Daniel shouted. "LaTasha is smart, she's interesting and she's not stuck up like some of the girls you think are so perfect for me."

"You're right. I don't know her and I don't want to get to know her. Do you think your father and I did everything we did for you just so you could end up with some little ghetto girl trying to catch somebody like you."

"I can't believe you would say that mom. She's from the same town that I was born in. I was a little ghetto boy when you got me. Have you forgotten that? By rejecting her, it feels like you are rejecting me too. I'm no better than she is and you obviously don't think she's good enough."

"Daniel, that's not what I meant, it's just that . . ."

"Oh, that's exactly what you meant. Maybe it's time for me to try to figure out who I really am and where I really belong. I want to meet my birth mother."

"I thought that might be something we could do after you graduate next year," Alexa said almost panic stricken.

"No, I want to meet her now, as soon as we get back home."

"Honey, let's talk about this later when we're both feeling a little calmer."

"Fine," Daniel said as he walked out the door and headed to the beach to run.

As he raced down the beach his heart beat faster and faster. He didn't want to cry, but he couldn't hold back his feelings. In a way he understood what his mother was trying to say, but it just didn't seem fair. By an accident of fate, his parents had chosen him and taken him away from the life that LaTasha lived into a world of society and privilege where outsiders were tolerated, but never accepted. How could his mother not see that her attitude made him feel unworthy. He sat down on the beach and cried. He cried for the birth mother he had never known. He cried for the father he had known all too briefly. He cried for the pain that he knew he had caused his mother that night and he cried for himself for the life he would never know. As he made his way back to the house that night, he didn't know what he would say to his mother, but he knew that it was time for him to meet his birth mother.

When Daniel opened the door, the house was dark, but he could see a light on under his mother's door. He approached the door and lifted his hand to knock, but he stopped short of knocking when he heard his mother crying. She was sitting in her room listening to a song that always made her cry, "Everything Must Change" by Quincy Jones. Why was she doing this to herself? He wondered if she just wanted to feel sad tonight. He knew it was a song that she played whenever she was sad about losing his dad. Was it going to be their song now too? In a way he felt bad that his mother was feeling so hurt, but he also felt irritated that she had devoted so much of her life to him that she couldn't let go and let him make his own decisions and lead his own life. It wasn't fair to him that she had made him the center of her life. He was mad at her, but he was also mad at himself for feeling that way. He finally decided that it wasn't a good time to talk to her right now because frankly, he had no idea what he wanted to say to her, so he turned and went to bed.

The rest of their time there on the island was strained. They avoided any conversation about the fight that they had or anything related to that topic. They gingerly danced around each others feelings being careful not to bring anything up that might sound like it was related to meeting his birth mother.

For LaTasha, the summer abroad had opened her eyes to an entirely new world. She had a sense of self confidence that she had never had before. She felt like the world was just waiting for her now. She could barely wait for the start of the school year so she could see Daniel again and tell Mrs. Walton all about the summer program. On the first day of school, she got off the bus hoping that Daniel would be waiting somewhere nearby, but she didn't see him. She scanned the cafeteria before school started, but it was lunchtime before she actually saw him. When she finally spotted him, he was sitting at a table with a couple of other girls that she had met before, Megan and Courtney. She wanted to approach them, but they were laughing animatedly and she felt like she would be intruding. Just as she was about to turn and find someplace else to sit, Daniel caught sight of her out of the corner of his eye.

"LaTasha, hey come sit with us."

LaTasha turned around startled. Megan and Courtney looked startled too. She really didn't want to join them—well she wanted to join Daniel and not the others, but it would be too awkward to say no, so she turned around and smiled and set her tray down on their table.

"Hi, Daniel, hi everybody," she said, forcing a smile. While she had grown comfortable with Daniel over the time she had been at St. Matthews, she had never quite felt like she fit in with the girls who seemed to be part

of his world. While Daniel's family was quite well off, he talked mostly of things that LaTasha felt she at least had a chance to relate to, art, history, world events. When it was just the girls, they invariably discussed designer bags and clothing and who had just acquired what and what the latest type of manicure or spa treatment was and where the best salons in town were to get your hair done. LaTasha wasn't any different from any other teenage girl who read magazines and dreamed about these kinds of things. But the difference was, these girls weren't just dreaming about them, they were living the dream and try as she might, she just couldn't relate to them.

"How was your summer? Tell me how the program was," Daniel asked enthusiastically.

"It was wonderful," LaTasha said, feeling a little self conscious now as all eyes looked at her. " I learned so much and met so many interesting people. I loved England."

"The food there is dreadful," Megan said flatly.

"It sure is," Courtney chimed in.

"It is, but after a while you get used to it," LaTasha said hopefully. She wanted to tell them more about her trip, but before she could speak again, Megan had already started.

"Yes, it's really bland, a lot like the food up in Martha's Vineyard where all of us spent our summer. Like the English, the folks in New England don't use a lot of seasoning in their food. But they do have great steamed clams and boiled lobsters. We really had a great time up there at some of the clambakes on the beach, didn't we Daniel?"

"Oh, I didn't realize you all had gone to Martha's Vineyard together," LaTasha said somewhat surprised.

Before Daniel could respond, Megan jumped in again, "Well, of course. That's where we all summer," Megan replied, using summer as a verb as only the well-to-do could do.

LaTasha looked at Daniel and he just sort of blushed and hung his head. He felt like he had been hiding something from LaTasha, but he really hadn't. It was just like Megan said, all of them did spend the summer in Martha's Vineyard, but they always had—ever since they were little kids. Their parents all knew each other and they made a point of all going up there around the same time so the kids could hang out together. They had all grown up together. It was tradition. It was what they did. But it didn't really mean anything.

LaTasha wanted to say something to him, but she didn't know what to say. Should she ask him if that was why he had been too busy to write or call this summer. She wanted to know if he had been thinking of her the way she had been thinking of him all summer, wondering if their relationship might turn into something more than a friend/mentor-mentee relationship. He had been so kind to her during her time at St. Matthews, and she appreciated it. But this year she had hoped that maybe their relationship could move to another level. She looked at Daniel expectantly, but he didn't say anything more. Finally, she decided to break the silence.

"So, Daniel, can you help me with the first writing assignment this semester."

"Absolutely, I've got some great ideas for you. Why don't we meet after school and talk about them."

"That would be great. Well, I've gotta run."

"Where you headin?"

"To my biology class in the south wing."

"I'm going that way. Come on, I'll walk you."

"Thanks," LaTasha replied picking up her tray and heading to the drop off area.

"Bye Megan, bye Courtney. I'll see you guys later," Daniel said over his shoulder.

"Bye," they said in unison.

After Daniel and LaTasha were out of earshot, Courtney turned to Megan and said," What was that all about?"

"Charity case," Megan replied. " She just got here last year and you know how Daniel always thinks he is supposed to save every stray cat in the neighborhood. Well, I think he's taken her on as his project. Sort of like Richard Gere did with Julia Roberts in Pretty Woman. I think he's determined to help a ghetto girl do good."

"Well as long as she doesn't think that she can help herself to Daniel," Courtney replied. "You know how those girls are. They try to find some guy like Daniel whose family has money and then they get pregnant to try to trap them. Have you and Daniel had sex yet?" she asked abruptly.

"No," Megan sputtered. " We don't exactly have that kind of relationship. It's not like I don't want it, but I think that we have both felt like our parents have always wanted to see us together so we have just resisted it. But, I'm starting to see that maybe I better go claim what's mine before somebody else tries to move in on him while I'm asleep at the wheel."

"And you better be ready to give it up, because you know little Ms. LaToya, LaTasha, La-whatever her name is, is probably giving it up already."

"You're probably right," Megan said, already thinking about what her next move should be.

Over the next few days, Daniel and LaTasha worked hard on their writing assignment. Each student was required to present an essay about their summer. LaTasha had worked very hard on an essay about her summer abroad. Daniel had really enjoyed reading her first draft and told LaTasha how her words made the experience come to life for him even though he had participated in that particular summer program already. He made LaTasha recite out loud to him over and over until her voice was stronger and more confident. He suggested that she watch herself in the mirror at home and he praised her progress enthusiastically. He taught her how to pause dramatically and how to breathe evenly so she wouldn't have to take a breath in the middle of a sentence. LaTasha hadn't realized that there was so much involved in public speaking before she started working with Daniel. Daniel had also suggested that LaTasha allow him to videotape her presentation so she could watch herself with a critical eye. That had made a big difference for her. In the video, she was able to see small gestures that were annoying and distracted from her presentation. She also noticed how she had a tendency to say um at the end of a sentence and repeat the words "you know" too often. That exercise had been just what she needed to polish up her presentation.

Daniel was working on a piece about the black families who summered on Martha's Vineyard. When he first told LaTasha about it, she really had no idea that there were black families that had actually vacationed on an exclusive island off the coast of Massachusetts for decades because they owned homes and property there. Many of them were doctors and lawyers and other business people whose families had passed the homes onto their families. Since race relations had always been good on Martha's Vineyard, there were black families who had vacationed and owned homes there for more than a hundred years. It was a rich history and he was excited to share it with his classmates.

Finally, the day arrived when they were supposed to present their papers. Daniel got to school early and then went to wait for LaTasha at the bus stop. Just like clockwork she was there at 7:35. LaTasha was half expecting he would be there and she was really happy to see him.

"Hi Daniel," she said excitedly.

"Hey LaTasha. Ready for the big day?"

"Why is this such a big day?" she asked playfully.

"I don't know. It's just the first presentation the semester, that's all."

"Well, thanks to you, I'm ready and I'm going to volunteer to be one of the first to present so I can get this over with."

"Good for you," Daniel said smiling.

When LaTasha got up that afternoon to present her paper, she was obviously nervous. Although she gripped her paper tightly, her hands were visibly shaking. As she started to read, her voice was barely audible. Mrs. Manford interrupted her and said, "LaTasha, you really need to project. Nobody can hear you."

Daniel bristled at the tone his teacher used and felt immediately that he just wanted to put his arms around LaTasha to protect her. He stared at her and willed her to project the way she had when they had practiced. together. He knew she could do it. He just wanted everybody else to know it too. He wanted them to see how far she had come, to understand the kind of obstacles she had overcome in her life, how hard it was for her to get up at 5:30 in the morning to be on a bus by 6:00 just to get here. He worried that nobody would see what he had seen, a bright, intelligent, articulate person with a depth of character and spirit that were often missing among many of his classmates.

And then suddenly she spoke. She still sounded a little tentative at first, but then her voice became strong and she began to project the way they had practiced. She paused dramatically at all the right points and she made eye contact with her audience. She described her summer in vivid detail, talking about the countryside, the food and the school itself. She talked about conversations with people she had met there and how they had all arrived with certain cultural expectations about the others and how they worked through them. Her presentation was so interesting that she literally had the other students sitting on the edge of their seats.

Even Mrs. Manford perked up with a show of genuine interest in LaTasha's presentation. She had done it. She had captivated them with the sheer presence of her words. She wasn't just reading. She wasn't looking down. She didn't stutter or say um. She was looking straight at them, with confidence and assurance. It was a great moment. And then she finished.

Several kids in the class stood up to applaud. Even Mrs. Manford stood up. Daniel stood looking at LaTasha proudly. But LaTasha, overcome with joy, could see no one through her tears. She knew she had turned a corner, that she was college material. She knew what kind of life she could have now.

Daniel was waiting for LaTasha in the hall after class. He could hardly wait to tell her how proud he was of her. She had come so far and now he knew without a doubt that she would reach her goal of getting to college. He could see that she had a new confidence that hadn't been there even a few months before. He had gotten her a little gift that he had hoped to give her to congratulate her for a job well done and now he knew he should give it to her. It was a book about Martha's Vineyard. She had seemed so interested in it when he talked to her about his paper, he thought she might want to read more about it for herself.

LaTasha was too excited for words as she gathered her things to leave the classroom. Before she could get all her things together, Mrs. Manford called her to the front of the room.

"LaTasha, you did very well today. I'm very proud of you," Mrs. Manford said. "Your presentation was great and you sounded so articulate today when you gave it. You would hardly know that this was only your second year at St. Matthews."

Although this was clearly only half a compliment, LaTasha realized it was probably as much as she was going to get from Mrs. Manford. It was the soft bigotry of low expectations, and she could choose to be mad or accept the compliment graciously. She chose the latter.

"Thank you, Mrs. Manford."

And with that she continued to gather her things to leave. She was excited to talk to Daniel after class and she hoped he would still be outside waiting. Not only did she want to talk to him about her presentation today, but she also wanted to give him an invitation to a barbeque that her mother was having for her that Saturday. Her mother had picked up some cute barbeque invitations from the drug store and she and LaTasha had carefully penned the invitations for Saturday's event. Daniel had never been to her house for dinner and she was really looking forward to having him there.

"Hey LaTasha," he said finally as she came out of the classroom. He was grinning from ear to ear.

"Hey, so how did I do?" LaTasha asked.

"You know you were great."

"What was your favorite part?" she asked anxiously.

Daniel opened his mouth to answer her, but before he could get anything out, Megan Smith tapped him on the shoulder to get his attention.

"Uh, hey Megan."

"Hey yourself, Daniel. Are we all set for the Cotillion this weekend?"

"Yes. I guess so. I got my tux. I'm getting a fresh haircut tomorrow."

"And what about my flower. I know you are getting me a corsage!" she said flirting.

"Of course I'm getting you a corsage. And my mom got us a limo so I can pick up Chase and Joy on the way to your house so we can all ride together."

"Are we going to grab anything to eat on the way in case the dinner at the banquet isn't any good."

"Oh, I think the food will be good this year. Joy went to the tasting dinner with her mother and she said it was great. Filet and salmon, mixed veggies, scalloped potatoes yeast bread, pecan pie with ice cream."

"That does sound good. But all that food! I won't be able to eat for a week, she said giggling.

Overeating was hardly an issue for Megan Smith. She was one of those girls who looked like she didn't weigh one hundred pounds soaking wet. Even in her school uniform she looked like a million bucks. Her hair was always freshly cut in the latest styles. It hung past her shoulders and was highlighted with auburn and darker brown streaks. Her makeup was so flawless she almost looked liked one of those women at a makeup counter. She came from a well known and well-off family. At the last school auction, her mother had paid more than $20,000 for the senior class quilt. She was to be presented at this year's cotillion and as the most popular girl among those to be presented, she had let it be known early in the year that nobody was to ask Daniel Pierce to the cotillion except her.

LaTasha rolled her eyes in disgust. Not only was Megan one of those girls that you just loved to hate, she had also stolen LaTasha's moment of glory. Daniel didn't even get a chance to tell her how well she had done today before Megan came up and interrupted them. That just seemed so unfair. It wasn't often that LaTasha had something so special to celebrate and now that she did, she didn't want anybody, especially Megan Smith, stealing her joy. And all of this talk of the cotillion was giving her a headache. She didn't even really know what a cotillion was and she certainly had no idea that Daniel was going to go with Megan. She knew that she and Daniel weren't dating, but even still she felt a twinge of jealousy. Listening to them chat so easily made her look uncomfortably at her own clothes. Her shirt was clean, but it was not pressed and starched the way Megan's was. They both had on the same skirt, but it was obvious that Megan had hers hemmed just about as short as it could go without violating the school's dress policy. Megan's tennis shoes were clean and new and she had completed them with blue and gold shoe strings to match the school colors. LaTasha felt self conscious as she looked down at her scuffed tennis shoes. She was still clutching an invitation she had intended to give to Daniel.

Before LaTasha and Daniel had a chance to resume their conversation, the bell rang for the next class.

"Oh wow, "Daniel said, finally turning toward LaTasha. "We didn't get to finish our conversation."

Finish, we didn't get to start it thanks to Megan, thought LaTasha. But instead she just shrugged her shoulders and said, "That's ok. I'll catch up with you later."

"Oh, I'm so sorry," Megan cooed. "Did I interrupt something?"

LaTasha opened her mouth to say yes, but before she could get anything out, Daniel said, "Oh no, that's ok. We were just talking about what happened in class today."

LaTasha was furious. They weren't just talking about what happened in class. They were talking about how well LaTasha had done in that class presenting her paper. They were talking about her moment in the sun and how she had shone and Megan had shown up like an eclipse to block the brightness of that moment. She turned on her heel and headed off to class. Her ears were ringing so loudly she could hardly hear, but she could still make out Megan's condescending tone as she asked Daniel what in the world was wrong with her. Even today's success in class hadn't made any difference. She was still holding the handwritten invitation in her hand that she had meant to give Daniel. Now she realized that Daniel had plans for Saturday night with Megan and she was glad she hadn't given Daniel the invitation to the barbeque her mother was having at their house. She would never fit in here. She didn't dress like them, she didn't talk like them and she didn't have enough money to compete with them. Talk of cotillions and limousines and corsages and tasting menus was a world she didn't understand and one that she was sure she was never going to have the chance to experience. As she turned to walk away, Daniel called after her and her heart lifted slightly.

"LaTasha, I almost forgot. I got a little something for you," he said reaching into his book bag.

LaTasha could tell from the packaging that it was a book of some sort. She had no idea what it would be, but she was so happy he had thought enough about her to give her this small gift. When she got to her next class, she opened the present and as she thought, it was a book. But when she turned it over to read the title she was shocked to see that it was a copy of a book about Martha's Vineyard. There were pages and pages of prosperous looking black people dating back to the 1940's standing in front of their grand Victorian homes on ths island. There were stories about their charmed lives and picture perfect families. LaTasha could hardly believe that Daniel had thought this would be a nice gift. There were so many things wrong with him giving her this book, she didn't know where to begin. It was clear to her that there was no place for her in Daniel's life and she needed to stop fooling herself. It was time to move on.

Chapter 18A

Birth Mother

When LaTasha told D'Andre she was pregnant, he felt a rush of panic set in that clouded all his thoughts. He knew he had not responded appropriately, but as LaTasha slammed the door behind her and walked toward her house, he couldn't honestly remember what he had said to her. He did know, however, what he had to do. At the end of the day he knew he and LaTasha had to be responsible for their choice to have unprotected sex. He didn't want a baby, but since he was obviously going to have one anyway, he knew he had to provide for his family any way he could. Without a high school education his job choices were limited. He would never make enough money working in the grocery store or at the auto shop to pull them above the poverty line. Even when he made a little extra money here and there, there was always some emergency, an illness a broken appliance that sucked that money up. Taking care of his mom and LaTasha was his responsibility and he had to do it by any means necessary. As he thought about what would be necessary, he stopped and said a silent prayer before he left his house.

He found the local drug dealers sitting on the same steps on the same corner that they always occupied. Like it or not, he knew that if he was going to have to support his mother, LaTasha and a baby, he was going to have to do more than sack groceries and work on cars. In thinking about the offer that the dealers had made to him time and again, he decided that he would try this hustle just long enough to save up some money to get ready for the baby and then he would quit before it got too good to him or he got in trouble. As usual, the same guys were sitting on the same corner talking about the same thing they always did, hustlin'.

"Hey young blood. What's up with you man?"

"Nothin' much. Just trying to figure out if it's too late for a young brotha' to make some money around here."

The oldest of the guys sitting there started to laugh. He had a hard weathered face with a scar down one side. When he laughed, the scar seemed to blend into his mouth making his smile long and contorted almost like the Joker's smile in Batman.

"Oh, you finally came to your senses and realized you weren't going to get rich sacking groceries, huh?"

"Somethin' like that. I just need more money, so what can I do for you?"

"Just like I said before, deliver some packages for me from time to time. In fact, you can make a test run tonight and run this package over to Eleventh Street. When you get there, ask for Georgy and get my money from him and bring it all back to me. When you do, I'll break you off a little somethin'."

"Awright, give me the address."

And with that, D'Andre had decided to throw in with the local drug dealers. He never thought it would come to this, but he also never thought he would be looking at having a baby at seventeen. His daddy had been a criminal, and his daddy's daddy had been a criminal too. And now, he was ready to subject himself to this same generational curse by working with these known drug dealers. But to D'Andre his situation was different because he didn't intend to become a career criminal like his grandfather had been. He just needed a short term hustle to take care of his business and unlike his father, he didn't intend to do anything stupid that would cause him to get caught. He just needed to get ahead a little bit so he could take care of his obligations.

For a while his hustle, as he called his drug dealing activities, worked very well. Until one night. He had gone to Georgy's house to make a delivery. He made deliveries to him two to three times a week. Usually, they just did their business in the garage. When he got there, he would back his car into the garage and once they closed the door, he would unload the cocaine right in the garage, put the money in the trunk of his car and take off. This night, Georgy insisted that he bring the delivery inside and count out the bricks of cocaine one at a time before he would give him the money. He assumed Georgy must have been shorted on an earlier delivery and was now being extra cautious. He carried the box from the garage to the house. Once inside, he opened the box and begun counting the bricks as Georgy requested. There were ten kilos all together. Once he had counted them out, Georgy opened a suitcase full of money and counted out $380,000 which was the grand total at $38,000 a kilo. Out of that take he would get about $3,800 for making the delivery. That wasn't bad for one night's work except that unbeknownst to D'Andre, the entire transaction had been captured on video tape. Georgy had been arrested earlier that week and had decided to cooperate with the authorities by completing some drug deals and turning in a few other dealers. As soon as D'Andre went back into the garage to leave, the door was opened by armed agents from the Drug Enforcement Administration yelling for him to raise his hands and hit the floor.

It was a nightmare. Before he knew it, they were all over him yelling and screaming and telling him he was under arrest. On one side of him an agent was reading him his rights and on the other side another agent was handcuffing his hands behind his back. He was so scared he wet his pants and his humiliation was amplified when they dragged him from the garage into the glare of the waiting television cameras. This was like some bad scene out of one of those police shows. Helicopters were swirling their lights overhead and dogs from the canine units were straining on their leashes to get into the house where the drug transaction had just taken place. He tried to hold his head down so his face wouldn't be seen on camera, but one of the agents jerked his shirt forcing him to look up into the camera just before he was pushed into the back seat of a waiting patrol car.

Back at her house, LaTasha was laying on the bed in her bedroom, watching t.v. with the sound off. She found that she needed a lot more rest these days now that she was almost six months pregnant and a full thirty pounds heavier. She wasn't really paying much attention to what was on until she saw D'Andre's face flash across the screen being dragged in handcuffs to a waiting patrol car. In the months since she had first told him she was pregnant, he had seemingly done an about face and had told her that he would do everything he could to support her and the baby. She had been skeptical at first, but he had begun showing up each week with money to help her. Her counselor was still trying to convince her to give the baby up for adoption, but D'Andre had made her feel confident that he would support her once the baby was born. Now his face was plastered across the screen, having apparently been arrested in a drug sting. Just as she realized it was him, her phone began to ring. Before she could answer it, her cell phone also started ringing. The first call was from her best friend, Nicole, "Girl, D'Andre on t.v. gettin' arrested."

"I know, lemme call you back."

Her cousin was on the cell phone, "Tasha, your man on t.v. in handcuffs. I knew he musta been dealing, all the money he been givin' you lately."

"Bye LaQuita, I gotta go."

She had no idea who to call. Finally, she thought she better call D'Andre's mother since she probably had no idea what was going on. She dialed the number and heard the phone start to ring. At D'Andre's house, his mother was sitting in the living room with her feet up on an ottoman having just gotten in from work, when the front doorbell rang. As she was walking toward the door, the phone started to ring. She was about to turn back for the phone when the banging at the door grew loud and more insistent and was accompanied by men yelling, "Open the door, police."

Erica froze in her tracks. The police had come to her house only once before in her life and that was to tell her that her husband was dead. Now they were here again, and D'Andre was nowhere to be found. She was paralyzed with fear and every movement seemed to be in slow motion after that. She looked at the door and then at the ringing phone and decided, for whatever reason, to answer the phone first.

"Mrs. Parker, it's LaTasha. I don't know how to tell you this but D'Andre's been arrested. It's on t.v. right now."

Before she could say anything in response, the police had broken the front door down after deciding she was taking too long to answer. She stood there with a receiver in one hand and her other hand covering her mouth.

"Mrs. Parker, Mrs. Parker ," LaTasha yelled into the phone. But one of the officers had already burst the door open and ran toward Erica.

Snatching the receiver from her hand. He yelled, "Who is this?"

LaTasha was scared to death, so she just hung up. The officer pressed the caller i.d. button and yelled the number out to another officer who was standing nearby with some papers in his hand.

"Mrs. Parker, we have a warrant to search your residence. Your son has been arrested for drug trafficking. Do you understand what I am saying to you?"

Erica looked up and tried to answer but no words would come out of her mouth. She stood there swaying back and forth in stunned silence. How could this be? She loved D'Andre and would do anything for him. He and LaTasha had a child on the way who needed his Daddy. D'Andre was young and had his whole life to look forward to. She went to church every week and she had faith and believed in God. How could he do this to them? She felt herself swaying the way she did sometimes when she had forgotten to take her blood pressure medicine, but she just couldn't keep her balance. And then she fainted.

When Erica was awakened by the smelling salts, she was on a paramedic's stretcher. She glanced around frantically. Her first thoughts were of D'Andre. He must be frightened. She had to get to him. She thought about the night the police had come to tell them that Andre had died and about how D'Andre had rolled himself into a little ball and started rocking until she could calm him down. She knew he must be so scared now and she wasn't there to comfort him the way a mother should. She tried to get up off the stretcher, but she was too weak. She had hit her head on the side of the coffee table and had a nasty gash. Blood had dripped all over the front of her bouse and little pieces of lint from the rug had stuck to it. She laid back down and watched as an army of DEA agents tore her house apart. Before she could say anything in protest, the paramedics had taken her outside and put her into the back of a waiting ambulance. The street was full of bystanders and gawkers pointing and looking. "They shot her," one said. "I knew her son was no good," another one added.. "Ms. Erica is always so nice to everybody—too bad she has such a thug for a son."

Erica wondered who were these people that called themselves her neighbors. How could they say such hateful things. As the paramedics wheeled her to a waiting ambulance, television cameras descended on them. A young female reporter managed to push her way past the police and jam a microphone in Erica's face.

"How do you feel about the fact that your son just got arrested for trafficking in cocaine."

Erica was appalled. That was the stupidest question that she had ever heard. She thought it would probably be better if she kept her mouth shut, but then she asked herself, what's the point. So she decided to let her have it.

"How you think I feel? How would you feel if your seventeen year old son, the son that came from your womb, started selling drugs because he had given up all hope and thought that was the only thing he could do to support his family. The boy that you raised, sat up with when he was sick, helped with his homework and invested all the time and money you had into. I mean really, how would you feel?"

"I would be devastated," the young woman replied.

"You white people come down here in our neighborhoods trying to shame us when our children do wrong because you think that we don't feel any shame or embarrassment about the crimes that our children commit. That we just accept this as part of what happens around here and that nobody feels bad about it. When those white business men commit crimes, the old white judges say that they are embarrassed in their communities but that we aren't. Well that's just not true. We have dreams and hopes for our children and they don't include going to prison."

At that point the paramedic pushed the stretcher into the ambulance and shut the door. The young reporter just stood there watching, but Erica had made her point. It was little satisfaction, however, because the pain she felt in her heart was overwhelming. She had lost her husband because he had felt that breaking the law was the only way that he could support his family and now her son had headed down the same path. She was desperate to talk to D'Andre and find out what was going on with him. To her great relief, LaTasha came to the hospital later that evening to tell her what was going on. D'Andre had called to ask her to help him post bond, but she had already spent all the money he had given her.

D'Andre had a lawyer appointed to him from the public defender's office. He was fortunate because the lawyer's from the public defender's office were dedicated, hardworking and committed attorneys. Since he was still a juvenile, he hadn't been placed into custody with adults. His lawyer met with him early in the morning the day after his arrest and quickly determined that he was completely green and unfamiliar with the criminal justice system. He assured D'Andre that given his lack of previous criminal history, he was sure he could get him a good deal.

D'Andre's head was spinning and his heart was racing so fast he felt like it was going to jump out of his chest. Despite his lawyer's calm and reassuring demeanor, he was scared to death. He didn't have any idea what was going to happen to him and he was terrified about what that might mean for his mother and for LaTasha, both of whom depended on him. He had been embarrassed when he had to call LaTasha to ask for help. To add to his humiliation, both his mother and LaTasha showed up that afternoon for his arraignment where he entered his plea of not guilty. They smiled at him and waved and LaTasha gave him a thumbs up sign. He could barely manage a smile in return. All he had wanted was to take care of both of them and instead he had dragged them into this nightmare.

D'Andre's lawyer had worked hard to try to get him the best deal possible. Because he was a juvenile and they had shown his face on t.v. that actually worked to their advantage. Additionally, his clean criminal record and his reputation as a local star basketball player had both helped a lot. Even though D'Andre was a very low level member of this drug conspiracy, he knew a lot of the guys who were involved in large transactions from around the neighborhood. As part of his deal with the government, he told them everything he knew in exchange for a recommendation from the prosecutor for a lighter sentence.

By the time that D'Andre had finally decided to plead guilty, the prosecutor had essentially agreed to recommend a term of probation based on the level of cooperation D'Andre had provided, the fact that he was a juvenile and the fact that he had no prior criminal history. He knew that his cooperation with the government meant he would probably have to leave town for a while and he didn't want to do that without LaTasha and the baby. He asked LaTasha to come visit him at the detention center so he could talk to her about their future together.

He hadn't had a decent haircut since he had been picked up and he was ashamed of the way he looked in prison clothing, but all that was forgotten when she walked through the door.

"Hey baby," he said grinning.

"Hi D'Andre. How you doin' in here?"

"I'ma make it ok. I just been worryin' about you and the baby. How you two feelin'?".

"We alright, I guess. It's just kind of hard, goin' through all this right now while I'm pregnant."

"I know, I know. And I'm gonna make it up to you. I promise. But look here, I had to cooperate with the government and give up some of those boys to get a chance to get outta here, so I know I'm not going to be able to stay in town when I get out. I need to know . . . . are you gonna come with me?"

"Come with you where? I don't want to leave here on the run, looking over my shoulder every minute. What kind of life would that be for me and a baby?"

"It wouldn't be forever. Just until some of the heat dies down. You know, until those guys are put away and everybody else has forgotten about me."

"D'Andre, I can't live like that. And it's not fair to bring a baby into this world to live like that either. Look at both of us. I come from a family where every girl has a child out of wedlock. You come from a family where every man ends up in prison or dead from a life of crime. At some point somebody has to be the one to say enough is enough. I think that it is up to us to break that cycle in both of our families. You got a chance to learn from this mistake and go on and make something of your life. And I have a chance not to be the next Washington girl to bring home a baby without a husband. I want to give the baby up for adoption, D'Andre and give our baby a chance to have a better life than the one that we would be able to give him. I don't want to keep this baby, and now that you have a record, no judge would give you custody of him. So I came here today to ask you to do the right thing by our child and sign these papers giving the baby up for adoption."

D'Andre was stunned. For the first time he was speechless. He just hung his head in shame. On the one hand he couldn't believe that

LaTasha was asking him to give up his own baby. But on the other, he knew she was right. What kind of life could they expect to lead if they were constantly worried about retaliation from one of the several people he had snitched on to get a better deal. He had done what he needed to do to get out of jail so he could be with his family but at the same time, he had done something that would make it impossible for him to live with his family in peace. In his heart, he knew that was no kind of life for them. He bit his lip to hold back the tears he felt forming in the corner of his eyes. It was hard for him to speak because of the lump in his throat, but he finally managed a hoarse sounding response.

"You're right. I hate to admit it, but you're right. Our baby deserves a better life than this. I just hope you believe that I really did all this for us so we could have a better life. It just didn't work out the way I had hoped."

"I know baby. But sometimes being responsible means having enough vision to see beyond what we might want today and to dream a bigger dream for our child. And saving the dream for him might allow us to save the dreams we have for our own lives."

Before D'Andre made his appearance in Court he had signed the papers allowing his child to be adopted. As a result, when he stood in front of the judge and was allowed to express his remorse for his involvement in the offense he was charged with, his testimony was genuine and heartfelt. He explained to the judge how his involvement in this criminal activity had resulted in him having to give up his child and how much regret he felt because of it even though he knew he had no other choice. To everyone's surprise, the judge told D'Andre that he too had been adopted and how grateful he had been that his birth parents had loved him enough to give him up for adoption so he could have a better life.

The judge then asked if anyone else wanted to speak. Erica stood up slowly in the back of the courtroom and raised her hand. As all eyes turned to look at her, she felt a knot growing in her stomach. The judge motioned for her to come forward.

"Yes, ma'am, and you are?", the judge asked.

"I'm Erica Parker, D'Andre's mother."

"What would you like to say?"

"Well, your honor. I've never been in a court before and I never expected to have to be in one. I heard you and D'Andre talking about adoption and I know that you think being adopted gave you a better life. When I was pregnant with D'Andre my counselor tried to talk me into giving him up for adoption, but I didn't want to."

D'Andre looked shocked as he heard his mother say those words, but she kept going.

"And even though life hasn't been easy for us since his father died, I think that I made the right choice to keep and raise my son. D'Andre may not seem like much standing here before you today waiting to be sentenced, but he is rich in every way that counts. He is kind, he is respectful and he cares about his friends and his family. In fact I think if he didn't care so much about me and LaTasha, he wouldn't be in the mess that he is in now. People love him because he has a good heart and he is a good person and he has a family that will help him make the right choices for himself and for us. I think if you give him a chance, that he can turn his own life around and he can help other young people too."

The judge was genuinely moved by Erica's remarks. He gave D'Andre a term of probation that required him to complete his GED as a condition. He also ordered D'Andre to perform one hundred hours of community service by speaking to young high school dropouts about staying in school. He knew that D'Andre had been a sports legend in high school and had dropped out after his injury. Like Erica, he thought that D'Andre would have a better chance of reaching young people than many adults would. The judge had seen many things in his days and felt that there was nothing worse than being possessed of an aptitude or ability and not having the opportunity to maximize it, but he hoped that D'Andre's story might make a difference to some other young person and he was sure that D'Andre wouldn't blow this chance he was being given.

Chapter 18B

Earth Mother

Daniel had been calling LaTasha for weeks, but he couldn't get her to return any of his calls. He really was at a loss as to why she might be avoiding him. They hadn't argued or had any disagreement and ordinarily they would have spoken just about every day. It had now been some time since they had last talked—right after LaTasha finished her presentation in Mrs. Manford's class. Now whenever class was over, she hurried away before he could catch up with her. She had done so well and he had tried to congratulate her but had gotten distracted by Megan. He and Megan had grown up together since childhood. They had met through Jack and Jill, the club for African American mothers. Their mothers were both doctors so they were very close and spent a lot of time together. Consequently, Daniel and Megan spent a lot of time together too. During the summers their moms packed them off to the national Jack and Jill conventions and to the convention of the National Medical Association for African American doctors. Then their families had started spending the summers together in Martha's Vineyard. It had been an idyllic life, and one that Daniel had very much thought of as the norm until he met LaTasha.

He had always known that everyone expected he and Megan to end up together eventually, but both of them had seemed to resist the urge to be pushed together against their will. This year something had changed. It seemed to start right at the beginning of the school year. Megan came after him aggressively and in a very sexual way. Even his mother seemed to be trying to force them together and had invited Megan and her mom to come spend the weekend at their beach house. One afternoon, when their mothers had gone into town to go shopping, he took Megan for a long walk on the beach to one of his favorite spots, a secluded area where the rocks came together and almost formed a cave-like structure. He just wanted to show it to Megan and have a nice picnic on the beach.

The warm sun was beating down on them and although it was a cool day their bodies were warm. It almost caught Daniel by surprise when Megan leaned over and kissed him hard, forcing his mouth open with her tongue. Then, she rubbed her breast against him. When it happened, he first assumed it was an accident, but sensing his hesitation, she left no doubt that it had been intentional. She grabbed his hand and placed it inside her blouse. Once he felt her stiff nipples he knew they were going to cross a threshold that they had never explored before. She left no doubt in his mind about it when she hiked up her short skirt and placed his other hand between her moist thighs. Although he had committed at church to remain celibate, he realized that promise was about to be thrown out the window.

His heart began to race and tiny beads of sweat formed on his forehead as he slipped his fingers under the edge of her panties. He'd had wet dreams before, but the sensation he felt after he touched her caused a throbbing so intense that it almost hurt. He paused for a second, trying to catch his breath, but Megan pushed herself closer. She let out a little moan and then she reached over and unzipped his trousers. He heard himself groan and tried to stop. He hadn't thought it would be like this. He wanted to keep his promise to wait for sex. He had always thought he would be in control, but Megan was taking him on this ride. He hadn't even had a chance to think about having sex with Megan or anyone else for that matter and it occurred to him that he did not have any protection.

"Megan," he said in a voice that was so rough and primal sounding, that it even startled him. "I don't have any condoms. I just didn't think . . ."

"Shhh," she said as she reached into her backpack with her left hand, while she still kept her right hand firmly on him, "I've got just what we need. And, I'm on the pill too, so we don't have anything to worry about."

"Damn, baby, damn, damn, damn," he said as she expertly rolled the condom on.

"That's just what I was thinking," she said. "Damn."

From that point on, it seemed that everyone assumed that they were an item. Even Megan began to act like they were betrothed in some way. *But as much as he was a part of this world, he felt a closeness to LaTasha that he had never experienced before. And even though it appeared that he was "..to the manor born" as the aristocrats of another time might say, sometimes he felt closer to LaTasha than he did to Megan or any of the other girls that ran in her little circle. It was something about LaTasha's unassuming and unpretentious manner that made her attractive to Daniel.*

Finally, one day Daniel decided just to wait for LaTasha at her bus stop after school. As she walked down the sidewalk toward the bus stop, she could see Daniel from more than a block away, but she had nowhere to turn. He clearly saw her and he was definitely waiting for her to get there. She had been avoiding him ever since the incident in the hall with Megan and she wasn't sure she was up to talking to Daniel yet, but it didn't look like she was going to have any choice. As she approached the bus stop, Daniel's face broke out in a wide grin.

"You can run, but you sure can't hide," he said teasingly.

"Why are you standing at my bus stop?"

"Waiting for you, and I am not leaving until you talk to me."

"I don't have time. I have to catch my bus."

"I'll take you downtown to get your transfer. And if I have to, I'll drive you all the way home tonight. But you and I are going to talk."

They walked together in silence for a while and finally Daniel said, "I'm sorry about what happened the day you presented your paper."

"It wasn't your fault. I just got my feelings hurt because Megan interrupted us."

"I shouldn't have let it happen. I really apologize. I've missed you so much."

"Me too," she replied.

"Are we alright," Daniel asked hopefully?

"We're alright."

"I got in early admission at Columbia."

"That's great. Although, I really don't entirely understand the whole early admission thing."

"I know, it's kind of confusing. It seems like it's a well kept secret that you only find out about if you're at the right school with the right counselors. It just means that I applied early to get preferential consideration for admission, but once they accept me I am committed to going there. There's an advantage if it's really the school you want and you don't need to wait to see about scholarship offers. Have you started working on your college applications yet?"

"Well, a little bit."

"Don't worry about it. I'll help you with them. My mom got me a consultant to help me with mine and I learned a lot in the process. There's no reason that I shouldn't put all that knowledge to work helping you with your applications."

"A consultant?" LaTasha asked.

"Yeah, somebody who helps organize your applications in a way that highlights what that particular school might be looking for. Who knows if it works or not, but most everyone I know uses one."

"Sounds expensive."

"Yeah, it is, about three thousand dollars. But my mom said she didn't have the time or the expertise to do it and she would rather pay somebody to do it for me. Come on, let's go to my house. I'll show you how to format your applications the way they did for me. It'll help you a lot."

Daniel had been grateful they had been able to repair their rift. He really liked LaTasha. They began to study together again occasionally after school and he wondered to himself whether they could ever be more than just friends. LaTasha wondered the same thing too, but knew that in the environment of St. Matthews, she was out of her league. But Daniel didn't seem to be bothered by all that. He liked LaTasha and he didn't treat her differently because of where she came from.

Over the next several weeks, Daniel helped LaTasha with her applications and together they located a pre med program that was looking for students who had come from disadvantaged backgrounds like LaTasha's. Daniel helped her write her admission essay in a compelling way and to her great amazement, she was offered admission to that program with a full scholarship.

LaTasha wondered what she could ever do to repay Daniel for all he had done for her. She also wondered what she could do to move him one step closer to her. While they were clearly the best of friends, LaTasha wanted more than that. She just needed to find a connection to help him take the next step.

One day when they were sitting in the park, she remembered Daniel once telling her that his birth mother lived somewhere in the area that she was from and she decided to ask him about it.

"Don't you ever wonder about your birth mother?"

"Sure I do. I look in the mirror and I wonder who I look like, whose nose do I have, whose eyes?"

"Is that all?"

"What do you mean?"

"I mean don't you wonder what your birth mother is like, where she lives, what she does, whether she thinks of you? You're almost eighteen years old. Don't you think it's time you went to meet her?"

"Actually I do sometimes, but just out of curiosity. Really, I can't imagine having a better mother than my mom. And even though my dad died when I was only eight, I still remember him and think about him all the time. In fact, he is the reason I've decided to go to law school. But sometimes I think about what it would be like to meet my birth mom. I tried to talk to my mom about it this summer, but I don't think she was ready for me to go meet her yet. I think that mostly I want my birth mother to see that I turned out alright."

"Do you know where she lives?"

"Yeah, somewhere in Pecos City from what my mom told me once."

"You know that's my neighborhood?"

"Yeah, I know. Just think, if I hadn't been adopted, we probably would have grown up together."

"Well, if you decide to go visit her, I'll have your back and go with you."

"Would you really?"

"Sure, why not."

After Daniel took LaTasha to the bus stop that night, he thought a lot about their conversation that afternoon. He did want to see his birth mother, to see if they looked alike, to hear from her why she had decided to give him up for adoption, to let her know that even though she wasn't able to raise him, that his parents had made sure he had a wonderful life. He remembered once looking at a scrap book that his mom had made for him. It had pictures of his birth mom in it, but he couldn't really remember what she looked like. Now that he was eighteen years old, he felt that it was about time he got a chance to meet her.

Later that evening Daniel asked his mother about visiting his birth mother. Without saying anything she went to her room and reached under the bed and pulled out a plastic box. He remembered seeing it before, but it had been a really long time and he couldn't really remember what was in it. As she began lifting the items from the box, a flash of recognition came over his face. First there was a plastic bag with a little white christening outfit. Then there was a little pair of shoes and a tattered blanket. Finally, Daniel's mom pulled out a photo album. Inside were pictures of his birth mother, the house she had lived in when he was born, pictures of him taken the day he had come home from the hospital, a letter from his birth mother and his adoption papers. Daniel noticed that as his mother was turning the pages of the album her hands started shaking. He didn't know what to say, but instinctively he got up and went and hugged his mother as tight as he could.

He wanted her to know that even though he was curious about his birth family that he would never leave her. He wanted her to understand that he was as afraid of losing her as she was of losing him—especially since they had lost his dad. He wanted her to know that he understood how much she loved him and how much she had sacrificed for him his entire life. Sometimes that made him worry if he was too much for her to handle. And he wanted her to understand that having the knowledge about his birth family would give him a sense of power over his own existence that he had always needed just as he was beginning to plan his future as an adult.

As he hugged her tight, his mother felt the same bond that she had felt the very first time she held him and the tension that had existed between them for so many months seemed to melt away. She wanted him to know how much she loved him and that she had been scared of losing him his entire life. She wanted him to know how much she believed he was a gift from God and that she would cherish him always no matter what he did in life. She wanted him to know that although she had devoted her life to him that she wanted to give him roots as well as wings to fly away. But most of all, she wanted him to know that she understood his need to connect with his birth family and that she fully supported his decision to do so. And without saying a word, the bond between mother and son was strong enough that they were each able to convey to the other exactly what they were feeling without saying a word.

Daniel looked through the papers his mother gave him. When he read the letter his birth mother had written him, he knew that it would be alright to contact her. There were addresses and phone numbers for his birth mother and grandmother. He couldn't believe that both of them were named Erica. He doubted the numbers would still be good after seventeen years, but he decided to give them a try. First he tried his birth mother's number and as he suspected, it was not a working number. Next he tried the number written down for his grandmother. To his surprise the phone rang and a woman answered.

"Hello," she said.

"Uh, hello," Daniel mumbled. "My name is Daniel Pierce and I am trying to locate Erica Jackson."

"This is Erica Jackson."

"Well, no offense, but I think I am looking for a younger woman. I am looking for my birth mother."

"Oh, my goodness, you lookin' for my daughter. Lord have mercy. You the baby that Erica gave up for adoption?"

"Yes, ma'am. I am. Do you know how I might find my mother?"

"She lives here with me. But she ain't home right now. Call back around six and I'll tell her you gon' call , ok?"

"Ok, I will. But do you think she'll be glad to hear from me."

"Oh, yes. I think she been waitin' for this call for the last eighteen years."

"Do you still live at the same address?"

"Yep, sure do. Nothin' much changes around here."

Daniel realized after he hung up that this woman who was his birth grandmother was younger than his mother—only forty seven years old, but she sounded like an old woman. He decided that instead of calling that he would just drive down there to see her. But he needed some support so he called LaTasha and asked her to go with him since it wasn't far from where she lived. As they turned onto the street where Erica and her mother Erica both lived, Daniel felt a knot in his stomach. There was row after row of 1950 era government housing with cement walls and flat roofs. Most of the buildings were surrounded by hard packed dirt, the grass having long ago disappeared. Finally, they came to the building that they were looking for. There were two old lawn chairs sitting out front. Daniel and LaTasha got out and approached the door. There was a screen door that was shut, but the front door was open so they could see right into the living room. They couldn't see anybody, but they could smell dinner cooking and hear women talking somewhere in the distance. The room itself was dark with an old oversized sofa against one wall and a matching love seat against the other. Both couches faced a small t.v. set and an oscillating fan moved slowly back and forth in another corner of the room. Daniel reached out and knocked on the door.

"Who is it?" someone yelled from the back.

Daniel hesitated. What should he say? It's your son. It's your grandson. It's me Daniel. Instead he simply said, "I'm looking for Erica Jackson."

Ricky knew immediately that it was the young man she had spoken to earlier and she began to shout, "It's him Erica, it's him!"

Both women came running to the front door. Daniel could see immediately that he was related to these two women. They both had his same strong features, the wide face, the bold nose, the same almond eyes and cinnamon colored skin. He was taken aback by how much he looked like them. But on the other hand, they both looked so old and beat down. He knew his birth mother was only thirty four and his birth grandmother was only forty seven, but they both looked years older. His mother threw the screen door open and ran to him and hugged him. He hugged her back tightly. When she backed away, she had tears in her eyes.

"Let me look at you. What a handsome young man you turned out to be. I am so happy to see you."

"Thank you," Daniel said blushing. "This is my friend, LaTasha. We go to school together."

"Well, how are you honey," the older Erica asked.

"Just fine," LaTasha replied softly.

"Well come on in, both of you," Ricky said.

"Momma, don't let the chicken burn," Erica said suddenly.

"Oh, yes, in all the excitement, I forgot we were fixing dinner. Be right back," Ricky said over her shoulder.

"Sit down, sit down and tell me all about yourself," Erica said.

"Well, I'm a senior in high school and I've been accepted to college at Columbia."

"Where is that?", Erica asked.

"It's in New York."

"New York?" his mother replied. "Why would you want to go way up there? Ain't they got perfectly good colleges right here in Texas?"

Daniel stared at her blankly, somewhat dumbfounded. He could think of nothing to say.

"Never mind, never mind," she finally said. "So tell me, you so big. Do you play any sports?"

"Yes, actually, I play lacrosse," Daniel said proudly.

"Lacrosse?" she asked "Why would you play that when you could play football. Isn't lacrosse for white boys?"

"Well, I'm playing, so I guess not," Daniel said sarcastically. He was a little taken aback by her reaction.

"I just meant, you're tall, you could have played basketball, maybe even gone pro."

"Well, I've been playing lacrosse since I was nine and next year I'm going to play lacrosse at Columbia. I'm going into law like my dad. I don't have any interest in playing sports professionally."

"Momma, did you here that," Erica yelled out to Ricky, without even acknowledging what he said, "he's going to be a lawyer."

"Hold on, hold on, I don't want to miss anything," Ricky said as she came running back into the room wiping her hands on a dish towel. "Now start over."

Both women listened in rapt attention as he told them about his life, where he lived and went to school, how long he had played lacrosse and that he also played the violin. He talked about his family and the death of his father, his mother's work as a doctor and their travels around the world. Over dinner, Erica told him about her life. She had dreamed of finishing high school after she gave him up for adoption, but had found it too hard to go back. She had gotten a GED and gone on to become a licensed vocational nurse. She had married once, but her husband had been killed and she never had any more children. Eventually she had moved back in with her mother and the two of them were content here. They didn't really have money to travel but they didn't have the desire either so it didn't really matter. They both agreed that they saw as much of the world as they wanted to see by watching the travel channel on t.v. After dinner, Daniel showed them pictures of himself from a small photo album he had made her. There were pictures from almost every year of his life. He had been careful to leave out any pictures of his family though. In a way, he needed to keep these two worlds separate.

As he got up to leave, he walked over and hugged his mother tightly. She made a little sound, half cry, half sigh that said so much about what she was feeling. She wanted him to know how hard it had been to give him up, but that she had done so out of love. She wanted him to know that he had become exactly the kind of young man that she had hoped he would be, strong, confident and self assured with a bright future ahead of him. She wanted him to know that even though she was glad to see him, that she didn't expect this to be the start of a new mother-son relationship because he had a mother, and that she understood in many ways this was not only hello but goodbye and that she was ok with that.

As he hugged his birth mother, he wanted her to know that he felt the bonds that were created between them when he was still in her womb. He wanted her to know that he understood how much of a sacrifice she had made to give him up. He wanted her to feel the strong arms that she had created and feel the heart that she had caused to beat. He wanted her to know that he was thankful that she had given him life and that she had wanted that life to be a good life. But he also wanted her to know that he had a mother, one who had also sacrificed for him and one that he would never leave.

In the end, what Daniel felt was an overwhelming sense of gratitude that he had found his earth mother and that his birth mother had loved him enough to let him go. He was glad to meet his birth mother because he was curious to see who he looked like and what his birth family was like. But now that he had met them, he was ready to go back to the life he knew, the life he had grown up with, the life he was raised to live.

Daniel rolled down the window as he pulled away from the curb and waved goodbye. In his heart he knew that it would probably be many years if ever before he saw her again. They were once one, but now they were of two different worlds. He would go back to his life and she would remain in hers.

They were connected and yet they would forever be separated by the very facts of their existence.

When Daniel pulled up to LaTasha's house to drop her off, he reached over and hugged her tight.

Daniel really admired LaTasha—her perseverance, her determination. He was also really grateful to her. Helping him reach the decision to visit his birth mother had really been a gift. He knew his mother probably should have been the one to initiate such a discussion, but he also knew that he was all she had left and that it was probably too difficult for her to do. For Daniel, he could clearly see that his birth mother had dreamed of a better life for him and he intended to go and live that life. As much as he admired LaTasha, he could clearly see that their worlds were too different. He knew that he would make a difference in this world, but it wouldn't be by going back to a world he didn't know just because he had been born there. He had been raised to understand that to whom much is given much is expected. But he had also been raised to be with someone like Megan and if he didn't end up with her, it was clear to him that he would end up with someone very much like her. With LaTasha he had felt of sense of connection to a past he was born into, but never knew, but with Megan he had a sense of tradition born from his upbringing that he couldn't deny.

LaTasha had somehow thought that seeing where he was from would bring him closer to his roots and ultimately to her. In that one hug, Daniel told her that he was releasing her in much the same way he had just released his birth mother. While she was grateful for the experiences that St. Matthews had brought her and fully intended to go to college, it was now her dream to come back home and do something productive in her own neighborhood. She tried to explain that to Daniel, and while he told her that he thought that was a worthy goal, it was clear that nothing like that could ever be a part of his future plans, even though his birth mother still lived in this neighborhood.

LaTasha understood that for Daniel, this neighborhood was no longer a part of who he was. For him, it represented only what he had been delivered from. She held on tight as he hugged her. She knew she had to let him go, but she didn't want him to see her cry. She was crying for all the things that she and Daniel would never have together. At the same time, she cried because she was so grateful for the things that he had already given her. She would never really be able to thank him for saving her dream of a better life.

Daniel had given LaTasha the love of learning, the understanding that education was the key that unlocked the whole world. She was happy to have had the chance to see some of the world thanks to Daniel's encouragement and she fully intended to see more. In many ways, big and small, he had been the catalyst she needed to unleash her full potential. But ultimately she saw her place as being back in her community. It was where she believed she could do the most good. She knew that Daniel would do all he could to be of help to others, but she felt that for him it was a sort of noblesse oblige—something he had to do in the same way the king had to take care of his subjects. For LaTasha, she had to share what she had learned by coming home and being a part of this community. She believed what Langston Hughes had said in his poem, "to save the dream for one, it must be saved for all". For her, that had to be done up close and personal and so in the end, she released him, once and for all.

Chapter 19

Earth Mother

Alexa woke up early one Saturday morning thinking about all the things that she and Daniel used to do together. They always had an abundance of activities to keep them busy, but on Sunday afternoons, they often just went to a movie or to the museum. Over the years they had managed to see every IMAX film that came out and had visited every interesting exhibit that had come to town. Going to the museums on a regular basis had been a learning experience for both of them. Together they had seen the dead sea scrolls, the mummies, the body exhibit, the gold exhibit, exhibits on energy, dinosaurs, bugs and butterflies. The experiences had been wonderful for both of them. But lately when Alexa tried to interest Daniel in going to see an exhibit, he showed little interest. She knew he was getting older, but she still hoped he would spend some time with her. It seemed like it was just yesterday when he started elementary school and she told Daniel how lucky he would be when he got to go away for college to begin life on his own. He protested then that he would never leave his mother because he wanted to be with her forever. But in her heart she knew that wasn't so.

"Daniel, let's go to the museum today," Alexa asked hopefully. "There's a new exhibit I want to see."

"Just me and you, mom?"

"Yes. Won't that be fun? Just like we used to do."

"No offense mom, but I need a friend to come too."

"Oh honey. But you'll be graduating soon and we hardly ever get to spend any time together anymore."

"Moooom," he said, dragging the word out like she was asking him to eat brussel sprouts or do something equally foul.

"Oh, ok, Daniel. Call one of your buddies to come too," she said reluctantly.

But she knew that meant was that she would chauffeur them around while they chatted in the back seat about their own lives as if she wasn't there. Then in the museum, Daniel and his friend would be dragging behind, talking in their teenage code about things that only they could understand. More and more these days she was dreading the fact that it would soon be time for Daniel to leave for college. She had built her whole world around him and his needs after his father died.

Because his father had died when he was so young, she had devoted her entire life to raising Daniel, feeling that she had the responsibility to serve as both mother and father and the obligation to set aside her own needs. Her commitment with Anderson had been to raise a child together and she had been determined after his death not to let him down. She was a den mother for the cub scout troop, a booster for the soccer team, an officer in Jack and Jill. She made sure Daniel attended every Jack and Jill teen conference and that he was active in church. She had insisted he become a good swimmer, learn to play golf and to speak Spanish. Thanks to her persistence he had also become an accomplished musician. But somewhere in there she had neglected herself.

And now, Daniel was grown and would be leaving her soon. She still thought of herself as an attractive woman, but she just didn't think she had the energy or desire to do the whole dating thing again. Oh, she had dated some over the years. One time she had even tried to have a serious relationship. One of her girlfriends had introduced her to one of her co-workers. His name was Edward Ship and he was tall, dark and handsome and recently divorced.

Dating him had been awkward for her at first. Before Eddie, she had been on a lot of first dates, but since it never progressed beyond that, she never had to think about bringing anyone home to meet Daniel. But Eddie was persistent and they went on a second date and then a third and finally they seemed to be dating.

Eddie had been kind and patient with her, melting away the icy barrier she had placed around her heart after Anderson had died. It was months before they slept together and when they finally did, it blew her away. Sex with Anderson had always been passionate and tender. But with Eddie, it was wild and exciting. He did things to her that straight-laced Anderson would have never thought of. He introduced her to all kinds of new things. He made her let her hair down. She really was having fun with him.

But she never saw the same carefree attitude between Eddie and Daniel. With Daniel, Eddie was stern and distant. He wasn't unkind, but he always talked to him in an authoritarian way. Eddie himself had a pretty rough childhood and probably didn't have much fun. It was almost as if he didn't want any other kid to have a fun or enjoyable childhood either. He was often critical of Alexa for what he called over indulging Daniel and being too lenient. He even scoffed at the fact that Alexa was paying $16,000 a year to keep Daniel in private school. Alexa had made it clear, however, that raising her child was her business and that she had made the choices she felt were best for him.

For a time, things seemed to go along smoothly, but one day Edward just said he wasn't ready for the responsibility of raising a child and didn't think he could be a good dad. As quickly as he had appeared in their lives, he was gone. For weeks afterwards Daniel asked about Eddie. Alexa had been determined that she wouldn't let Daniel meet anyone she went out with unless it was a serious relationship. She had thought the relationship with Eddie was serious and she had let her guard down and allowed him to become a part of their lives. After his abrupt announcement, Alexa vowed to commit herself entirely to raising her son without the complication of a relationship with anyone else.

Even now when Daniel was about to graduate, all she really wanted to do was be a mother. More and more these days she thought about what her life would be like when Daniel left. She was not ready to be an empty nester yet and her thoughts turned increasingly to adopting another baby.

Alexa found herself going on adoption web sites during the day to look at children available for adoption. Several times she had picked up the phone to call her old social worker. She still had the phone number of the adoption agency in her PDA. But she always stopped herself before she completed the call. As a woman of faith, she knew she had to seek God's guidance before making a decision of this magnitude.

One night the feeling that she should adopt was so strong that she got down on her knees immediately to seek God's guidance. She had long understood the power of dreams and that God often answered your prayers by revealing the answer through your dreams. Over the years, she had taken many dream classes and knew that the way to best make use of the information in dreams was to try to wake up and write as much as you could down as soon as you could. That way you could later go back and analyze the message. The message often came in code. The things, places and people were not ever literally those things, places or people. They were very often metaphors or symbols of other things. She had learned over the years how to interpret the symbols in dreams both for herself and for many of her friends.

Often when Alexa had a problem on her mind, she would pray about it before she went to bed and ask God to reveal a solution for her in her dreams. And often, He would do just that speak the perfect solution to her through her dreams. Tonight she wanted an answer about whether she should adopt another child and so she prayed for God to open her eyes so that she could see whether she should pursue that possibility.

That night she had an odd dream. She had been having problems with her Sunday New York Times being thrown into her flower beds and getting wet by the sprinkler system. In her dream, her New York Times was delivered to her home in a wooden box and placed gently on the top of her fence. When she woke up, she wrote the dream down and immediately began trying to figure out what it meant. The way she did it was to think about what all of the symbols in the dream were and what they meant to her. In her real life, the Sunday New York Times was one of the great pleasures of her week. She enjoyed coming home after church and sitting in her living room, listening to music and reading the paper while she had some coffee. It brought her a sense of peace and comfort and it was one of the things she counted on every week. This small ritual made her house feel like a home.

Of late, she had been upset that she was losing the chance to have this comforting Sunday ritual because the paper was getting wet by the sprinkler. In the dream, the paper had been delivered to her house in a box and set on top of the fence. To her that symbolized a special delivery of something that brought her a great deal of comfort and happiness. As she thought about it, she realized that the Sunday newspaper and the comfort of the ritual of reading it at home was actually a metaphor for the joy she felt from mothering and that the special delivery of a new paper was actually a metaphor for the need for her to reestablish that comfort by bringing a new child into her home. She knew that it was time to call her social worker at the adoption agency.

"Hi Agnes, it's Alexa Pierce."

"Alexa, oh my goodness, how are you? And how is Daniel."

"Great, I'm great. And Daniel is great too. You know he's a senior this year."

"Really? Time has really gone by fast."

"Yes, too fast. Actually, that's why I'm calling."

"What? What is it?" Agnes asked with a start.

"Well Agnes, I've been thinking of adopting another baby."

"Really, Alexa?"

"Yes, I know it may sound crazy to want to start over again after I've gotten Daniel through high school, but I've prayed about it and I think that having another child would be right for me. What do you think?"

There was a long pause. Alexa couldn't figure out if Agnes thought she was crazy or if she was seriously considering her question. After what seemed like an eternity, Agnes finally began to speak. Alexa wondered if she would just say something to placate her, but she had faith that everything would work out the way it was supposed to.

"Well," Agnes started. "You know I'm always looking for good homes for my children". She always referred to the babies waiting for adoption as her children. I would think that you were ready to have a life of your own at this point, but I don't have any doubt at all that you would make a wonderful mother to some child fortunate enough to get you as parent. In fact, if you are serious, I know of a young lady who is going to give her child up for adoption soon."

"Really?" Alexa asked.

"Yes. She's a high school student, and she's drug free and expecting a healthy baby."

"Wow. I was just calling to see if another adoption might be possible. I didn't expect you might have a baby I could consider already."

"Well, if you didn't want a baby, you know you shouldn't have called me," Agnes said laughing. "Think about it and if you decide you are really ready for a baby again, let me know and I'll start the process for you."

"Ok," Alexa said weakly, "I'll do that."

After she hung up, her hand rested on the receiver for a long time. Thoughts were swirling through her head about the possibility of adopting another baby. Could she, should she, take on that kind of responsibility. And what would Daniel think? Would he be accepting of the idea? She knew from her previous experience with the adoption process that she would have to have his support to make this happen because all family members were asked to weigh in on the possibility of a new family member.

That evening as she often did, she prayed before she went to bed and asked God for guidance on this most important decision. She knew that God would reveal the right answer to her as He always had. But that night, her sleep was fitful and no answer came to her in her dreams. The next morning she fixed a cup of coffee from the coffee maker that had brewed it to be ready for her by 5:30 a.m. As she sat on her back porch sipping the hot beverage, she contemplated whether she should seriously pursue the adoption idea. While she sat there thinking, she watched a small robin's nest . For the last several days she had been watching the male and female building their nest. After they had finished building the nest, the male had left and the female had laid her beautiful blue eggs. She had carefully snuck a peak one morning when the mother wasn't around. Now, finally, the eggs had hatched and this morning for the first time, she could see that the mother robin was pushing the babies out of the nest. As she watched, all three of them fluttered a little before they fell to the ground. Finally, two of them seemed to get the hang of the flying thing and took off on their own for short flights. But she watched with great concern as the smallest of the birds ran under a bush to hide. His cries for his mother were sad and pathetic, almost childlike. He cried and cried until finally, the mother went back to get him. The mother bird knew instinctively that this baby still needed her. As she watched this drama unfold in her backyard, Alexa thought of her own life and the similarities to this scene. She and Anderson had worked hard to build a life together and a home for their family. They had been blessed with Daniel, but Anderson wasn't there to help her raise him. He had left a good home, for them, however, and so it was up to her to raise him the best she could and get him prepared to make his own way in life. She had thought of Daniel when she watched the first two little birds make their way as they got pushed out of the nest. But there was still one more baby that needed a mother's love and she knew, just as the mother robin had known, that she had to go get that baby. She had prayed and asked God to reveal the answer to her prayers. She had expected to see His answer in her dreams as she often did, but this morning, God had revealed the answer to her in the bright light of day. She put down her cup and went back into the house.

"Agnes, it's Alexa Pierce, " she said when she got the social worker on the phone. "I'm ready for the baby."

OR . . .

Chapter 20

Earth Mother

"Hi Agnes, it's Alexa Pierce."

"Alexa, oh my goodness, how are you? And how is Daniel."

"Great, I'm great. And Daniel is great too. You know he's a senior this year."

"Really? Time has really gone by fast."

"Yes, too fast. Actually, that's why I'm calling."

"What? What is it?" Agnes asked with a start.

"Well Agnes, I've been thinking of adopting another baby."

"Really, Alexa?"

"Yes, I know it may sound crazy to want to start over again after I've gotten Daniel through high school, but I've prayed about it and I think that having another child would be right for me. What do you think?"

There was a long pause. Alexa couldn't figure out if Agnes thought she was crazy or if she was seriously considering her question. After what seemed like an eternity, Agnes finally began to speak. Alexa wondered if she would just say something to placate her, but she had faith that everything would work out the way it was supposed to.

"Well," Agnes started. "You know I'm always looking for good homes for my children" she said. She always referred to the babies waiting for adoption as her children. But I would think that you were ready to have a life of your own at this point, but I don't have any doubt at all that you would make a

wonderful mother to some child fortunate enough to get you as parent. I just wonder if you are more motivated right now by your fear of having an empty nest. If you are serious, I do know of a young lady who is going to give her child up for adoption soon. But I really want you to think about this. Have you talked it over with Daniel, your family, any of your close friends?"

"Well, no, not really?" Alexa said. In fact she hadn't talked it over with anyone. She was afraid her friends and family would think she was being ridiculous. After all, she was forty-eight years old, with an eighteen year old son and she had only allowed herself to have one serious relationship in the ten years since Anderson had died. She knew she should probably be thinking about having a life for herself, but she just didn't know how to go about starting a life that didn't involve raising a child.

"Well, I won't count you out, but I won't count you in right now. Talk to your family and friends and ask them to help you figure out if this is really what you should do right now. Most of all, pray about it. If it is the right thing for you, then you will know it."

"Ok, I will. And thank you."

"You're welcome. I'll talk to you later."

After she hung up, her hand rested on the receiver for a long time. Thoughts were swirling through her head about the possibility of adopting another baby. Could she, should she, take on that kind of responsibility? And what would Daniel think? Would he be accepting of the idea? She knew from her previous experience with the adoption process that she would have to have his support to make this happen because all family members were asked to weigh in on the possibility of a new family member. As she often did when she was trying to make a tough decision, she decided to call her friend and toughest critic, Andrea, and seek out her advice. As usual, Andrea picked up before the first ring even finished.

"Hey girl, what's up?" Andrea asked.

"Oh, you know, just trying to use you for some free life advice again and save myself some therapist fees."

"Well hold on, let me get a glass of wine so I can think. Alright, what life dilemma can I help you with today. You need some advice on some new drapes, a new car, where to go on vacation this year?"

"I need some advice on whether I should adopt another baby."

"Shit!"

"What happened?"

"You made me drop my glass of wine!"

"I'm sorry."

"What the hell are you talking about? Another baby? Nobody else knows the truth, but I remember how old your old ass is—forty eight! Am I right?"

"Yeah, you're right, "Alexa said sighing.

"What has ever possessed you to think that you should adopt another baby now?"

"Well, I've been thinking about it a lot and praying about it too. And I had this dream . . ."

"Oh here we go again with you and those damn dreams of yours. What was the dream and what did you figure out from analyzing it."

"Well I have been having a lot of trouble getting my Sunday, New York Times—and you know how much I love my paper on Sunday. In my dream, the paper was delivered to my house in a box and set on top of the fence. To me, that symbolized a special delivery of something that brings me a great deal of comfort and happiness. Another baby."

"Please tell me that is not it. You think that the newspaper in the box is a metaphor for a baby? Friend, how about this as an alternate interpretation for that dream—the universe recognizes that the only man you are likely to meet at this point in your life is the pizza delivery man, but a good man,

somebody who reads the New York Times, is somehow miraculously getting ready to be delivered to your doorstep. Surprise!"

"Andrea, you are crazy. Why can't it be a baby?"

"Why can't it be a man?"

"I just think I can be a good mother to a child who needs a home."

"Oh, now you're the savior of all children who need a good home, huh? Alright, my diagnosis is that you got a messiah complex. Girl, get down off the cross, we need the wood! You can't save the world. You already saved one child. It is your turn to let somebody take care of you. I think you're just scared to get back out there again and you're looking for an excuse not to have to do it. But don't worry honey. It's just like riding a bike. It will all come back to you."

"But when I became a doctor I thought that was my calling. Then I realized that parenting was really my calling and being a doctor was just a way for me to finance my calling."

"Ok, so now it's time for a new calling. There's no rule that says you only get one calling in a lifetime. Heck, you say you've already had two. Now I think that your calling needs to be, I don't know, maybe being a kept woman."

"But . . ."

"But nothing. At the end of the day, it's all about how you define yourself. And that changes at different times in your life. You have to decide, are you a mother who happens to be a doctor or a doctor who happens to be a mother?"

"At the beginning, when I first got Daniel, I think I was a mother who happened to be a doctor. Motherhood felt like my calling then, but as I've gotten older and Daniel doesn't need me as much anymore, I have started focusing again on my old dream of just being a great doctor."

"You know I really understand that. I've been single forever and always thought that I would have the chance to parent, but now I think that ship has sailed so I am singularly focused on my career."

"But why? You could adopt as a single mother. There are so many bright, intelligent, financially well-off single black women out here who would make terrific mothers if they would just think outside the box and realize that you don't have to have a husband to have a family. If you can't find prince charming, then at least adopt a future prince charming."

"I am perfectly happy with my life, miss thing and I don't want to find or raise a prince charming. I already have everything a girl could want."

"You're right about that Andrea. You have everything. But you know, you can't go around life all the time with a catcher's mitt on both hands. You have to throw something back. Don't be like all these women out there waiting for the right man who wake up one day in their forties and say, 'oops, I forgot to have a baby'".

"Uh, I thought we were talking about you here, not me."

"We were, but why are we leaving it to our uneducated, less fortunate sisters to raise the next generation of black children? Just think about it."

"No sweetie, you think about what I said—the man with the newspaper is coming. And you are going to have to pay for the advice. Since you made me spill wine on my carpet, you have to take me out to dinner this week."

"Ok, I will."

"Ok, then bye girl. And next time you have a dream, let me have first crack at telling you what it means."

"Ok," Alexa said laughing.

That evening as she often did, she prayed before she went to bed and asked God for guidance on this most important decision. Instead of asking for what she wanted, she decided to pray a new prayer that a friend of hers had suggested to her. This time she asked God to give her what He knew she needed. She knew that God would reveal the right answer to her as He always had. But that night, her sleep was fitful and no answer came to her in her dreams. The next morning she fixed a cup of coffee and went outside to get her Sunday paper. She was irritated to find that the paper wasn't there again. She plopped herself down in a chaise lounge on her front porch and began sipping the hot beverage. As she did so, she contemplated whether she should seriously pursue the adoption idea. While she sat there thinking, she watched a small robin's nest that was perched in a nearby tree. She had watched a male and female build the nest over a period of time. After they had finished building the nest, the male had left and the female had laid her beautiful blue eggs. She had carefully snuck a peak one morning when the mother wasn't around. Now, finally, the eggs had hatched and this morning for the first time, she could see that the mother robin was pushing the babies out of the nest. As she watched, all three of them fluttered a little before they fell to the ground. Finally, two of them seemed to get the hang of the flying thing and took off on their own for short flights. But she watched with great concern as the smallest of the birds ran under a bush to hide. His cries for his mother were sad and pathetic, almost childlike. He cried and cried, waiting for the mother robin to come and get him. Just as the mother flew down to help the little bird, the male robin came back to the nest. He whistled at her as if he was trying to summon her back to the nest. She looked up, but then looked at the little bird . She must have instinctively believed that this baby still needed her. As the mother bird moved toward the baby, the male whistled at her again, more sharply this time as if he was summoning her to come back to him. As she watched this drama unfold in her backyard, Alexa thought of her own life and the similarities to this scene. She and Anderson had worked hard to build a life together and a home for their family. They had been blessed with Daniel, but Anderson wasn't there to help her raise him. He had left a good home, for them, however, and so it was up to her to raise him the best she could and get him prepared to make his own way in life. She had thought of Daniel when she watched the first two little birds make their way as they got pushed out of the nest. But there was still one more baby that seemed to need a mother's love. But the male robin seemed to be trying to pull the mother in the other direction. Just as she was contemplating what all this meant, her telephone began to ring.

"Alexa, it's Agnes."

"Oh, hello Agnes. How are you?"

"Great. Did I call too early?"

"No, no. I was just sitting outside having some coffee. What's up?"

"Well I hadn't heard from you yet, but I wanted to talk to you about something."

"Really? Well . . . hold on a minute Agnes. Somebody is ringing my doorbell. Who in the world could that be this early in the morning? I'll be right back."

She sat the receiver down on the hallway table and opened the front door. A handsome man was standing outside her front gate holding the Sunday New York Times. Alexa was shocked. He looked to be about six feet four and athletically built. He had salt and pepper hair and a thick mustache and was dressed casually in a jogging suit. Alexa guessed that he was about fifty . She instinctively looked to see if he was wearing a wedding ring and he wasn't. Before she could get to the gate she caught her own reflection in the front window. She looked a mess in an old tee shirt with no bra and some faded sweat pants. She quickly ran her hand through her hair and did the best she could to suck her stomach in and stick her bare breasts out. She remembered something her friend Roseanne always used to tell her, tush in, torpedos out.

"Yes?" she said.

"Hello, I'm Adam Smith. I just moved in next door into the Green's old house," he said in a deep baritone voice.

Alexa was barely able to keep her composure. This handsome, sexy stranger was her new neighbor?

"Oh, hello, I'm Alexa Pierce. I didn't know that anybody had moved in yet."

"Yeah, well I closed a week ago, but my stuff just got here yesterday. I'm a doctor over at Bellaire General."

"You are? So am I. What's your specialty?"

"Pediatric oncology."

"You're kidding. I'm an oncologist too. This is too much of a coincidence."

"There are no coincidences in life I always say. Everything happens for a reason, I think. And today, it is my great fortune that somebody threw your New York Times to my house."

"Why does that make you lucky?"

"Because I got to meet my beautiful new neighbor and colleague too, it seems."

Alexa almost blushed. Now she really wished that she didn't have on her ratty old sweats.

"Well, would you like to come in for a cup of coffee."

"I don't' mind if I do," he said with a grin.

Back inside, Agnes, who had been patiently waiting for Alexa to return to the phone began to call out, "Alexa are you there. Helloooo. Helloooo."

By the time that Alexa and Adam came inside the house, Agnes had hung up and there was just a dial tone on the phone.

"Looks like your phone was off the hook. Did I interrupt something?"

Alexa thought about it for a minute and then she said, " It was a call that I thought I wanted. But I think I may have changed my mind. Let's go get some coffee."

"I'm following your lead."

Thank you God, she thought.

CPSIA information can be obtained at www.ICGtesting.com
Printed in the USA
LVOW130024071112

306181LV00001B/3/P